WHY SHE LIED

MARTINA MONROE BOOK 4

H.K. CHRISTIE

Copyright © 2022 by H.K. Christie

Cover design by Odile Stamanne

www.authorhkchristie.com

First edition: March 2022

ISBN: 978-1-953268-10-5

ANASTASIA - THE DAY SHE VANISHED

My heart warmed at the sound of Ryder's laughter. Moments like these made me grateful for each day. My son was five years old and the light of my life. He wasn't like me. Ryder was outgoing, gregarious, and always happy to meet a stranger and turn them into a friend. I grinned as he waved at the bottom of the slide before climbing off and scrambling over to a little boy wearing navy shorts and a green and white striped top. I couldn't make out what Ryder was saying, but I was sure that he was introducing himself based on the fact he held out his small hand for a shake. His father had taught him that. Demitri had told Ryder that whenever you meet a new person, you are to introduce yourself and shake their hand while looking them straight in the eyes.

Ryder was lucky to have such a wonderful daddy. Demitri was the best father that I had ever known. In the early months, he had woken up in the night to feed or change Ryder. As Ryder grew, Demitri read to him at night, taught him to use the potty, and played catch with him. He went to every one of Ryder's T-ball games and cheered him on. Demitri, the ever-proud dad, would stand up on the bleachers with his hands punching overhead, yelling, "Go, Ryder, go," as my little man ran to first base. I supposed it helped that Demitri was a huge sports fan, and I think he was determined to make Ryder one, too. I was never really into sports, but it was fine by me that my husband was and that he wanted our son to be as well. Life was good. Better than good — it was great. I had a wonderful husband, child, and career. Although, I had to admit, the last five years had been a whirlwind since Ryder was born. I was nervous about mother-hood, especially when I had fallen pregnant ten years earlier than I had planned. But as soon as I heard that first heartbeat, at the doctor's office, I knew I would do everything in my power to protect my baby, and I had.

An adult woman approached Ryder and his new friend. I stood up straight to get a better look. Based on the coloring of the woman with her bushy blonde hair and fair skin, it was likely the other boy's mother, but one could never be too sure. I stood up and waved so that she understood Ryder was my son. She waved back, and I watched as Ryder taught the boy how to climb up the stairs and ride the slide down. Ryder was a born leader. At barely five, he was strong and confident. He was my biggest accomplishment. I couldn't believe he belonged to me. I remained standing as the woman approached. "Hi, I'm Jenn. Is that your son?"

"Yes. That's my Ryder. I'm Ana."

"It's nice to meet you. He is adorable and sure likes to talk."

"That he does. He gets it from his father." Both Demitri and Ryder had been given the gift of gab. I studied Jenn and was sure I had never seen her at the park before. "Would you like to have a seat on the bench with me? This is the perfect spot to see the entire playground and keep an eye on the children."

"Sure." She smiled.

Unsure if I was paranoid or just an attentive parent, I wanted to be able to see Ryder at all times. I wouldn't be one of those mothers who said she had looked away for a second and her boy was gone. There was no way I could have lived with that.

As Jenn sat next to me, I started up a conversation but did not take my eyes off Ryder. "Are you new around here?"

"We are. We just moved into the neighborhood."

I said, "I think you'll love it here. It's so quiet and beautiful," as I admired the giant oak trees surrounding the playground.

"Do the two of you come to the park a lot? Are you a stay-at-home mom?" Jenn asked.

"Oh, no, it's my day off."

"What do you do for a living?"

"I'm a nurse. Right now, I'm working three 12s. That leaves four days to spend with my guy." The days I worked, my parents watched him in the morning, and he attended kindergarten in the afternoon. It was actually a nice balance. As much as I'd love to spend all my time with Ryder, it was probably good for both of us to be around people our own age.

"And what do you do?" I asked.

"I'm an accountant, but I don't start my new job until next week. Unfortunately, weekdays at the park with Kyle will be coming to an end."

Suddenly, a cry sounded.

Jenn sprang from the bench and ran over to her son, who had tumbled off the edge of the slide. From what I could tell, he wasn't hurt. Maybe just startled. I got up to do the obligatory check to see that everything was okay. Ryder ran up to me. "He fell. Do we need to call the doctor?" he asked.

Peering over at the little boy, I said, "I don't think we need to call the doctor. I think he might just need a Band-Aid and a kiss."

Ryder nodded, as if he understood. "Can I go on the swings?"

"Of course."

Ryder galloped toward the swings, and I followed behind. He hopped up on the seat and said, "Push me?"

"You got it." I walked behind Ryder to push, and a figure emerged from behind the trees.

"Hello, Anastasia."

My body froze. I turned to see the man I hadn't spoken to or seen in over five years. "What are you doing here? You shouldn't be here."

"Mommy!" Ryder called out.

"Sorry, honey." I pushed Ryder's back, and he soared through the sky.

I pushed him again, to keep him flying and not seeing the man standing behind me with a gun tucked inside of his jacket.

He said, "You need to come with me."

"I can't. You need to leave," I whisper-shouted at him.

Distracted, Ryder hopped off the swing. "Mommy, who is that?"

Their eyes met for the first time. They both seemed to be lost in the gaze and no longer focused on me. I said, "He's just a man who works here at the park."

In a low voice, he said, "Anastasia, the two of you have to come with me. I won't ask you again."

"Why are you here?" I asked.

"I can't get into that right now. Come with me now, or you both *will* die."

My heart thudded in my chest. Was this really happening? I held my breath and took Ryder's hand in mine. "Come on, honey. Let's go on a little adventure."

Ryder whined. "I want to go on the swings."

"We'll come back tomorrow. I promise."

Ryder fidgeted. "I don't want to go tomorrow. I want to go now."

I pleaded, "Ryder, we're leaving now. Please be a good listener."

He stared up at me with those big brown eyes and said, "Okay, Mommy," before we followed the man to the parking lot.

I gazed back at the playground and the children with their parents. A sinking feeling inside of me told me I was saying goodbye to the life I loved.

2

MARTINA

THE SUN BEAT DOWN ON THE BACK OF MY NECK AS I plunged the shovel back into the earth. Using the heel of my boot, I forced it down farther, filling it up and then tossing the soil to the side of the hole. Wiping my forehead, I was ready for a break, but we had too much ground to cover to stop.

Hirsch and I had volunteered to help with the big effort. After all, it was our case, and there were only a handful of other people who wanted to find Darla Tomlinson as badly as we did. We had started re-investigating the missing person case a few months back and had hit many roadblocks until we finally caught a break. It was a hard-fought break. It was our only break.

We'd set up an operation to get Andy Tomlinson's new fiancée alone to try and make her talk. Hirsch had devised a plan to stake out Tracy and arrest her on a minor charge and then go at her hard in the interrogation. Thinking she was facing jail time for shoplifting, Tracy told us everything she knew about Darla's disappearance. It was why we were out in a remote area of a state park in the San Francisco Bay Area with a team of ten crime scene investigators and a dozen volunteers. Andy's fiancée said she was with him the night he killed Darla and that he had buried her in the foothills of Mount Diablo, where he had assumed nobody would ever find her.

I stuck the shovel back into the earth and repeated the gesture. My back ached and my shoulders burned. I was in good shape, but we had been shoveling for two hours. My physical discomfort at that moment was probably nothing compared to Darla's last minutes alive. I thought of Darla's two children who had been without their mother for the last seven years since she had gone missing.

Brown, the head of the CSI unit, called out. "Over here."

I glanced up, and my eyes met Hirsch's baby blues. I said, "Let's go," and dropped the shovel. We hurried over to Brown, where his team had been digging. I stared down into the hole, and my heart sank. What looked like a black plastic garbage bag was visible. Tracy had explained that Andy had wrapped Darla in black garbage bags after he killed her and then buried her.

Brown said, "Now, we be careful."

Nodding, I said, "All right," and stepped back to let the professionals do their job and ensure the scene wasn't compromised. The team had been careful to preserve as much evidence as possible, and I didn't want to get in the way.

Hirsch stood next to me. On one hand, I was excited to bring answers to Darla's parents and her children, but it devastated the other part of me that the young mother's life had ended at the hands of her husband. It was a job well done, but I couldn't cheer the team on as they unearthed Darla's grave. Another victim who died at the hands of someone they had trusted. Someone they had exchanged lifelong vows with, promising to love and cherish in sickness and in health. This one hit me hard and filled me with a mounting sadness. Hirsch placed his hand on my arm. "We're bringing her home, Martina."

I forced a weak smile at my partner. "Yes, we are. Nice work on Tracy."

"I didn't feel great about it at the time, but it's looking like it led us to Darla's body, so it was worth it."

After working with Hirsch for the better part of the last year, we had become close friends. He was like the big brother I had never had. Truth be told, I had brothers - two - but we weren't close. Hirsch was a good guy who anybody would be proud to call partner or brother. He knew these cases hit me straight in the heart.

A few minutes later, our suspicions were confirmed, and Brown and his team uncovered the remains of a female skeleton in her early twenties who had given birth. There was a tiny chance this was not Darla Tomlinson, but I think everybody at that site knew it was.

Thankfully, we had enough circumstantial evidence and Tracy's testimony for an arrest warrant for Andy Tomlinson.

He had sworn he was innocent and had no part in his wife's disappearance, but I had a feeling his story would change when faced with the remains of his wife, exactly where Tracy had told us they would be.

"Hirsch, what do you say we go get Andy and show him his handiwork and see if he still denies what he did to Darla?"

"Let's do it." Hirsch and I trudged back to the makeshift parking lot full of cars driven by the volunteers, police officers, and CSI team. While we had dug, Andy Tomlinson had been sitting in the back of a black and white.

An officer stood outside the car. "How is it going out there?"

Hirsch said, "We found her."

I added, "We want to take Mr. Tomlinson over to the site to see if there is anything he'd like to say about it."

"You got it." The officer opened the back door and leaned

over. "Mr. Tomlinson, you're going on a field trip. It's good news. It sounds like they found your wife."

There was no word from inside the vehicle. The officer helped Andy out of the car. When Andy saw our faces, he snarled as if that would deter us. His helpful disposition at the beginning of our investigation was long gone.

Hirsch said, "'That's right, Andy. We found Darla. We thought you'd like to see your wife one last time."

Andy said, "I want my lawyer."

Hirsch said, "Don't worry, we'll get you your lawyer."

He shook his head but didn't resist as the officer led him to the dig site. As we approached Darla's grave, I watched Andy Tomlinson's expression. It wasn't sadness or regret. It was defeat. He knew we had him and that his life, like Darla's, was over.

HIRSCH AND I REENTERED THE SHERIFF'S DEPARTMENT TO complete paperwork, notify Darla's family, and likely prep for a press conference. The end of the case was bittersweet and exhausting.

Since Detective Hirsch and I started solving cold cases, we had become the poster children for the CoCo County Sheriff's Department Cold Case Squad. Detective Hirsch was the lead, and I was the contracted private investigator who worked beside him. It had been an interesting year working there.

Sometimes I missed my team back at Drakos Security & Investigations, but we kept in touch, and as time went on, Stavros and I had mended our broken fences. I thought when it was time to go back to the firm, I would know. I was still an employee of Drakos Security & Investigations but had an ongoing contract with the sheriff's department to help solve cold cases with Detective Hirsch. Neither of us knew how long the arrangement would last. We just knew that we both enjoyed the work and the two of us made an awfully good team.

As a private investigator, I never really had a partner. We had teammates, but not a partner where we worked each case together. I genuinely liked working with Hirsch and had even briefly considered a new career path in law enforcement. For the time being, that was off the table because I couldn't imagine officially leaving the Drakos team. We were a family, and it would be too hard to say goodbye, so I didn't. Stavros kept our biweekly meetings to check in on how things were going, and he had even helped Hirsch and me on investigations when we needed it. Stavros and my relationship had grown stronger since I had started with the Cold Case Squad, and for that, I was grateful.

Hirsch and I approached the receptionist. "Hi, Gladys."

The older woman with short gray hair said, "Hi, Martina. Hi, Detective Hirsch. You two sure are popular today."

"What do you mean?" I asked.

"A woman came by. She left several messages and a letter for you, Martina."

"Really?"

"Yes, she was here for hours. I told her I had no idea when you would be back. She finally left the station but left the note."

"Did she tell you her name?" I asked.

Gladys answered, "No, but it's likely in the letter."

"What did she look like?" I asked.

Gladys said, "Mature. Maybe in her sixties. She said she wanted to talk to Martina, but she wouldn't say what it was about. She only wanted to talk to you."

Gladys handed me a white envelope, and I said, "Thanks. We'll see you later."

Hirsch and I headed back to the Cold Case Squad Room. A

few of our team members were milling about, working on cases. Vincent was the first to ask, "How did it go? Did you find Darla?"

Hirsch said, "We need to confirm the remains against Darla's dental records, but Brown says the skeleton is a female, early twenties."

Vincent said, "Well done, you two. It sounds like you found Darla, and her husband Andy is exactly where he should be."

I added, "We just need to make sure he stays there."

Vincent said, "I'm guessing there will be a press conference."

Hirsch said, "Most likely."

Vincent offered, "If you need anything from me, let me know. I can stick around if you need me."

Vincent was the Cold Case Squad's top researcher. He was young and cocky, but he was good. Vincent was the go-to guy for searching records, both electronic and paper, and combing through backgrounds and social networks. Come to think of it, Vincent would have made an excellent private investigator, but he seemed to enjoy his work at the sheriff's department.

Hirsch said, "I don't think so. No need to stay late."

"All right. You two have a good night, and don't work too hard." Vincent sauntered off.

In the past year, the Cold Case Squad had grown to a dozen investigators, analysts, researchers, and crime scene investigators. Our solve rate was high, and since we got stuff done, we continued to receive funding to focus on cold cases - most that had been long forgotten. I was proud of the team. Like Vincent, each and every other member was always willing to lend a hand or stay late if needed.

I plopped into the office chair. Hirsch did the same. "How are you feeling?" he asked.

"Tired and sad, but I'm glad we could find Darla and bring her back to her family."

"I agree. It will be a good thing for them. At least they can finally start the grieving process and get to bury their daughter."

"Any idea when the media liaison's going to come find us?" I asked.

"I'm guessing soon after I tell Sarge. He'll notify the rest of the chain of command, and then she'll be here before you know it. Are you feeling camera ready?"

Hardly. "Do you think I have time for a shower and a change?" *And a call home to hear my little girl's voice.*

"If you're quick. This case took longer than anyone expected. The sheriff will be itching to let the public know that we finally found her."

I shrugged. "Well, if it were easy, Darla would've been found years ago, don't you think?"

I was beginning to think that Hirsch and I had lucked out on our past cases. We'd been able to close the previous cold cases at nearly record speed with the bad guys locked up or dead. The higher-ups had gotten a little too used to the quick turnaround. The truth was that most cases took quite a while - which should be obvious considering the cases we investigated had gone cold.

Hirsch said, "True. Maybe it's good it took us so long to solve this one, so it will reset expectations if the next one takes a while."

"I guess. I'm going to hit the shower. I'll meet you back here in thirty minutes."

"I'll go tell Sarge the news."

I waved and headed toward the locker room. I was happy they'd finally given me my own locker, so I would have a change of clothes in the event that a day's work led me to be a sweaty mess like I was today. It was late September, but it was hot as heck, and the sweat had already crystallized. If I didn't hit the shower soon, my own salts would rub me raw.

After a hot shower and fresh clothes, I reentered the empty Cold Case Squad Room. Hirsch hadn't returned yet from notifying Sarge about the discovery of Darla's grave. Maybe he had opted for a change of clothes, too. After all, he had been by my side, also shoveling for hours.

With a steaming cup of hot coffee in hand, I sat down at the table and stared down at the letter and stacks of messages the receptionist had given me. Curious as to whom had penned the note and waited patiently for hours, I picked up the lined paper but set it back down as the door creaked open. Hirsch entered with the media liaison. The letter would have to wait. It was show time.

3

MARTINA

ALONE IN MY BEDROOM, I SLIPPED A FIREARM INTO MY ankle holster. My outfit was now complete. Music emanating from the kitchen and down the hall into my bedroom told me the household was up and breakfast was being cooked. Since my mother had moved in with us several months back, she'd turned our household from a gloomy and rushed environment to one filled with music, home-cooked meals, and a puppy. Not only did Mom help take care of the house, she also helped raise my nine-year-old, Zoey. She loved having her grandma in the house, and, of course, she loved that dog, Barney. The three of them were like bright lights, a constellation of stars up in the sky. They were my life force. Exiting my bedroom, I walked down the hall and made out the sound of Zoey's voice singing along to the radio. In the living room, I spotted Zoey dancing around with Barney, our black-and-white Shih tzu yorkie mix who had more energy than any creature I'd ever known. The dog raced around her feet as if he were dancing with her. "Good morning, Mommy!"

"Good morning, Zoey."

Mom poked her head out of the kitchen. "Good morning."

"Morning, Mom, what are you cooking up?"

"Asparagus and goat cheese frittata. It's almost ready."

I said, "Sounds amazing."

Mom smiled and headed back into the kitchen.

"Are you ready for school, Zoey?" I asked.

"Just about. Grandma said we have to eat breakfast and then we'll be on our way."

"Anything interesting going on at school today?" I got home so late the night before, Zoey had been asleep already.

"Nope, just a normal day," she said, with disappointment.

"Well, sometimes normal days are nice."

"I guess."

From the kitchen, my mom said, "Breakfast is ready."

She was too good to us. I walked into the kitchen, and there was a plate set with the frittata and a cup of coffee already in my favorite travel mug. Mom knew I'd be leaving right after breakfast to get to work, and they'd be leaving to drop off Zoey at school.

Mom seated herself and said, "You got in pretty late last night. How did it go?"

Before I could answer, Zoey said, "Were you on TV?"

"I was. We solved another case."

Zoey said, "Cool."

"Yep, but it was a late night."

"What's your next case, Mommy?"

"You know, we haven't picked one yet. We still have to close out a few things with Darla's case, and then we'll pick the next one."

Mom said, "You should invite August over for dinner to celebrate the closing of another case."

My mother loved Detective Hirsch and preferred to call him by his first name. *August.* He had become a regular fixture in our household. He lived alone and didn't cook and, well, frankly, he mostly worked all the time. So, whenever my mom offered him a home-cooked meal, he jumped at the opportunity. He had become part of our family. Zoey loved to ask him things about detective work and homicide cases. Of course, Hirsch was smart enough not to give her any gory details but rather a sugar-coated version of the job.

I said, "I'll check with him to find out when he's available."

My mom said, "Tell him I'll make his favorite."

"I'm sure he'll make himself available."

Mom said, "I hope so. You know, I was talking to a friend of mine at bingo this week, and she has a daughter who sounds lovely. She's a schoolteacher. She's real cute and seems smart and nice, too. I bet she'd be perfect for August."

I was glad my mother had finally given up on the idea of Hirsch and me becoming a thing. I'd had to explain to her a few times we were strictly partners and that it was more like a brother and sister relationship than anything else. But I didn't know how Hirsch would feel about my mom setting him up with her bingo friend's daughter. Well, if anything, it would give me something else to tease him about.

"I'm sure you can tell him all about her when he comes for dinner."

Mom said, "Splendid."

I shook my head and took a bite of the asparagus and goat cheese frittata. It was creamy and fresh. "Mom, this is delicious."

"It's a new recipe. I used half egg whites and half whole eggs for extra protein," she said with a smile.

My mother had the chef gene, but she hadn't passed it on to me. The only genes she passed down to me were her eye color and alcoholism. Both of us were in AA, and she was even a sponsor. It was an enormous responsibility I wasn't quite ready for.

Life was going smoothly. *Knock on wood*. I hadn't been

attacked and hadn't landed myself in the hospital in months. The quiet existence was definitely a nice change of pace. Was I finally ready to give back and be a sponsor or volunteer at a drug and alcohol rehabilitation center? I knew how important my sponsor, Rocco, was to me and my recovery. It only seemed right that I return the favor to another soul in need.

Rocco and I didn't talk as much as we used to, mostly because of having a strong support system that I didn't have when I first entered sobriety. I think having a partner like Hirsch had given me extra strength that I hadn't realized before. He had my back, and it seemed that I didn't have to tell him I was about to slip. He knew and was there to catch me and seemed to sense my emotions and give me space when I needed it but then was strong and supportive when I needed that too. Rocco used to be all of that for me, but with Hirsch and my mom for support, Rocco and my calls had morphed into a catch up on how he was doing and to discuss any challenges I had faced since our last conversation.

Before Hirsch and before Rocco, I had a life partner. He was my rock, my crutch, and my sounding board. My every-thing. *Jared*. It was nearing three years since his death, and I still missed him. I wished he was there to see our daughter grow up, to discuss cases, and to feel his warm, powerful hugs again. He was gone, and he was never coming back. I knew that and that I had to continue life in a healthy way. After he died, I had spiraled downward and had depended on the bottle too much, and I had nearly killed myself in a drunk driving accident. It was the event that led me to turn it all around. That and my boss Stavros Drakos forcing me to put my life back together with the threat of unemployment and losing my PI license and my daughter. Thinking back to that time, I remembered being scared as heck. But I saw that my new normal had turned out to be pretty great. Still, was I ready for another commitment, like becoming a sponsor? Maybe not yet.

After breakfast, I hugged my little girl and said goodbye.

READY FOR ANOTHER DAY, I ENTERED THE COLD CASE Squad Room and waved to a few of the investigators, who had already arrived. Hirsch wasn't one of them. He usually beat me to the office; I'd have to give him a hard time about that. I chuckled at the idea. He was probably late because he was in some drive-through getting a fast food breakfast sandwich.

Seated, I glanced down at the letter Gladys had given me the day before. It had been such a long day, both physically and emotionally. I hadn't thought to go back to see what it said or who it was from. But the curiosity had gotten the better of me. I picked up the envelope and pulled out the folded paper, flipped it open, and read.

DEAR MS. MONROE,

Forgive my persistence. I am desperate. I am pleading with you woman to woman - from one mother to another. The ten-year anniversary of my daughter Anastasia Hall and my five-year-old grandson Ryder's disappearance has passed, and we still don't have any answers. Where are they? Are they cold? Scared? Calling for me? I believe the not knowing killed Anastasia's father, and it's been eating away at me to the point there is barely anything left. I have seen Detective Hirsch and yourself on the news solving cold case after cold case, and I'm begging you to please take a look at Anastasia and Ryder's disappearance. I'm begging you. I have nowhere else to turn.

Sincerely,

Dorothy Fennelli

AT THE BOTTOM, DOROTHY HAD INCLUDED HER PHONE number and information regarding her daughter and grandson's missing persons case. *Poor woman*. Her relatives had been missing for ten years. I couldn't imagine what I would be going through if my daughter had gone missing ten years or one year or one week or even a day ago. It would be agonizing. When Zoey had entered kindergarten, it was difficult, and I'd known she'd be okay in school and later with my mother, to care for her after school. But not knowing who she was with or where she was or if she was safe or hurt or if she was crying for me...I think it would eat me up too. I didn't think I would be any different from this Dorothy Fennelli, who not only was missing her daughter but her grandbaby too.

Something about this letter, the desperation and the heart-break, tugged at my heart.

Vincent approached. "Good morning, Martina. Everything okay?"

With a forced grin, I said, "I'm fine. I'm just a little weary. I received this letter from a parent of a missing woman and child."

"Is it someone you know?" Vincent asked.

"No, it's not someone I've ever heard of, but the mother is begging us to take her daughter's missing persons case."

"Do you want me to pull up the file for you?" he asked.

"Could you?"

"You got it. Give me a minute, and I'll be back with every-thing you need on..."

I said, "The letter says the missing woman's maiden name is Anastasia Fennelli, but her married name is Anastasia or 'Ana' Hall, and her son is Ryder Hall, aged five years. They both went missing ten years ago from Danville."

"Anastasia and Ryder Hall. I'll find them." With that, Vincent rushed off.

Hirsch sat the end of the table. "What's that about?"

"A case."

He cocked his head. "A case?"

I handed him the letter. "From the woman Gladys told us about. She waited for hours yesterday and then left a note."

He accepted the letter and read the words on the page. When he finished, he said, "Well, I guess we found our next case."

I explained, "Vincent is pulling the file now."

"No rest for the wicked," Hirsch said with a smirk.

I grinned. "Never."

4

HIRSCH

AFTER I TURNED ON THE OVERHEAD PROJECTOR, I SCANNED the Cold Case Squad Room, ready to start the morning briefing session, but we had a missing person. Vincent. I knew Martina was excited to get started on the next case, even though it had been less than twenty-four hours since we found Darla Tomlinson's body. There was still paperwork, forensics, and statements to be given before the case was fully closed out. But I knew from the look in Martina's eyes when she handed me the letter from Dorothy Fennelli that the decision was made.

Martina was someone who, once she was determined to do something, nothing that would stop her. Not me. Not a badge. Not a bad guy - *no one*. As her partner, I would help her find Anastasia Hall and her son, Ryder. Despite officially being the head of the Cold Case Squad for the CoCo County Sheriff's Department, Martina, the private investigations consultant, really was the woman running the show. Except she didn't have to do the paperwork or manage the rest of the staff, although she had helped. She had this keen instinct on which cases to take and which ones had a chance to be solved in a relatively short amount of time. Her growing frustration over the length of time it took to find Darla Tomlinson had begun to wear on her, even though she said it hadn't. I could see why the letter from the mother of the missing woman and child would get her going, and I hoped we would find Anastasia and her little boy sooner than the three months it had taken us to find Darla.

I never enjoyed letting a family know we found their loved one buried and reduced to bones, but after seven years, Darla's family had said they were certain they would never see her again. Still, I think there had been a small glimmer of hope that it wasn't true. Last night when I called Darla's family and then later stopped by the house, they weren't smiling because they were excited that we were bringing their daughter home. They were grief-stricken with having to accept their daughter was gone and never coming back. I didn't envy Darla's parents. Her ex-husband, obviously not surprised, didn't shed a tear. At least not for Darla. But I felt terrible for Darla's children, who no longer had a mother or a father - because I would make sure that Andy Tomlinson went to jail for the rest of his life. The forensics team said that, between the collected physical evidence and Andy Tomlinson's fiancée's testimony, we should be able to have a pretty airtight case against Andy Tomlinson.

Would it be too much to ask for this latest missing person to be found alive? I knew it wasn't statistically probable, but stranger things had happened. A few cases back, Martina and I found three missing women alive who I would've never thought would still be breathing. Layla, Willow, and Raquel. Those three names would always remind me to not give up hope.

The door swung open, and Vincent entered, his face flushed and his blond hair tussled. He lifted up a file in his hand. "I've got it. The file on Anastasia, a.k.a. Ana Hall, and her son Ryder."

I said, "Thanks, Vincent. Why don't you have a seat? We're about to start."

Martina and Vincent both ignored me, and Martina grabbed the file folder from Vincent, who only then sat himself right next to her. I was about to speak when I thought better of it and turned to Martina. "Do you want to start with the Hall case? Or do you want to wait until tomorrow?"

She scanned the pages and then said, "Let's go through the other cases first, and then we'll go over this one. I'd like to get the rest of the team's input before we get started."

I knew better than to argue. "You got it." I began the debrief and listened intently as the other investigators provided updates on their cases. The team was making good progress, and we were happy to report to them we had found Darla. There were cheers, hoots, and hollers like every time we solved a case.

Celebrating our success was important. We needed to keep our momentum and our winning streak to maintain funding for the Cold Case Squad. I'd learned over the last year that funding was iffy at best. The brass only guaranteed us the budget for the rest of the year. The budget review for next year was in process, which meant we had to earn our keep and solve cases to make sure our team remained intact for next year too.

When it was time to go over the Hall case, I asked Vincent to pull up the information on his computer and then project from his laptop. I turned to him. "Why don't you also lead us through the case, Vincent?"

"You got it, Boss."

Vincent was one of the best researchers we had. Actually, I wouldn't say it to his face because he was confident enough on his own, but he was *the best* we had. He didn't usually lead the meeting. The investigators typically presented their cases and discussed the challenges they were having. But seeing as he got the information on Ana Hall so quickly, I thought he might like the new opportunity to show off his skills. As his supervisor, I needed to ensure I challenged and provided all the team with new opportunities to foster their career development and add to their resume. Sarge *might* have nudged me a time or two to do so.

Vincent presented a picture of a woman with dark hair, dark eyes, and a wide smile kneeling down next to a boy of five with similar coloring but slightly darker skin. They were in a park and looked happy. Vincent began, "This is Anastasia, aka 'Ana,' Hall, maiden name Anastasia Fennelli. The boy is five-year-old Ryder Hall, son of Anastasia and Demetri Hall. They both were reported missing ten years ago. The original investigators said the last known whereabouts were at a local park near their home. There is no evidence suggesting that she left on her own or by force. Except that her vehicle remained in the parking lot of the park, and she's made zero contact with any family members since their disappearance."

Detective Ross asked, "What about the husband? Was he investigated?"

Vincent said, "He was a person of interest early on. But there was no physical evidence or motive indicating that he was involved or that Ana had met with foul play. The original team searched the Hall house and Ana's car and found nothing."

I glanced over at Martina, who was studying the woman's face while still clutching the letter from Anastasia's mother in her hand. "Did they question any people from the park they disappeared from? Any witness statements?" Martina asked.

Vincent said, "When the officers went back to the park, nobody had remembered seeing Ana or Ryder, but by the time they went there, it had been several hours since they were suspected to have been there. No security cameras in the area."

"How did they know she was at the park when she disappeared?" Martina asked.

Vincent said, "She told her mother that she was going to take

Ryder to the park. She was on the phone with her right before she left for the park, and her car was in the parking lot."

"Were either of the Halls having extramarital affairs? Anyone have any enemies or vendettas?" I asked.

Vincent explained, "The file says they were both well-liked. They had been married for almost six years and no affairs were reported. From all accounts, they were a happy couple."

Happy couple? Married under six years? Five-year-old son? A shotgun wedding? Maybe they weren't as happy as everyone had reported. I made a mental note to check into the husband and find out what the actual story was with their marriage. "Any other important details about the disappearance?" I asked.

Vincent shook his head. "Not that I can see. No forensics and apparently no motive. Vanished without a trace."

Every single person in that room understood that nobody vanished without a trace. I looked over at Martina. She nodded. We would find Anastasia and Ryder Hall.

After thanking the team, I closed out the morning session. This was the part of the day the team scattered and got back to work on their investigations.

Vincent shut his laptop, and I said, "Nice work. You did a great job leading the new case."

He grinned. "Thanks, Boss."

Martina added, "Yeah, nice work, Vincent."

Vincent was great at research, but I had a hunch he'd be an excellent investigator as well. I made a mental note to see if we could use him in the field - assuming he was interested.

Turning to Martina, I said, "Well, what do you think?"

She smirked. "Nobody vanishes without a trace."

"Who should we talk to first?" I asked.

"The husband."

"Let's take a ride."

A smile crept onto Martina's face. "I'll drive."

After packing up my things, I followed Martina outside to the parking lot. She was rarely wrong about these things, which gave me a renewed sense of hope that we would in fact find Anastasia and Ryder, and hopefully soon.

5

MARTINA

STARING OUT AT THE CRYSTAL BLUE WATER OF THE SAN Francisco Bay, I said to Hirsch, "How would you like it if every day this was our view from work?"

"Wouldn't be too shabby. Certainly nicer than digging up dead bodies."

"You ready?" I asked.

"I was born ready."

We headed toward the tall office building on the edge of the bay, sitting amongst several others. It was the biotechnology hub of the Bay Area, and there were dozens of biotech and pharmaceutical companies in the area. We had learned from Vincent that Demetri Hall was a scientist at Oranto Biotech Laboratories in South San Francisco.

We had not informed Demitri we were stopping by his place of employment to discuss his wife's and son's case. Hirsch and I had both agreed it was better to get the visual of his reaction when he learned the case was being reopened. Would he be shocked? Surprised? Happy? Worried? We'd find out soon enough.

We walked down the path and couldn't help but continue to

admire the breaking waves against the city landscape. I wondered if Demetri took long walks at lunch each day or if he stayed holed up in his laboratory. Hirsch opened the door to Oranto and said, "After you."

After entering the swanky lobby, I strutted up to the receptionist. "Hello, I'm here to see Demetri Hall. My name is Martina Monroe, and this is my partner, Detective Hirsch, of the CoCo County Sheriff's Department."

"Is Mr. Hall expecting you?"

"No, sir, and we would appreciate it if you didn't let Demitri know who is here to see him. Please ask him to come down to the lobby so we can have a talk."

"Do you have a warrant?" the young man asked.

Hirsch said, "No, but we're here to discuss the disappearance of his wife and child. We think he will want to talk to us."

The receptionist said, with a slightly shaking voice, "No problem. May I see a badge?"

Hirsch removed his badge and handed it to the man. He held it in his hand as if it might bite him. He then handed it back to Hirsch and said, "I'll get him down here for you."

Hirsch said, "Thank you."

Hirsch and I moved over to the side of the lobby, where there was a bank of chairs. The building was modern and clean, with large windows - impressive by most standards. I whispered to Hirsch, "What do you think? Is it the husband?" I was half teasing.

"Maybe. This guy is smart enough to be a scientist working in this big, fancy building. He could probably cover up a murder pretty easily. But it's not usual that he would also kill the child, right? Unless, of course, he's one of those people who wanted a fresh start. If that's the case, I would expect that he has a girlfriend or serious love interest."

I said, "I agree, and it would've come out right after she disappeared. It always does."

"Yep. The file didn't say anything about him having a girl-friend back then. I wouldn't be surprised if he did now. Ten years is a long time."

I nodded. "Hopefully, he remembers as much as possible from then. If he didn't do anything to his wife and son, maybe he'll be able to help us find out who did."

The receptionist called out to us. "Ms. Monroe. Detective Hirsch, this is Demetri Hall, as you requested."

We both swiveled in our seats to study the man who was our number one suspect. He was of average height and build, with floppy brown hair and hazel eyes. He didn't look menacing or like a monster. But then again, the monsters rarely looked like monsters. They usually looked just like everybody else. It was how they got away with their crimes, but if this monster or this man did something bad to his wife and child, he wouldn't get away with it.

Hirsch lifted out of the seat and stepped forward. I did the same. Hirsch said, "Mr. Hall, my name is Detective Hirsch. I'm with the CoCo County Sheriff's Department, and this is my partner Martina Monroe. We would like to speak with you about your wife and your son, Ryder. Do you have a few minutes?"

Demetri's eyes widened. He was obviously surprised that we reopened the case. He stammered. "Yes, of course. Have you found them?"

Hirsch shook his head. "No, Martina and I have reopened the case, and we are re-investigating Anastasia and Ryder's disappearance."

Demetri placed his hand on the wall to steady himself. "But you haven't found anything yet?"

"No, we haven't. We just started. We need you to walk

through that very last day that you saw Anastasia and Ryder. Can you do that?" I asked.

Demetri surveyed the room. "Maybe we can go into a conference room to talk about this."

I looked over at Hirsch and gave him a nod. Hirsch said, "That would be really helpful, Mr. Hall."

"Of course." Demetri hurried up to the receptionist. "We're going to go up and use one of the conference rooms. Do they need to sign in?"

"Yes, please."

Demitri said to us, "You need to sign in. It's protocol. Sorry."

"It's fine. Not a problem." I stepped up first to the sign-in sheet and gave the receptionist my ID. Hirsch did the same before we followed Demetri through the building and were brought into a small conference room. Hirsch and I sat across from Demetri Hall. I said, "Okay, we need you to tell us everything about that day."

Demetri nodded. "It was Ana's day off. She wanted us to call her Ana - not Anastasia. She didn't like being called Anastasia." He paused. "She worked as a nurse. She had a three-day work week with twelve-hour shifts. It worked out. She got to spend more time with Ryder. She loved Ryder so much. I had talked to her that morning over breakfast. She made cheese omelets, and we sat around the kitchen table as if it were a vacation day. My job schedule is pretty flexible, so I can go into the office a little later sometimes. We had a nice breakfast. I asked what they were doing that morning, and she said that they were going to go to the park."

"So, you were at work when they went missing?" I asked.

"Yes."

"It says here you live in Danville - that's quite a commute," Hirsch commented.

Demitri nodded. "It is."

"Did Ryder have school that day?"

"Yes. Ryder had just started kindergarten. But he was in the afternoon session. He didn't start school until one o'clock."

It suddenly shifted me back to when Zoey had started kindergarten and remembered that she was in school only half the day. Zoey had a morning class, which she was happy about because she was very punctual and liked to get up early. I couldn't imagine her going missing at that age or any age. "Did you speak to your wife after you left for work?"

"Yes, I called after I arrived. They were about to leave for the park. She sounded happy."

Before I could say anything in response to Demetri, his head fell into his hands. I wasn't convinced of his innocence, but on the surface, it certainly looked like he was grieving the loss of his wife and son. "Did you speak with Ryder on the phone as well?" I asked.

He lifted his head. "Yes, he was talking about animals. Zebras, I think. He loves animals." Demetri shook his head. "He'd be a teenager now. I always thought that by the time Ryder was at this age that I be sitting in the stands of his high school baseball game, and we'd be starting to tour colleges." He paused and stared at me and then Hirsch and then back at me. His eyes widened. "You two were on the news. You have solved some pretty high-profile cold cases."

I said, "That's correct."

"So, then, do you think you'll find them?" Demitri asked, with a hint of hope in his voice.

I glanced at Hirsch before saying, "We hope to find them and will do everything in our power to find them. Anything you can tell us will help us find them. Did you have any enemies? Did Ana?"

Demetri shook his head. "No. Everyone loved Ana. She was a caring nurse. A wonderful mother and a great wife. And I don't have any enemies. I go to work every day, go home, and would spend time with Ana and Ryder. We lived a quiet life. We enjoyed the little things." Demetri looked out, as if remembering the fond memories of his family.

Hirsch asked, "Is there anything you are working on at Oranto that could catch the attention of any unsavory characters?"

Demetri shook his head again. "No, I don't work on anything top-secret or revolutionary, to be honest. I'm working on seasonal allergy vaccines. No one's coming after me for those."

Hirsch nodded. "How long were you married?"

"We had celebrated five years a few months earlier - it was five really great years." Demetri lowered his head once again.

He certainly wasn't screaming guilty.

"And Ryder was five years old, but you just celebrated five years of marriage. Did you get married because Ana was pregnant?" I asked.

He gave a weak smile. "I would've married Ana the day I met her. She just had this life force. This light about her. When I found out she was pregnant, I proposed right away. So, I guess in a way, but I loved her, pregnant or not. I wanted to be with Ana for the rest of my life. There was no question about that."

I tried to assess if he was being sincere. If he wasn't, he was one heck of an actor. "Was there any infidelity in the marriage on your side or Ana's?" Hirsch asked.

"No. Ana and Ryder were my world."

"What about Ana?" Victims weren't always innocent. That didn't mean they deserved what they got. Assuming Ana was a saint, at this point in the investigation, would have been foolish.

"I don't think so. She worked long hours at the hospital and when she wasn't working, she was home with Ryder or working in the garden. Honestly, I don't think she would have had an affair. She never changed her routine or sleep patterns or eating or started new exercise routines. Nothing was out of the ordinary. But then they were gone."

Definitely strange. No change in her routine could mean that she hadn't intended to leave, which meant she and Ryder hadn't left on their own but were helped along with that journey. But by whom? "Did Ana have any ex-boyfriends who would come around or may have wanted to harm her or hadn't let go of the relationship?"

Demetri shook his head again. "She never mentioned anyone. I met her a few years after she graduated from college. She went to NYU and had moved back to California right before we met. She said she didn't date much and not anyone seriously, so I assumed there was no strange ex-boyfriend. When we started dating, she never mentioned anyone who made her concerned about her safety. Although..." Demetri hesitated. "It's not that she was worried about her safety, but she was always really cautious. Like when we moved into our first house together, she insisted on getting a security system right away, and she always had her eyes on Ryder. Sometimes I think maybe someone tried to get Ryder, and she got in between them or something awful, and that's why they had vanished. Now they're both gone. I don't know. She was always really cautious. I don't know why," he said sadly.

Had Ana been cautious for a reason? Were there things she had never told her husband? Probably.

"Is there anything else you can tell us that might help us find out what happened to Ana and Ryder?" Hirsch asked.

"I can give you the names and numbers of friends, family members. Anybody you want to talk to. I'll do anything. With no answers, the last ten years have been really hard. I'm so grateful you're reopening the case. I can't explain it, but I feel they are still out there. It's probably stupid - blind hope."

"Have you met anyone new? It's been ten years. Nobody

would fault you if you have a new girlfriend or someone special in your life," I added.

Demetri remained grief-stricken. "No, I would never. A lot of people pushed me to move on and to date again. But in my heart, I'm Ana's."

"You haven't been on a single date since Ana disappeared?" Hirsch asked.

"No. I guess... maybe it's stupid or naïve, but part of me feels like she's not gone and that she and Ryder will come back. Part of me feels they are still alive, even though it's not probable, but I don't want them to come home and find me with someone else. I just want Ana and Ryder back."

There were tears in Demetri's eyes. My heart ached for him. My gut was telling me he didn't do this, and my brain was saying that if I was wrong about this guy, he wouldn't get away with it, and he would pay for what he did to his wife and son.

Hirsch thanked him for his time, and he escorted us out of the building. We walked back on the path along the bay. "What do you think?" Hirsch asked.

I stopped and turned to him. "I don't think he has anything to do with Ana and Ryder's disappearance."

"I kinda got the same feeling."

"Yeah, and if we're right, this case just got a lot tougher."

6

ANASTASIA - SIX YEARS BEFORE SHE VANISHED

Marcy dragged me into the club. "Come on, Anastasia, you're going to meet a man tonight."

I wasn't opposed to dating, but I wasn't so sure I was going to meet the love of my life in a New York City nightclub. Sure, I could meet some guy to dance with and buy me a drink, but I had been in New York six years and knew the dating scene wasn't exactly set up for happily ever after. Which was fine for now. I'd always dreamed of having a loving husband, children, and a white picket fence. It sounded silly, but it was true. I was two years out of college working as a nurse in New York City - the greatest city in the world, or so the natives claimed. There was a new club to go to every night and the best restaurants in the world, but it still didn't feel like home. I missed the suburbs. The parks. The fresh air. I knew I wouldn't live in New York forever, but I was still young and having fun. My dreams were career and family, but that didn't need to come to fruition for a few more years. Which was why I had agreed to go out with Marcy. There was nothing hotter than the New York City club scene, and I was only twenty-four years old. I was living it up.

"Oh, Marcy, I may not find Mr. Right, but I'm okay with finding Mr. Right Now."

Marcy threw her head back and laughed. "You got it, girl."

Deep in the thick of the club, we moved our way up to the bartender and over the beat of the music yelled our order for two cosmopolitans. The music was loud, and the lighting was dark and hypnotizing. Squeezed in between two patrons, Marcy and I were face-to-face. "So, what do you want your Mr. Right Now to look like?" Marcy asked.

"Is it too much to ask for tall, dark, and handsome?"

Marcy said, "Not at all. We got this."

"What about you? What are you looking for tonight?" I asked loudly.

"I don't know. I had tall, dark, and handsome last time, and I'm not saying that's not nice, but I like a little variety, you know. Maybe one of those preppy stockbrokers." She giggled.

I laughed. "You're so funny."

The bartender returned with our cosmopolitans. We clinked glasses, and a splash of pink cocktail dripped over the side of mine. Marcy said, "To being young and in New York City."

"Cheers."

I turned around and stepped forward, and before I knew what was happening, I rammed into another person. With the bump, I spilled my cosmopolitan onto his white button-down shirt and down the front of my black sequined dress. Mortified, I said, "I'm so sorry."

He looked me up and down. "Nothing a little soap and water can't fix." He smiled widely and stared into my eyes. "I'm Jay. What's your name?"

Tall. *Check.* Dark. *Check.* Handsome. *Double check.* "I'm Anastasia."

"You seem to have lost your drink, Anastasia. Can I get you another?" he asked.

I glanced over at Marcy. She was giving me a big thumbs up. "Okay."

He went up to the bartender and raised his hand. The bartender was there in a flash. He must be a regular to get that kind of service. After he ordered me another drink, he turned back toward Marcy and me. "So, what are you two ladies doing out tonight?"

I said, "Just having fun."

"Is that right?"

"Yeah, do you like to have fun?" Marcy said it rather flirtatiously. Something in my gut stirred. Almost like I had bumped into him, and he should be mine. He was gorgeous, generous, and had thoughtfully ordered me a drink after I spilled mine on him. I thought I definitely found my Mr. Right Now.

The bartender returned with our drinks and Jay said, "Put it on my tab."

The bartender said, "You got it, Jay."

Definitely a regular. *Caution.* He probably did this for all the ladies. He handed me my fresh drink. I smiled. "Thank you."

Marcy and I exchanged glances again. Before we could say another word, two other gentlemen - both tall, dark, and handsome, walked up. "Hey, Jay, we're heading up to the VIP lounge. Are you going to join us?"

The VIP lounge?

Jay said, "I'll be there in a minute."

The bulkier of the two guys said, "Cool. Bring your new friends."

Jay said, "Yeah, this is Anastasia, and you are?"

"Marcy." She grinned, extending her hand to shake.

The bulky man said, "Plenty of seats up in VIP."

Jay glanced down at the two of us. "You ladies want to join us in the VIP lounge?"

No need to ask Marcy. I knew she absolutely wanted to go. I said, "Sure."

Marcy and I clutched onto each other as we followed the three men upstairs. Surely, the night would be epic. We weren't exactly poor, but this was New York City, and there was no way we could afford bottle service. But somehow, we snagged three who could. Marcy must have been in heaven.

Inside the VIP lounge, Jay motioned for me to sit next to him. I didn't mind. There was something about him I couldn't put my finger on, but I knew I wanted to be sitting next to him, talking to him. Strangely, I wanted to know everything about this man. "Tell me about yourself, Anastasia."

"Well, I'm a nurse, and I just graduated two years ago from NYU."

He said, "I had a feeling you were smart. You're beautiful, but I can tell by the look in your eyes there's a high level of intelligence behind them."

This guy was turning me into butter. "And what do you do, Jay?"

"I'm a student at NYU law. I'm in my third year."

"Really?"

"That's right."

"What type of law do you want to practice?"

"I'm considering going into criminal law. I think I'd like to be a defense attorney."

"Oh, that sounds interesting."

"You think so?"

"I do." I really did. This man was fascinating and making me feel all the feels.

Jay sat back and studied me again. "You know, if I didn't know better, I would say this isn't really your scene."

"Well, I like to have fun, and I love to dance, but you're right. I'm not necessarily into the club scene, per se. I don't have a tab or anything like that," I teased.

"It's my family's tab, actually. But I don't come here often either. Law school keeps me pretty busy."

"I would think so."

Jay cocked his head toward me. "What do you do for fun when you're not healing the sick?"

"I like to dance. I also like to read and go to Central Park and run or just stroll through. There is so much to take in."

"Where are you from?"

"California."

"Cool, I've never been. I've always wanted to go, though."

"Where are you from?"

"New York City, born and raised."

"You're one of those! A real New Yorker."

"Is that bad?" he asked.

Sipping my drink, I said, "No."

"You don't like New York?"

"Well, I'm not sure I want to stay here forever. I'm definitely having fun in New York, but to be honest, I kind of miss the simple life in the suburbs of California. Eventually, I'd like to settle down and have a quiet life."

Jay didn't say anything for a minute. He just studied my face. "Really?"

"Really." Was that a stupid thing to say to a guy I just met? I was terrible at this whole concept of the Mr. Right Now thing. Sure, I had visions of a one-night stand like everybody talked about. I hadn't done it in college and thought these were my early twenties and it was a time be free and wild and crazy, but it just wasn't me. I still couldn't get the vision of a husband and children out of my head.

Plus, there were criminals everywhere. How could I

possibly trust a stranger to go into a room in a house with locked doors where nobody was around to hear me scream? My attempts at being wild and crazy had officially failed. And here I was talking to a law student from New York who had captivated me.

"A quiet life?" he asked.

"Is that lame?"

"Not at all. To be honest, I can't imagine anything better. The quiet life out in the country with a couple of kids and a brilliant wife."

This man was the smoothest talker I'd ever met. We continued to talk the rest of the evening, and before I knew it, four hours had passed. It was as if I had hung on every word, and he hung on every one of mine. I didn't go home with him that night because I just didn't have it in me, but he asked for my number. Something inside of me knew he would call. There was something about Jay Castellano that I couldn't shake. It was like he was already a part of me.

7

MARTINA

Nodding, I said, "Great. That will be very helpful. We'll see you soon." I ended the call and tucked the phone into my backpack. "I just got off the phone with Mrs. Fennelli, and she said she will have her daughter Sophia at the house so we can question them at the same time but hasn't heard back from Anastasia's best friend yet. Mrs. Fennelli said she would keep calling the friend. Anastasia's father, Mr. Fennelli, died a few years ago. She says from a broken heart over the loss of Anastasia and Ryder, but the official cause was a heart attack."

"That's awful about Mr. Fennelli. But it will be nice to have the others together. It'll save us some time. Hey, do you need coffee before we go?" Hirsch asked.

"No, I'll be all right. You?" My adrenaline was still pumping from diving into the new case. It was one of those rare afternoons I didn't need a caffeinated pick me up.

"I'll live. But if Mrs. Fennelli offers me coffee when we arrive, I'll gladly accept."

"All right, then let's get ready to go. You want to drive this time?"

Hirsch grabbed his keys from the conference table and shoved them in his pocket. "Sure. Let's go."

After I slipped the strap on my backpack over my shoulder, I followed Hirsch out to the parking lot. It would be interesting to hear what Anastasia's family had to say about her marriage to Demitri. The spouse was always the first person to speak to and to suspect when a wife went missing.

Inside Hirsch's car, he started the engine and headed off toward the Fennelli residence. The time was as good as any to bring up my mom's plans for a love connection. I said to him, "My mom wants to invite you over for dinner."

"You sound apprehensive. If you don't want me to go, I can tell her I'm busy."

"I'm not tired of you - yet. I'm more than happy to have you over. But I need to warn you she wants to set you up with one of her bingo friends's daughters."

Hirsch laughed. "Oh, really?"

"I told her I didn't know how you'd feel about being setting up, but I figured I'd give you proper warning that she had an ulterior motive."

"I appreciate that. Who is this person, anyway?" he asked.

"I have no idea, and I don't think my mom has ever met her either."

"What is she making for dinner?" he asked.

"She said if you agreed to the dinner and to hear her pitch about this woman, she would make your favorite."

"If that's the case, I'll be there any day – anytime."

I had figured that. Hirsch hadn't dated much since his divorce, and from the little dating experience he had, he decided to take a break from it. He and I were in a similar boat when it came to dating. The idea of me dating seemed so foreign. It was something I didn't want to be bothered with and when would I have the time? My hands were full between work and Zoey. But

I thought Hirsch might like a romantic partner or at least someone to date or go to dinner with. He would never admit it, though. Maybe Mom's setup wasn't such a bad idea after all. As it was, he didn't get out much. I mean, I wasn't one to talk, but I had a daughter and a dog and a mom who lived with me. I had school events and Girl Scout events to attend that took up most of my social time. Hirsch, on the other hand, mostly worked, and he rarely went out with friends. Yep. The set-up was a good idea, but before Hirsch came over for dinner I'd try to get more of the scoop on this woman.

We arrived in front of the Fennelli home, a ranch-style house with beige stucco walls and a terra-cotta tile roof. The front yard was well kept, with a green lawn and flower bushes. No cars in the driveway. I wondered if they were the type of people who had a clean garage and could park their cars inside. Wouldn't that be nice? I had so many old things in our garage; I didn't know if I'd ever be able to park in it again. Between all of Zoey's baby stuff and Jared's things that I still couldn't bring myself to go through, it wasn't likely. Then again, even if I was ready to let go of his things, I wasn't sure if Zoey would want some of them. She was far too young to decide whether to get rid of her father's belongings or not. I would wait until she was an adult to make that decision. Considering that it would be all she had left of him, I couldn't bear to part with it.

We exited the car and hurried up the path to the front door. I knocked lightly and stood back. Hirsch gave me the typical shrug, like here goes. The door opened, and a woman of about sixty-five with dark hair and silver roots wearing red-framed eyeglasses smiled. "Ms. Monroe. Detective Hirsch. Thank you for coming. Please come in."

Hirsch and I exchanged glances. She obviously knew who we were from the news, as I'd gathered from the letter that she sent me. But I supposed she thought we would know who she was, as well. My guess was she was Anastasia's mother. She led us into a sitting room with a set of cream-colored sofas with plastic covering them. In the room sat another woman on the edge of the seat, but she stood up when we arrived. The older woman said, "This is Sophia, Anastasia's sister. Her best friend Helen wasn't able to make it, but I will give you her contact information so you can talk to her. I'm not one of those mothers who thinks that her daughter tells her everything. But I know girls tend to talk to other girls, you know?"

I nodded. "Sophia, it's nice to meet you, and I'm assuming you're Mrs. Fennelli?"

The older woman covered her mouth with her hand. "Oh, dear, yes, I'm so sorry. Yes, I'm Mrs. Fennelli. You can call me Dorothy, or my friends call me Dottie."

We both shook her hand.

Dottie said, "May I offer you some coffee or some tea or some ice water? It's pretty warm out."

I looked over at Hirsch. He suppressed a smile. "I'd love a cup of coffee."

"I'll take one too." What the heck. I didn't think I'd need it, but it wouldn't hurt.

"How do you take it?" Dottie asked.

Hirsch said, "Cream and sugar. If you have it."

"And you, Ms. Monroe?"

"Please call me Martina, and I take it black. Thank you."

Dottie said, "Boy, that'll be easy. I'll be right back. Please sit and speak with Sophia."

We advanced toward Anastasia's sister and introduced ourselves more formally. From the photographs of Anastasia, I could tell the two were sisters. They had the same curly dark hair and wide brown eyes. We sat across from her, and I asked, "Were you close with Anastasia?"

"Yes, we were only a few years apart."

"Do you have any reason to believe Ana would want to leave on her own? Or to run away with Ryder?"

Sophia shook her head back and forth. "No, I really don't think so. She loved Demetri and Ryder, and her job. They have a beautiful home in a nice neighborhood. It just doesn't make any sense that she's gone."

I thought that was interesting. Her own sister, who I'm guessing Ana was pretty close to, believed she had a happy marriage, loved her husband, her child, and her life - was nearly convinced that Anastasia did not leave on her own. Who would abduct both a mother and her son? It was peculiar. I made a note to have Vincent run some background on what kind of serial murderers were running around in the area and see if there were other similar disappearances at the time. "Was there anything out of the ordinary that happened before they disappeared? New routine or hobbies or anything?"

"No. Nothing," Sophia insisted.

"Do you like Demetri? Was he a good husband and father?" Hirsch asked.

Sophia said, "Yes. After Ana came back from New York, they met, and within weeks, she had fallen hard for him. He treated her like a queen. But not in a way that he babied her or treated her like she was a little girl. He knew she was a strong woman and respected her and supported her dreams. When they got engaged, it wasn't a big surprise. It was fast, but anybody who saw the two of them together knew they were in love."

Hirsch said, "Do you think either Ana or Demitri had ever been unfaithful?"

"Well, you never really know for sure, right? But I really don't think so. Ana never mentioned any kind of marital problems or that Demetri had been cheating. He just isn't the type. Not in a bad way, but he's kind of a nerd, not exactly a ladies' man. As far as I knew, when he wasn't spending time at work or with Ana and Ryder, he liked to play video games or just putter around in the garage. He didn't go out to bars, and he rarely had business trips. I just can't imagine either would cheat, and I know marriages are complicated and from the outsider's perspective, they could look different from when the doors are closed. I wasn't in it. I just saw from the outside and what Ana told me. From that point of view, they were a happy family."

Dottie returned with two cups of coffee set on porcelain saucers. I said, "Thank you, Dottie."

"You're welcome, dear."

Hirsch said, "Thank you, Mrs. Fennelli."

She gave Hirsch a warm smile. "You're welcome, Detective. Please call me Dottie."

He nodded as if in agreement. Hirsch was more formal with the witnesses than I was. I think it was his law enforcement training that kept him more laced up.

Dottie sat next to her daughter. "What did I miss?"

Sophia said, "They were asking about Ana and Demetri's marriage."

Dottie said, "He is such a lovely man. I know everybody suspects the husband, but Demetri is such a kind, quiet soul. He really loves Anastasia and Ryder. My gosh, at the hospital when Ryder was born, he had tears in his eyes and told me he'd never been so full of love in his whole life. I just can't believe he would have done something to them."

We would continue to dig into Demitri Hall's background. Vincent was already pulling financial records to see if there was anything that would give Demitri motive to want to get rid of his wife and child. Absent that information, we needed to find a new suspect or a motive for Anastasia and Ryder's disappearance. "It sounds like Ana had a wonderful marriage. What about her job? Did she ever mention she was having issues at her job?

Maybe somebody was harassing her, or things weren't going well?"

Dottie shook her head. "No. She was doing great at work. She loved her coworkers and the flexible schedule so that she could spend more time with Ryder. And the hospital had just approved her tuition request to go back to school so she could become a nurse practitioner. They were going to pay for it and everything."

I said, "It sounds like Anastasia had a great life."

Dottie nodded. "She did. She really did. That is why it is so unfathomable that she would just disappear."

"Can you think of anybody who might've wanted to harm Anastasia or Ryder? Anyone from her childhood or her college years? You said she went to school in New York?" I asked.

Dottie said, "Yes, she went to NYU. She got her bachelor's degree in nursing and stayed in New York for a few years before she came back to California. She liked New York, but I think she was tired of the hustle and bustle and was looking forward to a more relaxed pace."

"Was she working while she was in New York?" Hirsch asked.

"Yes, she worked as a nurse right after she graduated from the program. She had a job at a nearby hospital in New York City. She had friends, and she'd go out. She seemed happy there, too. To be honest, I was a little surprised she moved back so quickly. Before that week, she didn't give any indication she'd planned to move in the near future. Although she seemed so happy when she came back, and then she met Demetri almost immediately. She never seemed to regret coming back or ever showed that she missed New York."

"Did she have any boyfriends in college?" I asked.

Dottie said, "Nobody serious."

I glanced over at Sophia to check her reaction. The sister

probably knew a lot more than the mom when it came to the romantic life of a college student. "How about you, Sophia? Do you recall anybody special in Ana's life when she was in New York?"

"There were a few guys she liked that she had dated more than once. But nobody serious. I think when she started working, she was so busy she didn't date very much. As a new nurse, she worked all the worst shifts, so her schedule was flip-flopped from most. When she went out, it was usually at the urging of her friends."

"Did she have a roommate in New York?" Hirsch asked.

Dottie said, "Yes, she did. Marcy was her roommate. They lived together for the last couple of years of college and while she was working at the hospital. I have her name and phone number somewhere. I can get it for you."

Hirsch said, "That would be really helpful."

"Did she have any other good friends in New York? A coworker or boyfriend?" I tried one more time, having a hard time believing Ana didn't have a single boyfriend in the six years she lived in New York.

Dottie said, "No, not that I know of. Sophia?"

Sophia said, "No. Maybe ask Marcy when you talk to her."

This case might be a lot tougher than I had imagined. Missing persons cases were hard to investigate when there weren't a lot of clues or evidence to follow. All we had learned from her husband and her family was that Anastasia and Ryder had a wonderful life and no enemies. It made little sense. Had Anastasia and Ryder been taken by a stranger? It didn't happen very often. You only heard about stranger abductions in the news because it was so rare. Most people were abducted or murdered by someone they knew. If this was a stranger abduction, it was going to be a tough case to solve.

8

HIRSCH

Leaning back in my chair, I watched as the Cold Case Squad busied about. We finished our morning briefing, and the rest of the team was hot on the trail of a murderer and a rapist. Martina and I were the only ones who didn't have a solid lead. It was frustrating. I could only hope that Vincent's research came up with something or *anything* on Demetri Hall to provide us with a potential motive for him to get rid of his wife and child. Even as I thought the words, I knew it didn't sound right.

Martina returned with a cup of coffee in one hand and a file folder in the other. "You look deep in thought," she commented.

"Just envious of all the other investigators with actual leads."

Martina's amber eyes sparkled. "Fear not, Detective. This may be our toughest case yet, but we will get to the bottom of it. We will find Anastasia and her son."

"You think so?"

"I can feel it, Hirsch. I know we have nothing pointing us to what happened to them, but something tells me Anastasia didn't tell her family or her husband everything about her past. Between the fact that her husband said she was always cautious and her seemingly sudden return to California, I have a feeling Anastasia had secrets."

"You don't think it's a stranger abduction after all?"

"That was the direction I was thinking after we left the Fennelli house yesterday, but after a good night's sleep, I think digging into her past is what will reveal the reason for their disappearance. Plus, Vincent said there weren't any similar crimes in the area around the time they disappeared."

"I sure hope you're right."

"So, are you going to call Kim?" Martina asked with a sly smile.

I could feel my cheeks burning. The previous night, at Martina's house, Betty, gave me the phone number for her bingo pal's daughter Kim, who apparently was a catch and would be perfect for me. I was skeptical, but I didn't want to offend Betty, and it had been a while since I tried out the dating scene. "I'm thinking about it."

Martina's eyes lit up. "Oh, yeah?"

"Sure. Why not?"

"I can't think of a reason and who knows, maybe you'll find lucky Mrs. Hirsch number two."

Ouch. "Hardly. I'm just hoping she's somebody who likes good food and maybe likes to catch a movie once in a while. I'm certainly not looking to meet anybody at the altar."

That made Martina laugh. "I'm only teasing you."

"I know, I know. My disastrous dating life is quite humorous." Humorous. Nonexistent. Whatever you wanted to call it. I missed the company of a woman. I saw Martina every day, but she didn't count. At this point, I was practically part of the Monroe family. Zoey used to like to refer to me as Detective, but Betty had recently instructed her to call me Uncle August. It sounded so weird, like I was an old man. Uncle August. Martina had a great family—mother, daughter, and dog. I knew she missed her husband even though he had been gone a while. I had offered to set her up with some friends of mine, but she said she couldn't imagine dating anytime soon. If she did, I could tease her right back. Before I could pretend like I had the perfect match for her, Vincent approached. I said, "I have a feeling you've got something good." That feeling was hope. I hoped he had something good.

He cocked his head. "I found a few interesting things."

Martina said, "Let's hear it."

"It's not exactly a smoking gun, but I got back the financials on Demetri and Anastasia Hall. They didn't have any money problems. From what I could tell, the only debt they have is the mortgage on the house. No credit card or student loan debt. They lived within their means. Unlike most people," he said with a bit of snark. "But there was one sort of interesting thing I wasn't expecting to find. Anastasia has a life insurance policy worth five million dollars. The sole beneficiary is her husband, Demetri."

Martina's eyes widened. "Five million is a lot of money, especially when you have no debt or any kind of financial problems."

"Agreed. Could Demitri have five million dollars worth of motive?" I asked.

Martina said, "I suppose."

Vincent said, "Do you need anything else?"

I said, "Just let us know when you track down Marcy Blanchard." Unfortunately, the contact information Dottie had given us for Marcy was out of date.

"Will do," Vincent said before he left.

Martina tapped her pen on the table and then stopped. "But why would someone get rid of their wife and child for five million dollars when they didn't need any money? Simply greed? Maybe he just didn't like them?"

"I admit, it doesn't seem to fit, but it's something. I think we should talk to Demetri again and ask him about the policy."

"Yeah, I mean, what would motivate him to have a five million dollar policy on her?" Martina asked.

"I don't know."

She said, "What do you say we go find out?"

With that, I grabbed the keys to my car. Martina and I headed back out to South San Francisco to ask Demetri about the policy. On the way, Martina called Demitri to give him a heads up so he could meet us outside to talk. We already got the element of surprise the first time. This was a simple conversation. It was okay to let him know. Because if he was innocent, we didn't want him to lose his job over the inquiry. It wouldn't be right to lose your wife, your child, and your job.

Standing outside with Demetri Hall and Martina, I watched the waves as they crashed against the rock wall. "What else did you want to ask me about?" Demetri asked.

"Just a few follow-up questions. We've done a bit of looking into your background. It shows here that you've worked at the same job for twenty years. Is that right?"

"Yep. I've been here for twenty years. I like my coworkers and my job."

The Halls seemed to have it all - until they didn't. It made Anastasia and Ryder's disappearance even more strange.

"Do you have any money problems now or in the past?" I asked.

"No, we were quite comfortable. I've been here so long, I've got a healthy retirement account. Plus, I get a pension once I decide to retire. Ana loved her job too and made good money. We weren't hurting for anything."

I looked over at Martina, who wasn't doing a good job of hiding the puzzled look on her face. She said, "Our researcher found that you have a life insurance policy for Anastasia."

Demetri cocked his head. "I almost forgot. Yes, we both bought life insurance policies after Ryder was born. My job provides life insurance and so did Ana's, but she said it wasn't enough. She wanted us to have extra."

"We noticed that the policy amount is five million dollars. That's quite a bit, don't you agree?" Martina asked.

Demetri nodded. "Yes, it's a lot. It's excessive, but Ana insisted. She said if anything ever happened to her, she wanted to make sure we were taken care of for life."

Anastasia had insisted. I said, "Did she ever give you a reason she thought you would need that much money? It sounds like you're financially set, whether or not Ana was around."

"You're right. She had insisted and didn't give a reason, but I didn't push her too hard. She wanted it, so I got it."

This case was getting more and more bizarre. I wondered if Martina knew this would be a tough case. She had a knack for finding those. It was as if she liked the challenge. Me, I just liked bringing closure to families. Not knowing could be absolutely worse than knowing the truth, even when it was an awful truth. "You can't think of any reason she thought you would need that much money?"

"No. It was just how she was. She was overly cautious, like I mentioned before. She was so cautious. A lot of good that did." Demetri stopped and stared out at the bay. He returned his focus to me. "It was almost as if she knew something bad was going to happen."

Martina raised her brows. She said, "And there's absolutely nothing you can think of — anyone who may want to hurt Ana or Ryder?"

Demetri shook his head. "I wish I knew. The not knowing keeps me up at night. I just want them found and for them to come back home."

"You've been very helpful, Demetri. I appreciate it. We

won't take up too much more of your time, but we'll let you know if we find anything."

"Thank you. I don't know if I thanked you last time, but thank you for looking into the case again. It's as if I once had everything and now I have nothing. You know?" His voice held deep sadness.

Martina stared at him. "I know."

He nodded and headed back to his office building. I stepped toward Martina. "Well, what do you think?"

"I think Anastasia definitely had secrets."

I agreed. But what were they? What was Anastasia hiding?

9

ANASTASIA - SIX YEARS BEFORE SHE VANISHED

ACROSS THE CANDLELIGHT, HIS EYES TWINKLED. THAT night in the club when I had sworn that I was only looking for a fling, I never would have imagined that I would have met *him*. Since that night, I'd talked to Jay every single day. It was like we were soulmates.

He flashed his killer smile and said, "Happy birthday. I hope you like the restaurant. It's one of my favorites."

"It's so beautiful. And romantic. I love it," I gushed. The restaurant from the outside didn't look like much, but inside, they'd outfitted it in rich reds, golds, and green. It was quaint, with only two dozen tables. We were sitting in the back of the restaurant, where there were only a few other patrons.

Jay said, "Wait until you taste the food. It's life changing."

"I can't wait. I love Italian food."

"They have a veal parmesan that is to die for."

"I'm more of a fettuccine Alfredo kind of gal."

"Then you'll love theirs. They make all their pasta in house - it's the best in the city."

How had I gotten so lucky? He was handsome. He was going to be a lawyer. He seemed to adore me. It was like a fairytale. We'd only known each other a few months, but I could tell this man was going to change my life. I had already felt changed - since that very first night. Had I become a sappy romantic?

Every part of my being knew this was the man for me. Sitting in one of the best restaurants in New York City, his generosity and thoughtfulness overwhelmed me. I had expected little, since we hadn't been dating long, but he had surprised me.

"How do you feel now that you're twenty-five? A quarter-century."

I smiled. "You know, I don't really feel any older."

"Well, you look gorgeous." He slid a box across the white tablecloth. It was long and white with a red bow on it. "I got you a little something. It's certainly not as beautiful as you are, but I hope you like it."

Jewelry? He bought me jewelry? I took the gift and carefully removed the top of the box. Inside was a black velvet case that I removed from the outer box. My heart raced as I opened up the case. Stunned, my mouth dropped open as my eyes fixed on the most beautiful sapphire and diamond bracelet I had ever seen. It was too much for a law student. I couldn't accept it.

"This is too much, Jay."

"Nonsense. You deserve the best, Anastasia."

"I don't even know what to say." I couldn't take my eyes off the bracelet. It was shiny yellow gold with clusters of diamonds and sapphires in the center.

"Let me help you put it on." He got up from his seat and came over and removed the bracelet from the case and wrapped it around my wrist before fastening the clasp. I stared down at my new glittering jewels. I glanced up at him. We were so close I could kiss his lips. "Thank you."

"You're very welcome." He bent down farther and gave me a tender kiss. Goosebumps formed on my arms, and my whole body tingled. He retreated and looked deep into my eyes. "I love you, Anastasia."

My heart fluttered. "I love you, too."

A server wearing a three-piece suit approached, and Jay retook his seat. The server said, "Mr. Castellano, good to see you. What can I get you this evening?"

"It is my Anastasia's birthday. You will have to ask her."

The man stared down at me expectantly. "Miss?"

"Do you have cocktails?"

"Of course."

I said, "I'll have a cosmopolitan."

"Coming right up. And, sir, what can I get you?"

Jay said, "I'll have a bottle of your best chianti."

"Yes, sir."

I stared across at Jay. My heart was still beating fast from that kiss and our verbalized exchange of love. I had known I loved him, but I was too afraid to say anything. It was too soon. I thought he loved me, and I was so glad he said it because I was bursting with emotion for him.

After the best fettuccine Alfredo I'd had in my life, Jay and I walked hand in hand out into the bustling streets of Little Italy. Practically walking on air, I had never felt more alive.

10

MARTINA

Pacing the empty conference room, I waited as the phone rang and rang. "Hello?"

"Is this Marcy Jamison?" I asked.

"Yes, who is this?"

"My name is Martina Monroe, and I'm an investigator at the CoCo County Sheriff's Department in California. I got your name from Ana Hall's mother. She said you were roommates in New York. It would've been about fifteen or twenty years ago."

"Ana Hall? Are you sure you have the right Marcy Jamison?"

We'd learned Blanchard was Marcy's maiden name, making the search for her a bit more challenging. "Oh, I'm sorry, her maiden name was Fennelli. Ana Fennelli."

"Do you mean Anastasia Fennelli?" Marcy asked.

"Yes, Anastasia Fennelli." I made the mental note that Ana hadn't gone by the name of Ana while she lived in New York.

"Yes, of course. My gosh, we haven't talked since she left New York."

Oh jeez. This call was gonna take a turn. I disliked giving notifications of a missing person or death. I didn't think I would ever get used to it. Delivering bad news damaged my soul and made me sick to my stomach. I explained, "Well, actually, she's been missing for the last ten years."

"What? She's been missing?" Marcy asked, exacerbated.

I then explained to Marcy about the disappearance of Anastasia and her son Ryder and the subsequent reopening of the case.

Marcy replied. "My gosh, that's so terrible."

"Yes. I'm reaching out to you because we are trying to learn more about Anastasia's past to see if there's anything that could explain her disappearance or determine if there was somebody who may have wanted to cause her or her son any harm. Do you remember if there was anybody who may have stalked her, or was too friendly, or anybody that she complained about while she was in New York?" It was a lot for Marcy to have to answer after so much time had passed. Waiting patiently for a response, I said, "Take your time."

Marcy said, "No. I can't think of anyone. Anastasia was well-liked and although she had the attention of a lot of men, especially when we were in college and when we'd go out to clubs, nobody ever harassed her. She didn't have any problems. And if she had, Jay would've taken care of them for sure."

"Jay?" I asked.

"Yeah. Jay was Anastasia's boyfriend. No, not boyfriend - fiancé. They broke up right before she left New York."

Fiancé? "Do you remember Jay's last name?"

"Castellano," Marcy said matter-of-factly.

"Can you tell me about Jay?"

Finally, a lead. There *was* something Anastasia had been hiding from her family and her husband, but why?

"Jay was in law school when they met. Tall, dark, handsome - rich family - the whole nine yards. They met when we were out at a club. They hit it off right away. It was love at first sight. Well, according to Anastasia, anyhow."

"How long were they together?" I asked.

"Oh, I don't know. Six months? Maybe a little less."

Why would Anastasia have not told her family about Jay - a man she had fallen in love with almost immediately and had planned to marry? "Did they have a good relationship?"

"Yes, they were so happy and in love. She was gushing when he proposed. It was nauseating. I was so surprised when they broke up."

"Do you remember when they got engaged? Was it close to the break-up?"

"It was a few months before, which is why it was so surprising they broke up."

"Do you remember if she told her family she was engaged?" I asked.

"I would assume so, but I can't actually remember Anastasia saying she'd told them."

Because she probably hadn't. Or had she and they weren't telling us everything? "Did Anastasia say why they broke up?"

Marcy said, "She said they wanted different things and that it was very sad, but it was over."

I hurried over to my notepad and pulled out a pen and wrote down *Jay Castellano in New York.*

"Are you still in contact with Jay?" I asked.

"No, I left New York a while ago. I'm settled in Connecticut with my husband and children."

"And you haven't heard from Anastasia over the last fifteen years?"

"No. I hope she's okay. I can't imagine her just disappearing like that and her five-year-old too?"

"Yes. And you can't think of any reason anybody would want to hurt her or abduct her?"

"No. But she kinda left New York rather suddenly. I just thought she was so heartbroken over the end of her relationship with Jay. It seemed kind of sudden, you know. But she was a great nurse, and she got a job right away in California. She gave her notice and within a week - not even a week after the breakup - she moved back to California. She had paid through the end of our lease, but she said she didn't want to stay. She missed home, and she was looking forward to the next chapter of her life."

"Did you believe her?"

"She was devastated. I think she just couldn't handle being in the same city with Jay anymore."

"Is there anything else you can tell me about Anastasia or Jay that you think might be useful?"

"Not really."

"You said Jay came from money? How did you know his family was wealthy?" I wondered if he was from a polit-ical family. I had learned firsthand that those types would stop at nothing to cover up secrets they didn't want getting out.

"Anastasia told me he didn't have any student loans and that his parents were footing the bill for undergrad and law school. You have to be pretty loaded to do that. That and when they'd go out to dinner and to clubs, everyone seemed to know Jay and his family."

Hmm. "Any idea how his family made their fortune?"

"Anastasia said Jay's father was an entrepreneur - concrete or construction or something - but I'm not sure."

Hmm. "All right, well, let me know if you can think of anything else that may be helpful." I gave her my contact infor-mation and hung up the phone.

Anastasia had a secret fiancé. Why had she kept a secret like that from her family? It didn't make any sense. I went over to the whiteboard and wrote down everything I had learned about the case so far.

Happy marriage
Loving family
No money problems
Five million dollar life insurance policy
Secret fiancé - Jay Castellano - New York
Sudden departure from New York

I tapped the end of the marker on the whiteboard. What could it all mean?

Hirsch walked in. "What did I miss?"

Pointing at the name Jay Castellano on the whiteboard, I said, "Anastasia had a secret fiancé."

"Really?"

I explained, "Yep. They broke up days before she left New York."

Hirsch stared at the board as if in thought. "Let's get Vincent to find Jay Castellano. He may be the key."

"Exactly what I was thinking." Who was Jay Castellano? Had they really broken up because they wanted different things? What were those things?

11

MARTINA

I waited by the pickup counter as Hirsch finished ordering his specialty latte. He smiled at the young blonde cashier before meeting up with me.

"She's cute." I commented.

"Please, she's practically a teenager."

"Did you call Kim?" I asked. My mother's set-up was supposedly a perfect match.

"I plan to call her later tonight or tomorrow if we get too swamped."

"Really?" I acted more surprised than I was.

"What's the worst that could happen?"

I knew better than to ask that question. Things could always be worse than one could imagine. "True. Plus, maybe you'll get a little of that R&R you need."

He chortled. "I don't recall dating being anything like rest or relaxation. More like stress and heartache."

"True, but still less stressful than having to question a missing woman's family about why she kept a secret fiancé from them."

"Unless Anastasia didn't keep the secret, her family did."

"Why would they do that? I don't think they knew. Considering her best friend Helen hadn't heard of Jay either. But Helen had said that they hadn't met until after Ana left New York."

Hirsch shrugged. "Do you think Helen would change her story if we interviewed her in person? It's pretty easy to avoid eye contact over the phone."

I had spoken with Helen Russo on the phone for over an hour since she was out of town on business, but I didn't get the sense she was hiding anything. "True, we can re-interview her when she's back from her trip next week, if needed."

"Maybe they forgot?" Hirsch contemplated.

"I don't know if I buy that. Her friend Marcy made it seem like she told her parents. Most people would tell their parents when they got engaged, unless something was off about the whole thing. Maybe she thought they'd be upset about the engagement? If so, why?"

"If Anastasia was keeping a secret fiancé, even way back then, it does make you wonder why. Why would she keep it a secret? It wasn't like she was sixteen and dating a 50-year-old. She was a grown woman."

"Maybe after we get Jay Castellano's background check complete, it will give us some insight into why she might've kept their relationship quiet."

Hirsch's name was called out, and he stepped to the counter and picked up his fancy coffee.

We headed back out to the car, and I thought about what Hirsch had said. I had a feeling Anastasia didn't tell her parents about her engagement to Jay Castellano, but the why would be the most interesting part. Or it was a complete red herring and maybe had nothing to do with her disappearance. Assuming she hadn't seen Jay in more than six years before she disappeared, why would he come after her at that point? None of it seemed to make sense or point to why a woman with a picture perfect life would just disappear unless - I really hoped it didn't come to this - it was a stranger abduction or maybe a serial killer who was just getting started.

Vincent had pulled all the records of unsolved crimes in the area to see if anything matched or would fit the profile of an unknown subject who had been preying on mothers with small children. He hadn't found any, but that didn't mean it hadn't happened - it could be the perpetrators were never caught or law enforcement had never linked the crimes. It wasn't out of the question. Nothing was out of the question at this point.

BACK AT THE FENNELLI RESIDENCE, HIRSCH LED THE WAY up the path to the front door. We explained ahead of time that we'd be returning to ask a few follow-up questions, hoping Ana's sister, Sophia, could join Dottie. Somebody had to have known about Jay Castellano other than her roommate, right?

The door opened and Dottie Fennelli greeted us with a warm smile. "Please come in. Detective and Miss Monroe."

"Please call me Martina."

Dottie nodded. "Martina. Can I get you two anything to drink?"

"Nope, we're fully caffeinated. Thank you very much," Hirsch added.

She led us into the living room where we had met before. Sophia sat on the large chair, appearing more relaxed than during our previous visit.

We took a seat, and I began, "We don't want to take up too much of your time, but we've learned something from Marcy, Anastasia's old roommate, in New York. Something that surprised us." This had the Fennellis' interest. Both looked surprised. I continued, "Marcy said that Anastasia had been engaged to a man named Jay Castellano when she lived in New York. Did you know about Anastasia's relationship?"

I didn't need them to speak for me to understand the answer. Dottie's eyes were wide, and Sophia shook her head in disbelief. Sophia said, "No, I have never even heard this man's name before. You said they were engaged? That can't be right. She would've told us."

Dottie said, "I agree. She would've been so excited. She told me all kinds of things. I can't believe she would keep an engagement from us. I just can't believe it."

Had Marcy lied about Jay Castellano? If so, why? "Marcy seemed pretty sure about it. She said Anastasia and Jay broke up right before she left New York. More specifically, they broke up the week she left New York. Marcy thought it was why Anastasia decided to move."

I leaned back to watch their expressions and give them time to let the information sink in. Maybe it would spark a recollection or a memory that would align with Ana and Jay's relationship. Dottie turned to her daughter. "She did come home rather suddenly."

Sophia agreed. "She did."

"Did Anastasia give you a reason for returning to California?" I asked.

"That she was homesick and got a really excellent job offer."

That was believable. "How did she seem when she returned to California? Was she happy? Was she excited, sad?" Hirsch asked.

Sophia said. "She seemed tired."

Dottie asked, "Wouldn't you be tired if you just moved across country?"

Sophia responded, "Yes, but Ana was usually happy and chipper and energetic. But when she came home, it was like her light had dimmed. She said she was fine, and that it was the move and the jet lag, but I don't know. I guess part of me wondered if she was depressed. Maybe that was why she came home, you know?"

"And how soon after she returned to California did she start dating Demetri?" I asked.

Sophia said, "I think they met within a month."

Dottie said, "Exactly. That's why I think her energy wasn't different at all. She was already going out and meeting new people, like Demetri. Have you spoken with him? He was so good to her. Over the years, we've lost touch, but I know he loves her. She loved him. They were such a beautiful family." Dottie teared up.

Hirsch said, "We will do everything we can to find out what happened to Anastasia and Ryder."

Sophia spoke for her mother and herself. "Thank you."

After our goodbyes and ride back to the office, shooting theories back and forth, Hirsch and I stood next to the whiteboard where we had penned the details of the investigation. We both agreed we needed more information, especially regarding Jay Castellano. Vincent was on it, but we still hadn't heard the research was complete.

"I hope this one doesn't take as long as the last. It's very puzzling, don't you think?"

"I agree. If we don't get anything soon on Jay Castellano or if that ends up turning out to be a dead end, I'm not sure what else we can do. There's nothing to explain their disappearance."

As if reading Hirsch's thoughts or listening to our conversation, Vincent rushed into the room. "I'm so glad you're here. Have I got some news for you."

Hirsch and I exchanged glances. Did Vincent have the clues we needed to bring Anastasia and Ryder home?

MY HEART SPED UP. "WHAT IS IT?"

"I got some information back on Jay Castellano for the Anastasia Hall missing persons case."

"Yeah, we know the case. Vincent, what do you have?" Martina asked, rather impatiently.

Vincent seemed unfazed and said, "Get this. His name is Jay Alberto Castellano, born and raised in New York City. He went to school in New York and graduated from Columbia undergrad and New York University Law School. He currently works for a very prominent New York law firm in Manhattan."

There were shiny beads of sweat on Vincent's temple, and his cheeks were flushed. That couldn't be all he had found. "And? You've gotta have something else."

"Does he have a criminal record?" Martina asked.

Vincent shook his head. "Nope. Squeaky clean."

Martina looked as annoyed and puzzled as I felt. "Can we get to the punchline?" I asked.

Vincent smirked. "Get this. Jay is clean. Not even a parking ticket - his whole life. He's unmarried and lives in New York City - Manhattan, to be exact. Owns a penthouse. He's loaded, but that's no surprise. He grew up rich. His family has a country home in upstate New York worth millions and a brownstone in the city - where little Jay grew up."

Martina said, "So, he's rich and clean? Not exactly helpful."

Vincent smiled. "I know, right? So, that's when I expanded my search to his family members and hit the jackpot. Do you wanna guess what I found?"

"They're bad?" Martina asked with a look like she wanted to throttle Vincent.

"Well, if you think the fact that Jay Castellano is the eldest son of a suspected, or rather known, mafia boss named Sal 'Big Sally' Castellano, head of the Castellano Crime Family, then, yes."

"Wait, what? Are you saying that Jay's family is in the mob?" Martina asked, no longer annoyed with Vincent.

"No. They *are* the mob. The Castellano family is the most powerful crime family in the U.S. We're talking about one of *the* five families of the New York City organized crime scene. We're talking roots back to Sicily and bootleggers, racketeers, and union knee cappers. These guys are even credited with fueling the abuse of heroin in the U.S. in the fifties. These are not folks you want to mess with."

Anastasia was engaged to the eldest son of one of the most dangerous men in America. "But you say that Jay is completely clean?" I asked.

"I don't think you can be part of that family and be completely clean. I looked a little closer and read a few head-lines. You see, Big Sally has consistently made the news over the last twenty years. But the last story published was interesting. It includes a statement from his lawyer..."

Before Vincent could continue, Martina said, "Let me guess. His lawyer's name is Jay Castellano?"

"Yep. Jay is not only the golden boy and eldest son of a mob boss, he represents the family and a few other wealthy clients, but the Castellano family is his biggest client."

I shook my head. "This is all interesting, but..." My speech drifted as I gathered my thoughts. Something still wasn't adding up.

Martina said, "Jay's mob ties could be why Anastasia didn't tell her family she was engaged."

"Maybe? If she knew."

Vincent shook his head. "I doubt she knew. From what I've read, mobsters don't talk about being mobsters. They don't even call it that. They use a different name - a code rooted back to Sicily. To them, they're the Cosa Nostra or CN. From what I found, mafiosos don't talk about their illegal dealings. It's all very hush-hush. Each mafioso has some other front. It's almost like they're living double lives. For example, Big Sally owns a successful, legitimate cement company, which is how he justifies his lavish lifestyle. But in reality, the borgata, what they call their organization, is secret. By the way, the term 'family' was made up for Hollywood, but anyway, the borgatas are run like a large corporation where the boss is at the top - like a pyramid. The little guys are doing the dirty work, but the profits flow up to each level. It keeps the bosses looking clean - most of the time."

Wow. No wonder it had taken Vincent a minute to bring back the information on Jay Castellano. He had also been researching organized crime.

I said, "Okay, so maybe Anastasia didn't know Jay was affiliated with organized crime when she met him, but then she found out and they broke up? That doesn't explain why she didn't tell her parents she was engaged if she didn't know Jay was a mobster's kid until later. Even so, I'm not sure how Jay's mob family is connected to her disappearance. Don't get me wrong, I definitely think there may be something here, but she hadn't talked to anybody from New York in almost six years at the time she disappeared."

Martina said, "That we know of. She hadn't spoken to Marcy. Maybe she kept in touch with Jay? But why? We need to check her phone records. Can we do that, Vincent?"

"We can find out if she was in contact with Jay after she left New York - if she used her phone. I'll get right on it."

I said, "Thanks, Vincent."

With that, Vincent left the squad room. I turned to Martina. "So, the only thing that doesn't align with Anastasia's perfect life is that before she moved back to California from New York, she had a secret fiancé who was part of the mob. And let's, just for the sake of argument, assume she had no contact with him after their breakup. Why would she go missing almost six years later? Or if they were in contact - why would she go missing? Was there a reason the mob or Jay would come after her? And Ryder?"

Martina said, "It's a good question. I bet our pals over at the NYPD could help us out. Do you have any FBI buddies in New York, or should we give Special Agent Deeley a call?"

"I've got buddies all over the place, but I'll start with Deeley. He mentioned some work with the Philly mob when we met with him about the Henley case."

Martina nodded. "Maybe something happened ten years ago that would've prompted the Cosa Nostra to come after Anastasia or Ana. Once she returned to California, the only one who called her Anastasia was her mother. Demetri, her sister, and her friend Helen called her Ana."

I said, "And isn't it a little odd that when she came back to the Bay Area, she was married to Demetri within a year of returning, despite being so devastated over her breakup with Jay?"

Martina softened her gaze. "Wait a second."

"What?"

"Give me a second." Martina grabbed the case binder and started flipping through pages and pages of notes. I sat quietly as she was clearly in a desperate search for something that she'd seen. I knew better than to disturb her when she was in that state of mind. She pulled a page out of the binder and set it aside before she continued to flip through the contents of the binder. She stopped and then traced the paper with her finger and then halted and glanced up at me. "I think I know why Jay and Anastasia broke up."

13

ANASTASIA - SIX YEARS BEFORE SHE VANISHED

My jaw dropped as he drove up to the circular driveway in front of what I could only describe as a mansion. This was his family's *vacation* home? I could only imagine what their home in the city looked like. I knew it was a three-story brownstone and was in a good neighborhood and that Jay's parents were wealthy, but I'd never seen anything like this, at least not outside of TV or the movie theater. He drove stoically before parking near the entrance of the white palace. This was how he grew up. I wondered what his parents would think of me and my more humble family. We didn't go without, but my family's wealth was nowhere near that of the Castellanos. Would they think I wasn't good enough for Jay?

My heart beat faster, and a fluttering started in my belly. How did somebody so humble and sweet come from so much money?

Jay grabbed my hand. "What's wrong? Are you okay?"

"I'm fine, I'm just... I hadn't realized how..."

"How rich my family is?" he said with a smile.

"Yeah. My family doesn't have this kind of money. Not even close. Like maybe that part." I gestured over to what look like a freestanding building that maybe was a garage or maybe it was for the help. I didn't know.

Jay said, "It doesn't matter. It's just money. And don't worry, my family is going to love you."

I stared at the glittering diamond on my finger. "Are you sure?"

"Of course, I'm sure. I love you, and they will, too." He gave me a quick peck on the lips. "Come on. I can't wait for my parents to meet you."

I wished I had Jay's confidence. What would I say to people who lived like this? I had no idea. We were a blue-collar family until my sister and I had graduated from college. This was a whole new world, and I couldn't even imagine what it would be like to be a part of their family.

Jay had proposed just the night before at the restaurant where we had our first date. After the main course, he had gotten down on one knee while violins played in the background. Holding a black box with a sparkling diamond ring tucked inside, he'd asked me to be his wife. I'd jumped out of my seat and wrapped my arms around him, exclaiming, "Yes!"

It made me tear up just thinking about it. I had never been so happy in my entire life. It was like I was floating on air, and nothing could go wrong. He led me by the hand up to the front door, but before he could pull out a key to unlock it, the door opened, and a woman wearing a gray and white maid's uniform grinned. "Jay, it's so good to see you."

He led me inside and said, "Maria, it's good to see you too. I'd like to introduce you to my fiancée, Anastasia."

Maria said, "It is lovely to meet you, Anastasia. Welcome."

Maybe not a housekeeper? Jay continued to lead me through the hall, and my mouth dropped open. The house was massive, with fresh flowers on a pedestal and a winding staircase. It was as if I just stepped inside the *Lifestyles of the Rich and Famous* TV show. Jay turned to me. "That was Maria. She was my nanny, and she's the housekeeper. She's like a second mother to me. You'll love her. She's the greatest."

Nanny. Housekeeper. Is that how our children would grow up too? Would we have a nanny and a housekeeper? Maria returned to the foyer and said, "Your mother and father are around back on the patio waiting for you."

Jay said, "Thank you, Maria."

I was still trying to process the grandness of Jay's world as he led me through the opulent home to the back patio, which was the most gorgeous space I'd ever seen. There was a brick patio with tables, chairs, and planters filled with colorful flowers. And a sparkling pool with lush landscaping that looked like it was the garden of Eden. It seemed as if the Castellanos had created their own version of paradise.

We approached the table where an older gentleman and mature woman - who looked considerably younger than the man - sat. The man abruptly stood up. "Jay, my boy."

Jay let go of my hand and embraced who I presumed was his father. His mother followed suit, giving him kisses on his cheeks and a tight squeeze. "Oh, Jay, it's so good to see you."

"It's good to see you too and Mom, Dad, I want you to meet Anastasia. Anastasia, these are my parents Sal and Edna Castellano."

I extended my hand to shake Mr. Castellano's hand. "It's nice to meet you, sir."

He glanced down at my hand. "You can call me Sally." And then he gave me a bear hug.

I turned to his mother, and she gave me a kiss on each cheek before a light embrace. "Welcome, Anastasia. We're so happy to finally meet you. Jay has told us all about you, and I'm so excited to get to know you. I've always wanted a daughter."

My heart fluttered. "Thank you. I'm looking forward to getting to know you, too."

"Aren't you a doll? I can tell Jay lucked out the day he met you. Well done, Jay," she said to her son. "Please have a seat and join us. Maria is going to be serving lunch soon."

I glanced over at Jay. He gave me a wink.

Sitting down to eat with my future mother- and father-in-law, I couldn't wait for Jay to meet my mom and dad too. It wouldn't be as spectacular as this scene, but I thought my mom and dad would really love Jay.

We had decided to keep our engagement quiet until they could meet in person. Jay was a little old-fashioned and said that he wanted to ask my dad's permission to marry me before officially announcing our engagement. He was so sweet and thoughtful like that. He said he didn't want to upset my dad, but he couldn't help but propose when he did to make sure that I wanted him for the rest of his life. It was so romantic.

Over lunch, I learned all about the Castellano family. Sally ran a cement company and had a few construction companies, too. Edna was a homemaker and loved to entertain. I had been concerned I wouldn't fit in with their lavish life, but they were so warm and welcoming it was as if I was already part of the family.

I woke up the next morning in the Castellano guest house with a horrible feeling in my belly. I looked over at a sleeping Jay before I ran into the bathroom and released all the contents of my stomach.

Within minutes, Jay had rushed into the bathroom. "Are you okay?"

I groaned. "I think I have food poisoning."

"Maybe, but I feel fine, and we ate the same thing yesterday."

"I don't know what it is, then."

"Can I get you anything? Water? Crackers?"

"Water, please."

As I sat on the cold bathroom floor, hunched over the toilet, I glanced around the bathroom and fixated on the cabinet. It looked a lot like the cabinets in the bathroom in my apartment. The cabinet where I kept my... And then it hit me. Maybe this wasn't food poisoning at all. It couldn't be - could it?

14

MARTINA

After performing the mathematical calculation in my head, I knew it was true. "Anastasia left New York in October. Ryder was born in May of the next year."

Hirsch said, "Eight months later."

"Exactly. Ryder isn't Demetri's biological son."

"Unless Anastasia and Demetri actually met in New York. And that's why Jay and Anastasia broke up. But if that were true, wouldn't Marcy have told us Ana had met a new guy or that she was pregnant?"

It was a good point. Unless Ana had kept things from her roommate, too. I pulled out the photo of Ryder from the binder and then one of Demetri and slid it over to Hirsch. "Maybe. Maybe not. Ryder shares no physical characteristics with Demetri. It's possible but unusual for a biological parent and child. He definitely resembles his mother and has the same olive skin, dark hair, and brown eyes that are typical of an Italian like Jay."

Hirsch countered again. "But Anastasia's family is also Italian."

I conceded. "True."

"If what you say is true, it still doesn't explain Anastasia and Ryder's disappearance. Unless you think Jay came back for his son and took them both? And then did what with them?"

"Or maybe she never told him about the baby and then he somehow found out and came for him. They struggled, and she died, and he took Ryder. Or he didn't want the baby, and that's why they broke up, and then maybe five years later, he rethinks everything. Now that he's older and finished with school, he decides he wants his son." Both scenarios seemed far-fetched. Although, I'd bet my morning coffee Ryder was Jay's biological son.

"It's possible," Hirsch said, skeptically.

"We need to talk to Jay Castellano."

Hirsch said, "Does Vincent's report have Jay's contact information?"

"Yep. It has the law firm phone number, but it says the home and cell phone numbers aren't listed."

Hirsch said, "I'll call his office now and see if we can get Jay on the phone. Maybe he'll provide insight into why his ex-fiancé went missing ten years ago."

I pushed the paper that had the name of Jay's law firm and phone number on it over to Hirsch.

He dialed the number, and I watched as he straightened his posture. "Hello, my name is Detective Hirsch, and I'd like to speak with Jay Castellano, please."

Hirsch nodded before giving his contact information and ending the call. Setting the phone back down on the table, he reported, "The receptionist said Jay is out of the office and didn't know when he would return."

"That's strange." Wouldn't the receptionist of a major law firm know a partner's schedule? Or had they instructed the receptionist to lie?

Hirsch nodded. "It is."

"We need to find Jay Castellano." Like yesterday. I knew in my gut that Jay was somehow connected to Ana and Ryder's disappearance, but I didn't know how. Or was I grasping at straws since there weren't many other likely scenarios?

Hirsch said, "It may take more than a phone call to get Jay to talk to us. I'm guessing he's pretty close-lipped talking to a police officer, and he may dodge all our calls in order to thwart any attempts at us interviewing him about Anastasia and Ryder or any other illegal thing he might be mixed up in."

"Sounds like we're going to New York."

"Yep. We need to call our buddies at the FBI to get more information before making arrangements. Maybe they could get eyes on Jay before we head out."

"Works for me. I'll leave you to it. Zoey has a Girl Scout meeting tonight, and I said I would be there."

"Well, you can't miss that."

I was lucky to have such an understanding partner. Zoey had wanted me to be a Girl Scout leader from her first year in the Brownies. Not having the time, we compromised, and I attended all the events parents were invited to. "I certainly can't. Let me know if you find anything interesting about Jay Castellano. I'll have my cell on me."

"You bet. Tell Zoey and your mom I said hi."

"Will do." I grabbed my backpack and exited the station. I contemplated how difficult it would be to find Jay and then get him to give us the answers that we needed to find Anastasia and Ryder. Assuming, of course, that he knew where they were. But considering his underworld connections and the secretive nature of their relationship, I was highly suspicious of Jay and the Castellano family.

Or had we gotten it all wrong? Maybe Jay had nothing to do with Anastasia and Ryder's disappearance. Maybe Demetri found out Ryder wasn't his biological child and that Anastasia had tricked him into marriage. Had Ana told Demitri Ryder was his biological child? I turned around and hurried back into the station. Inside the squad room, I found Hirsch studying his laptop.

He glanced up. "Back already?"

"We need to re-interview Demetri."

"Do you think he didn't know that Ryder wasn't his biological child? He found out and then did something to Anastasia and Ryder?" Hirsch asked.

Maybe he had already thought that? Was I losing my touch? I said, "Anything's possible. It's strange he didn't mention that Ryder wasn't his. I mean, both he and the family said they didn't know that Anastasia had a significant relationship in New York. Yet she was most likely pregnant when she left."

"And we're sure Ryder wasn't premature?" Hirsch asked.

It was a good point. I looked up at the clock. Shoot. "Can you ask Vincent to pull Ryder's birth certificate? And the Halls' marriage license? I have to go."

Hirsch said, "I'll request the birth certificate, the marriage license, and I'll call Demetri to let him know we need to talk to him again. You go to the Girl Scout meeting - I don't want you to have an angry Zoey on your hands."

"Thanks. Call me when you get an appointment time for a meeting with Demetri."

"Will do. Now go."

I waved and hurried back out to the parking lot. I needed to solve the case, but I also needed to make it to the Girl Scout meeting because my Zoey was the most important thing in my world. Hirsch had helped me prioritize her. He knew how important it was for me to be there for her when I could. He seemed willing to step in and take on the extra hours if I needed to leave early. Maybe that's why I was pushing him to go out with Kim - so he could have some personal time. And maybe I felt a little guilty too. I would be happy to cover for him, like he did for me countless times before. I didn't want to think our partnership was unbalanced. It was nice to have a partner so that I could see Zoey's face light up when I was with the other moms plotting out the annual cookie drive or the next campout. With my village of Hirsch and my mom, I was becoming the mom that I needed and wanted to be for Zoey.

15

HIRSCH

AFTER I TOOK A DEEP BREATH, I PICKED UP MY PHONE. Every day, I dealt with criminals, murderers, and drug dealers. So, why did I find this to be so scary? I stared at the screen. Three letters K-I-M. KIM. Martina's mom's bingo buddy's daughter. Betty swore that Kim and I would be a perfect couple. Not that she had ever met Kim, but Betty said she was quite fond of her mother.

Everything I had heard about Kim from Betty seemed pretty good, but you never knew the real story until you met a person. Despite dating a lot in my twenties and then getting married and divorced in my late thirties, I never thought dating felt natural. Part of me thought that when you met the right person, it would be effortless and just happen, like in one of those stupid romantic comedy movies. Not that I'd ever admit that to anyone.

I didn't feel lonely, but all I did was work, and I knew that wasn't healthy. Plus, I did like the company of a woman. It wouldn't kill me to try dating again. It had been several months since my first attempt after my divorce. The woman and I both decided it wasn't a love match and went our separate ways, amicably. Would things end that way with Kim?

Come on, Hirsch, you can do this. I pressed call and held the phone up to my ear. Listening to the ring tone, I wondered what Kim looked like. Of course, Betty said she was a knockout, but who knew what that meant, anyway. And looks weren't the most important thing anyhow. If I were being true to myself, I'd like to meet somebody I could have a pleasant conversation with – that didn't include reality TV or murder.

"Hello?"

"Hi, is this Kim?"

"Yes, who is this?"

"My name's August. I got your phone number from Betty Kolze. She plays bingo with your mom." That sounded much more lame out loud that in my head.

"Oh, yes, the detective, right?"

"I am."

"Oh, I'm glad you called. Based on what my mother said, I'd assume at this hour, you'd still be at work. She says you work all the time."

I glanced around the Cold Case Squad Room. It was empty except for me, which was usually how the day ended for me. Alone in the office, working late, while others went home to their families or had fun with their friends. "Well, I'm actually still at the office, but I wanted to call you to see if you'd like to have dinner. Maybe this weekend?"

"I'd love that."

"There's this great tapas place that just opened. I heard good things. Would you be interested in meeting there?"

"That sounds great. I love tapas and sangria."

A casual dinner with a little red wine sangria sounded great. It had been a while since I'd been out to the bar after work. Martina was a recovering alcoholic, so usually our post-work socializing was at her house when Betty made us dinner or grabbing a coffee or lunch during the day. I realized maybe I ought to ask some of the non-alcoholic folks out for a drink once in a while. Vincent sure had earned one this past week. He'd been a dynamo on the Hall case. Of course, I could invite Martina too. I wasn't sure about the protocol there. But she also had a child and a dog at home to spend time with.

Actually, I was looking forward to going out with Kim. It would be nice to have a conversation that wasn't about work or people who were missing or kidnapped or murdered. "Great. I look forward to meeting you, Kim."

"Me too."

After we exchanged additional details, I hung up the phone and realized I was smiling. We didn't have a long conversation, but Kim seemed upbeat, friendly, and somebody who may like to have fun or go hiking or play Scrabble. Did I really want to meet someone? Maybe I did. Maybe I had been hiding away at the job instead of moving on with or, more like, *getting* a personal life. Sure, buddies invited me to their house for barbe-cues and dinners and to football games. But they were all family men. I was the only single and divorced man among my group of friends.

Admittedly, watching Martina with Zoey, I was a little jeal-ous. Zoey was a great kid. Despite how young she was, she loved to have conversations with adults and always wanted to know more about our cases and what it was like to be a detective. Insightful, energetic, and youthful. What would it be like to have my own child? I thought I didn't want kids, with an aware-ness of all the atrocities in the world. How could I bring a child into that? Not to mention a daughter. All the horrific things that happen to women, I'd have to put a GPS device on my child. I didn't think I could handle it if something bad happened. As it was, I'd lost a brother to violent crime and wasn't sure I could survive losing a child, too.

Enough contemplation for one night. I should at least go home and heat up something from the freezer. My phone buzzed. I recognized the number but was surprised by it. "Hey, Agent Deeley."

"Hirsch, how is it going?"

"Pretty good. How are things in Pennsylvania?"

"Not too shabby. I was calling you back, and it's good timing because I need to follow up with Martina and you on the Henley case."

"Oh?"

"Everything's pretty much wrapped up, but there were some open questions on the Henley estate, and I need a statement from you and Martina. It doesn't have to be right now, but if you have some time, I'd be happy to clear it up. I'm guessing you're with Martina now?"

"No, she went home already. She's at her daughter's Girl Scout meeting."

"Okay, well, if the two of you could call me back, I just have a few questions regarding some things you learned about Senator Henley when Martina and you came out to Pennsylvania earlier this year. I can set up a conference call sometime this week."

I said, "Sure. No problem. So, I was calling because..." I explained the Anastasia Hall missing persons case and the ties to the Castellano family in New York. "I was wondering if you have contacts at the FBI office in New York or if you're familiar with the New York mob scene?"

"Oh, I am familiar."

Exactly what I was hoping to hear. "Martina and I want to go out to New York to question Jay Castellano in person. If there is a crew watching him, it would be nice to get eyes on him to make sure he's there before we hop on a plane."

"We do. It's some highly confidential stuff, but we have a joint task force that I'm on. We can meet with you when you come out to New York. PA is only a forty-five minute drive into the city. It might be good for the two of you to meet here in Pennsylvania first. I can talk to the agents working out of the Manhattan office and get you the information you need. We have our monthly meeting coming up anyway. We can coordinate it, so the meeting is scheduled for when you and Martina are in town."

Adrenaline pumping, I said, "That would be awesome. Thanks, Deeley."

"No problem."

"I'll call you back when Martina is in the office tomorrow, and we can set up details to go over what you need on the Henley case and schedule our trip to the big apple."

"Excellent. You take care, Hirsch."

"You too and if you see Callahan around the office, tell him I said hi."

"Will do."

After ten years and zero leads into the whereabouts of Ana and Ryder, we now had a potential lead into what may have happened to her. Not to mention an FBI task force to help us find the truth.

Had Demetri found out that Ryder wasn't his biological son and took revenge on both of them? I doubted it. Or had Ana's past caught up with her and the mob had something to do with her disappearance? Or had Jay Castellano found out Ryder was his biological son and come to reclaim what was his and took Ana in the process?

16

MARTINA

STANDING IN FRONT OF THE HOME OF DEMITRI AND ANA Hall, I couldn't help but feel a little sad. A mother and father and a child with a perfect life had it all taken away in nearly an instant. Based on our previous conversation with Demitri, it did not surprise me he hadn't moved from their home after Ana and Ryder went missing. He had claimed he was waiting for them to come back. He had never given up on them, so we wouldn't either. I, for one, was interested in finding out if he knew Ryder wasn't his biological child, assuming he wasn't. The only way he could be the boy's father was if Demitri and Ana had met while she was in New York or Ryder had been born significantly premature.

After finishing his call in the car, Hirsch met me at the curb. "You ready?"

"Almost. How did he sound on the phone when you told him we wanted to talk to him again?"

"Eager to help in any way he could. He sounded hopeful that we had new information."

"Which we do, but I'm not sure we should share it all yet."

Hirsch agreed. "No, we shouldn't. I say we ask about paternity of Ryder and leave it at that until we have more information about Jay Castellano and the possible connection to her disappearance."

"Okay. Before we go in. What do you guess? Do you think Demitri knows Ryder's paternity?"

Hirsch nodded. "My guess is he knew Ryder wasn't his biological child before he married Ana."

It was always interesting to get Hirsch's male perspective. "Why?"

"As a scientist, he's smart and could have put the timeline together. I'm guessing he can subtract from when he met Ana and when she gave birth to Ryder."

"I agree, but maybe it's deeper than that. Maybe he was fine raising another man's son, as long as nobody else knew. Maybe the biological father came back in the picture and wanted to be part of Ryder's life, and Demitri didn't like it."

Hirsch squinted. "I'm skeptical."

Boy, Hirsch certainly seemed to have a high opinion of Demitri. I said, "You don't think Demitri had anything to do with Ana and Ryder's disappearance, do you?"

"I don't. That doesn't mean we can rule him out yet, but my gut is saying Demitri had nothing to do with their disappearance. I think he's deeply sad and still grieving that they have been gone for the last ten years. I believe he is, in fact, standing vigil and waiting for their return."

"That's interesting though, isn't it? That after ten years, he still thinks they are alive and not that they're dead, which is the most likely outcome." Unfortunately, the statistics didn't lie.

Hirsch said, "You're right. Probably most people would assume the worst, but I would think that you of all people would know that despite the statistics, there is always hope. Until you know for sure there isn't."

Hirsch was right. Even after more than a decade had passed,

part of me had still believed we would find my best friend who had gone missing after high school, happy and living her best life somewhere. On the outside, I had told myself she was most likely dead, but when her death was confirmed, I realized how much I had still believed or hoped that she would be alive. "Okay, let's go talk to Demitri and get his side of the story."

Hirsch led the way up to the front door. Before he could knock, the door opened, and Demitri stood there in sweatpants and a T-shirt. "Detective Hirsch, Ms. Monroe, please come in."

I looked over at Hirsch, who shrugged. Demitri must've seen us outside talking, and it made me wonder if he was nervous about today's interview.

He led us into the home, sitting us down at the dining table. "Can I get you anything? I think I have coffee, tea, water, and I might have some orange juice."

Hirsch said, "I'm fine. Thank you."

I said, "No, I'm fine too. Thank you, Demitri."

He mindlessly sat down in front of us. The two times we had interviewed him before, he was at his place of work wearing a button-up shirt and trousers, looking professional and put together. But the man before me wasn't that. He was pale with dark circles under his eyes and there was a haunted look about him.

"What is it you want to ask me about? Did you find out anything new?" he said, with hope in his voice.

"We've re-reviewed the case file and the notes about how you and Ana met, and then we looked at Ryder's age." Hirsch paused.

Demitri shut his eyes and reopened them. It was as if he knew why we were there and what we were asking. "Yes, when I first met Ana, she was pregnant with Ryder. He isn't my biological son, but he *is* my son."

Good thing I hadn't put a wager on Demitri's response. I

would have owed Hirsch a coffee. "You were okay with raising another man's child? Or being married to a pregnant woman?" I asked, somewhat skeptically.

"I love Ana and, even then, there was something about her and the baby that I had a deep connection to. I knew there was always a chance that Ryder would find out I wasn't his biological father, but I did everything a real father does. You know, like getting up in the middle of the night with him when he cried or needed a bottle or a diaper change. I helped coach his T-ball team, and I took him to his first day of kindergarten. I taught him how to catch frogs and tadpoles. When he had an ear infection, I gave him medicine. No, ma'am, we didn't share DNA, but we had something stronger. And no, I didn't mind because of how much I love Ana and then Ryder. I'm sure you can see that I'm a bit older than Ana. Before I met her, I had given up on the idea of having a wife and children. But when we met, and I found out she was pregnant, I was more than happy. I'd always hoped for a family, and the fact that there wasn't a biological connection no longer mattered. We were happy. Really happy."

Wow. Had Jared loved me like that? I mean, I knew he loved me, but it was easy back then. We were young and in love. Would he still have married me if I were pregnant with another man's child? How many men would do that? So far, my count was at one - Demitri Hall.

Hirsch's expression was thoughtful, as if Demitri reminded him of the things he didn't have either. That reminded me, I needed to ask him about his upcoming date with Kim. I could definitely see Hirsch as a father. As much as he said he wouldn't bring a child into this disturbed world, I was not sure I bought it or he did either. "Okay, so you knew Ryder wasn't your biological child going in. Do you know who Ryder's biological father is?" I asked.

He shook his head sadly. "No. Ana said Ryder resulted from a one-night stand. A wild night in New York."

"Did she give you his name or a description of what the man looked like or where she met him?" Hirsch asked.

"No. She didn't like talking about it. She said it was a mistake and that she was embarrassed because she had been drunk and let things go too far. The first time she told me about Ryder's conception was the only time we ever spoke of his biological father. She didn't like talking about it, and I didn't press the issue."

Hirsch side-eyed me. *Yeah, yeah. He was right. Demitri had nothing to do with the disappearance of his wife and child.* He *was* a good man who had lost the love of his life and his only son. "Is there anything else you can tell us about Ryder's paternal biological family that you think may help?" I asked.

"You think maybe his biological father did this?" Demitri asked.

I said, "We don't know. We're following all leads."

"You have other leads?" Demitri asked.

"We have a few avenues that we're going to explore. But for now, that's all we can tell you."

"I understand. If there's anything else I can help with, please don't hesitate to stop by. I just want them to come home."

I nodded as I tried to maintain my composure. I understood his grief, and I knew it well. The poor man had been grieving for ten years. It made me question if it ever got better.

We thanked him for his time, exited his home, and returned to the confines of Hirsch's vehicle. I said, "Okay, you were right. My gut is screaming that he had nothing to do with their disappearance."

"Told you. Now we just have to prove it."

"Exactly. I think it's interesting that Ana refused to discuss

Ryder's biological father." Assuming Demitri was telling the truth about that. At this point, I was inclined to believe him.

"You caught that."

I said, "The secrecy around her relationship with Jay Castellano and Ryder's paternity can't be a coincidence. Who knows? Maybe Ana cheated on Jay with the one night stand and that was why they broke up?"

"Maybe. Let's call Deeley and set up the meeting. My gut is saying our answers are in New York City."

I nodded. Unfortunately, I agreed with Hirsch. The unfortunate part was that if we were right and Ana's disappearance was related to organized crime in New York City, it didn't seem likely there would be a joyful reunion for anybody.

17

ANASTASIA - SIX YEARS BEFORE SHE VANISHED

Hands shaking, I reached out to pick up the stick, but I was too afraid to look. I yelled out, "Marcy!"

She barged into the bathroom and said, "What is it?"

"I can't look. Will you look at it for me? Please."

Marcy nodded and stepped toward the counter and glanced down at the stick before picking it up with just her pointer finger and thumb. "It's positive."

My heart dropped. How could this have happened? Jay and I had been careful, hadn't we? There was that one night. Oh, and that other night I slept over. How did I think this wouldn't happen? There was something about once Jay got me started, I couldn't stop. He was intoxicating, and I was helpless to his embrace. Those few times I had missed taking my pills when I'd stayed over at his place had most likely contributed to the situation. "Are you sure it's positive?"

Marcy gritted her teeth and said, "Sorry," before handing me the stick.

Taking it, I hoped she was wrong, and she didn't know how to read these very easy to interpret tests. *Dang.* There was no mistaking it. Two lines. The test was positive. But this was just an at-home test. Surely a blood test would be more accurate than a test I bought at the drugstore. "I'm going to take another test just to make sure it's accurate. Sometimes these things can be wrong." I knew the tests were 99.7% accurate, but there was still that 0.3% chance that the test was wrong.

Marcy left the bathroom and said, "Good luck," and waved as she closed the door.

How had I been so careless? I was a nurse and knew what could happen if I missed more than one pill in a month. I had been so swept away by Jay's loving embrace and our plans for the future. For the two of us. Eek. The three of us. Oh, jeez, what if it was multiples? Twins? Triplets? Would that be my luck? No, that couldn't happen. The test had to be wrong.

I squatted down over the toilet and retested midstream, one test after another. Good thing I had purchased a three pack of tests. It's more statistically significant to do three tests. One test could be wrong, but three tests couldn't be wrong.

When I was finished, I set them down on the counter next to the positive one and paced the bathroom as I waited for the tests to reveal my fate. Was I too young to be a mother? I certainly felt too young, and I didn't feel ready. I had always planned on having children one day, after I was married for a while, and then boom, maybe have one or two children. It was a dream, a far-off dream, not a right now dream. Not a living in New York City, engaged to a handsome, successful soon-to-be lawyer dream. No, this was too soon. Too early. This was five, ten years too early. How would I tell Jay? How would he react?

I gathered up my courage and walked back over to the vanity counter and glanced down at my three tests. My three identical tests with matching results. A wave of nausea flowed through me. It was true. I was pregnant. *Pregnant.*

I was going to have a child. Scratch that, Jay and I were

going to have a child - a human baby. A baby who wiggled and cried and relied on us to be their parents. I had to tell Jay.

A light knocking on the door drew me out of my fit. "Everything okay in there?" Marcy asked.

Sucking in my breath, I decided I was going to be brave because I was going to be a mother. *A mother*. I twisted the door handle and opened the door. "They're all positive."

Marcy sank into her shoulders. "Congratulations?"

"I guess?" I asked the universe.

Marcy asked, "When will you tell Jay?"

Feeling faint, I said, "I don't know. Tonight, he's picking me up and taking me out to dinner. Please don't tell anyone - ever. I'm not sure what we'll do, and if we keep the baby, we may decide to keep it a secret until after we're married."

Assuming Jay would still want me. What would he say?

"Your secret is safe with me. Are you okay?" Marcy asked.

"I don't know. I kind of feel numb. Is it normal to feel numb? Shouldn't I feel something?"

"Paralyzed with fear?" Marcy asked.

That was it. Fear. I was afraid. Afraid of how Jay would react to the pregnancy. Afraid of telling my parents. I was going to be a mother, and I wasn't married yet. "I think that's probably right."

"Any idea how far along you are?"

"My guess is maybe two months, if that."

My period had been a little over a week late, so I was likely only six to eight weeks pregnant with the baby. There was going to be a little Jay or little Anastasia. I didn't know what we would do. But suddenly, something came over me, and a warm feeling flushed through my body. *My baby*. I was going to have a baby. Tears streamed down my face, and it was as if the world stood still. Marcy wrapped her arms around me and squeezed. She let go and looked into my eyes. I said, "I'm having a baby."

"Yes, you are. And you're going to be the best mother I know. The best."

I nodded. I had to tell Jay.

A few hours later, I was freshly showered, dressed, and sitting on the sofa with Marcy waiting for Jay to arrive to pick me up for dinner. I had decided to tell him that night because I didn't think I could keep something like that from him, and I'd rather know his response right away instead of having to wait hours or days or weeks. I needed to know how he felt about the baby. Would he love it and move forward with our plans to be married? I wasn't sure. A knock on the door caused my heart to race. I said, "I'll get it."

"All right, I'll go in my room. Let me know if you need me, okay?"

"Thanks, Marcy."

At the front door, I took a deep breath before opening it. With the door open, I smiled at Jay. He said, "Hey. You look amazing," before leaning in for a kiss. He pulled back. "Are you ready to go?"

"Actually, there is something I want to talk to you about. Can you come in?"

"Of course. What is it?"

Without answering, I led him over to the sofa and sat facing him. I said, "I got some news today."

"Oh?" he asked, looking concerned.

It's now or never. "Jay, I'm pregnant."

His eyes widened, and he covered his mouth with his hand. He shook his head and then dropped his hand before grabbing mine. "You're sure we're having a baby?"

"Yes. I took three tests."

He grinned. "We're having a baby. I'm the luckiest man on Earth."

"So, you're happy about it?"

"Yes. I mean, it's a little soon, but we're already getting married and plan to be together. We'll work it out. This is just God's way of letting us know we're meant to be and that there's going to be three of us."

Through my tears, I chuckled. "I hope there's only one. I'm not sure if I could handle twins."

He pulled me close. "Anastasia, I'm so happy."

I said, "I'm glad."

He leaned back. "Are you happy? Or are you freaking out?"

"Yes, and yes. I'm freaking out, but I'm happy too." And when I said it, I knew it was true. The love I felt for this baby already was so immense, and I had this man. This wonderful man. I should've never doubted how he would respond. Yes, I was scared to be a parent but also excited to have a partner - a husband - a wonderful man by my side. What else could I possibly ask for?

18

HIRSCH

WITH A SIGH, I HUNG UP THE PHONE. IT WASN'T GREAT news but there was nothing I could do about it. All I could do was look forward to and think about the good things in life. Like trying to figure out what happened to Anastasia and Ryder. And like Kim. Like having dinner conversation with her that didn't include murder or forensics. It was fast and sudden and surprising, but I was smitten with her. Tapas and sangria had been such a hit that neither of us wanted the night to end. I invited her back to my place where we talked half the night and then woke the next morning, still in our clothes. We had drifted off on the couch while chatting and pretending to watch a movie. She had agreed to stick around while I went out to buy breakfast and then we ate at my dining table for the first time. It was easy and light and engaging. I had even snagged a goodbye kiss on her way out. Man, she was great. It had been a long time since I meshed with someone so well and so quickly. Kim was smart, funny, optimistic, and *gorgeous*. It was probably a good thing Martina and I were leaving for New York because I thought my big crush on Kim would lead me to do stupid things like asking her out again - for that night. If Kim were a drug, I'd be an addict. Man, I needed to slow it down and take my time. It had only been one - kind of two dates.

Maybe one day I would owe Betty a thank you, but I planned to give it some time before sending flowers. I didn't want to jinx the situation. As much as I was enamored with Kim, I wasn't sure how she felt about me. Wasn't that the worst part about dating? I finally found someone I liked and then I wasn't sure how she felt about me. And if I were to ask her, I would come off as needy or insecure. This ball of anxiety was all Betty's fault. No flowers for Betty. Lost in my thoughts, I didn't even notice Martina walk into the Cold Case Squad Room. "Hey, Hirsch. How's it going?"

"Neutral to better than neutral."

She sat her coffee cup down on the table and then slid onto the chair. "Do tell."

"I just got off the phone with the DA. Andy Tomlinson is out on bail. His lawyer and Tracy's lawyers claim that her confession was coerced, and they had absolutely nothing to do with his wife's death."

"Then how did Tracy know where her body was buried?" Martina asked.

"The lawyers claim that Tracy guessed."

Martina shook her head. "No way."

"Forensics aren't back yet, so we haven't linked him physically to the crime. All we have right now is Tracy's word against his. And, get this, now she's saying she won't cooperate."

"Where is Tracy now?" Martina asked.

"She's out on bail, too."

"What about the kids? Are they still with Darla's parents?"

"Yep."

"Small favors. Anything we can do to get them both behind bars for good?" Martina asked.

"The DA says to sit tight and wait for the forensics to come back. Chances are, Andy left some physical evidence behind. They are going back to search the house again, as well."

"Great."

"Are you ready for our trip to New York?"

"My bags are packed. Literally, they're in the trunk of my car."

Of course they were. She easily could have taken thirty minutes to swing by her house to pick the luggage up on the way to the airport. Our flight didn't leave for another five hours, but leave it to Martina to be ready to jet at a moment's notice. "I hope we get lucky and get the answers we need for Ana and Ryder in New York. Our meeting is set with the FBI tomorrow?"

"Yep, we'll meet Deeley and his colleagues from the New York office, bright and early."

"It's a good thing you have friends just about everywhere."

I chuckled. "You're one to talk. The last time I checked, your Rolodex was getting pretty full."

"I suppose I've made a few friends here and there." Martina studied my face. "Hey. How was your date with Kim?"

My cheeks burned, and I couldn't wipe the stupid smile from my face. "It was good."

"Oh, really? Do tell!" Martina said, with a sparkle in her eyes.

"I saw her the next day too..." Despite my embarrassment over my boyish crush, I told Martina about what a great night we had.

"So, you're going to see her again?"

"I sure hope so."

"Have you asked her out again?"

"Not yet. I figure I'll call her when we get back from New York."

"Oh, come on, Hirsch, call her now, and ask her out for

when we're back from New York. You don't want to go too long without talking to her. She might think you're not interested."

Not that I didn't think Martina was wise on relationships, but I guess I hadn't occurred to me to ask for her womanly advice. She didn't date, and she had been married for quite a while before she became a widow. "You think?"

"I absolutely think so. Come on, you must be better at dating than this."

"I don't know. I've started to question my judgement."

Martina shook her head. "Look, it's normal to be a little scared. But if she's as great as you say she is, you want to make sure she knows how you feel about her. You don't want to come back from New York and some other guy has swept her off her feet. You snooze, you lose, buddy."

"Okay, I'll call her when we get to the airport."

Martina grinned at me. "Good man."

Later that afternoon, we were about to leave for the airport when Vincent approached. "Hey, Hirsch, Martina."

"What's up?" I asked.

"I continued searching through Jay Castellano's digital trail and found some interesting things."

"What did you find?" Martina asked.

"Well, I called over to your contact at the FBI to get the okay to check into Jay Castellano's credit card statements."

"And?" Martina asked.

"From there, I checked for airline reservations and other unusual purchases. Our friend Jay Castellano not only bought an airline ticket approximately ten years ago, but he has also been buying the same airline tickets at least once a year for the last ten years."

"Where are the flights to?" I asked.

"Bay Area."

"Which airport did he fly into?" Martina asked.

"San Jose."

I glanced over at Martina. "Deeley said that there's a sizable organized crime presence in San Jose. Jay could've been providing legal counsel to borgata members on the west coast."

Martina said, "Maybe. Are there records of where he stayed?"

Vincent said, "No hotel reservations that I could find."

That was peculiar. Business trips usually included car rental and hotel. Maybe one of the mafia family members picked him up from the airport and he stayed with them. It wasn't terribly unusual from what I understood about how the borgatas operated. "Thanks, Vincent. Anything else interesting in his statements?" I asked.

"Just one. A big purchase at a jewelry store before his last trip."

"Really?" Martina asked.

"Yep. It was such a large purchase, I called the store and asked what they had in that price range."

"And?" Martina asked

"They gave me a hassle, and we did a bit of back-and-forth before they would give me information about what Jay Castellano purchased, but finally, they told me what *somebody* bought on *that* day for *that* price."

Martina and I looked at each other. Vincent had a way of keeping us on the edge of our seat when he was giving us news, but he was really dragging this one out. "Okay, Vincent, give it to us."

"The last time he was in California, Jay Castellano bought an engagement ring."

"An engagement ring?" I asked the room. According to the FBI, Jay was single. Maybe they didn't know as much about him as they thought. Or maybe he had a girlfriend, but she wasn't in New York.

Martina said, "Maybe the FBI was wrong. Even though their intel doesn't indicate any women or a family or girlfriend, maybe he does have someone."

"Interesting. Thanks, Vincent." I turned to Martina. "We have one more question for Jay when we get to New York." Who was Jay Castellano planning to marry? Perhaps we needed to track down the lucky lady while we were in New York.

19

MARTINA

STANDING ON THE CURB OUTSIDE OF JOHN F. KENNEDY airport in New York City, I watched person after person climb into yellow taxicabs. The air was cool with a slight breeze, a nice reprise from the warmer weather back in the Bay Area. It wasn't my first time in New York, but it was the first time since I'd visited with Jared. It had been a quick trip when we were on leave from the Army. Both of us were young, wide-eyed, and optimistic. The memory made me smile. I supposed that was progress, that thinking of Jared made me thankful for the fond memory instead of filling me with sadness.

Hearing Hirsch gush about his date with Kim, I could tell he had it bad for her. I could hardly remember what that first rush of love and attraction was like. Would I ever feel that way again? It wasn't something I thought of much, but seeing that extra spring in Hirsch's step reminded me what it was like in those early days of falling in love. I was happy for Hirsch and who knows, maybe one day, far - far away, I would have that again. I knew Jared wouldn't have wanted me to be alone or lonely. He would have wanted me to be happy in a relationship, and maybe I would be one day, but I couldn't imagine that happening any time soon.

Hirsch said, "The shuttle is right up there."

"All right. Let's go."

We hurried with our luggage down the sidewalk toward the hotel shuttle. We were about to cross the street when two men stopped us. "Hey, yous. Aren't yous the guys on the TV looking for the missing lady and her kid?" the portlier of the two said, with a distinctly Italian accent.

Before I could answer, the other man said, "Yeah, yous two are from California, right?"

Hirsch and I exchanged glances. My adrenaline pumped. This wasn't normal. Not that Hirsch and I didn't get noticed occasionally when we were out. We had been on the news for press conferences. Our faces were recognizable by some who followed the news. And yes, we had announced when new cases were being reopened, especially when it was a missing person, in the hopes that someone would come forward and give us information they weren't comfortable giving us ten years ago but were okay with it now. However, I wouldn't have expected to be recognized in New York and within moments of touching down. We needed to discuss this with Sarge and the department media liaison. After less than a year, we were now being targeted due to our familiarity. The letter from Mrs. Fennelli to reopen her daughter's case was one thing, but being stopped three thousand miles from home by who I could only describe as a couple of old school thugs didn't sit well with me. Our notoriety needed to end. I said, "Yeah, that's right. Do you have any information on the case that could help us?"

The bigger guy said, "Oh, no. We don't know nothin'."

Glancing over at Hirsch and then back at our welcoming committee, I said, "Well, then, we'll be on our way."

"Yous two have a real good time in New York, and be safe," the skinny one said, with a menacing grin.

The other one snickered as they sauntered off.

Hirsch and I didn't speak again until after we hauled our luggage onto the shuttle and seated ourselves away from the other passengers. "What do you think of those two? My gut says they're either the NYC welcoming committee *or* they were two members of the Castellano borgata, letting us know we're being watched."

Hirsch said, "I'm going to guess the latter, and I didn't like it. Not one bit."

"I didn't either."

Did the mob have our airline itinerary? How would they know that? And why did they care? I watched as Hirsch pulled a notepad out of his blazer pocket and began sketching.

"Drawing our new friends?" I asked.

"Yep. While it's fresh in my mind."

Smart. I sat there quietly as the bus motored on. If organized crime was involved in Anastasia and Ryder's disappearance, maybe they were also following the investigation. But why? Why would the mob want to get rid of Anastasia and her five-year-old son? I suspected that's what we were about to find out from our pals at the FBI.

By the time we made it to our hotel, Hirsch had sketched the two men who had stopped us at the airport. The images were surprisingly accurate. "I didn't know you could draw."

Hirsch shrugged. "I doodle."

"You're full of surprises, aren't you?"

"I am. You want to grab a bite to eat in the hotel restaurant before turning in?"

"Sounds like a plan."

THE NEXT MORNING, WE SAT IN A LARGE CONFERENCE room at the FBI's Philadelphia office waiting for the New York FBI members of the organized crime task force to arrive. We chitchatted with Deeley as he explained his latest case and how it connected to the FBI's organized crime task force.

"Never a dull moment for the feds, huh?" Hirsch asked.

"I'm not sure you'd say that if you had to listen to tens of hours of audio recordings. Why? Are you thinking of joining up? We'd be happy to have you," Deeley said with a wide grin.

Deeley was a funny and brilliant special agent we'd met when Hirsch and I worked our first case together. At first glance, you'd think, "I wouldn't mess with him," considering he towered well over six feet tall and had a muscled physique.

Hirsch said, "It may have crossed my mind once or twice."

Hirsch *was* full of surprises. I knew he'd considered the FBI route when he was in college, but I wondered if he had considered it more recently.

Deeley said, "We're always looking for good people. If either of you are interested, just let me know. I'll put in a good word."

I said, "We'll keep that in mind," and hoped Hirsch wasn't seriously interested. If he was, it would be the end of our partnership.

A knock on the door caught Deeley's attention. "That must be them." He got up and opened the door. A group of five people, both men and women in dark suits, entered the conference room. After introductions, we all sat down at the conference table and got right to the task at hand.

The head of the Castellano task force, Special Agent Brosco, a middle-aged woman with dark hair and dark red lips, said, "We understand you're looking into Anastasia Hall's disappearance?"

I said, "Yes, and her son, Ryder. He was five years old at the time, and he'd be fifteen now."

Two of the agents assigned to the Castellano borgata gave each other knowing looks. "You know the kid is Jay's, right?" Special Agent Costanza asked.

Hirsch nodded. "We pieced that together. It's one thing we want to ask him about. We have one theory that maybe he reclaimed his son - if he knew about him."

Brosco said, "I'm fairly certain he knew."

"Why is that?" I asked.

Brosco explained, "We have records on the family going back at least twenty years. It was big news when Jay and Anastasia got engaged. The mob loves a good wedding. They use them not only to celebrate the happy couple but for business, too. Anastasia's sudden departure and the broken engagement were not spoken of... which is strange."

"That doesn't prove Jay knew, but for argument's sake, if Jay knew he had a son, do you think he would've come out to California and snatched the two of them?" Hirsch asked.

Costanza shook his head. "It's not Jay's style. Despite his bloodline, he's a pretty good guy. He keeps his hands pretty clean, but he provides legal representation to his family. Jay also does pro bono work for the Innocence Project. He's like a mobster with a heart of gold."

"Is he a made man?" I asked.

Hirsch gave me a quizzical look. *That's right, I did some research, Hirsch. I can be surprising too.* Becoming a 'Made Man' is only for males of Italian heritage that have proven themselves. From what I had read, the candidates are vetted and have to be sponsored by other made men. They even have a secret induction ceremony that includes rituals and an oath to the borgata. Once you've become made, you can't be killed without the permission of the head of the borgata. Serious stuff.

Brosco said, "No. Jay has stayed clear of any illegal activity.

Rumor has it, it's how his father wanted it. He didn't want Jay to be a criminal."

Hirsch smirked. "Ironic."

Costanza said, "We always want better for our kids, right? Big Sal was no different. He knows the life is dangerous. He loves Jay and is proud he's a college grad. Most of the borgatas are made up of high school dropouts. Big Sal brags about Jay all the time on the tapes."

"Tapes?" Hirsch asked.

Brosco said, "We have bugs all over the city. We planted most of them in their favorite spots to eat and talk business. The borgatas have no idea. So, we hear a lot about what's going on with the five families."

"Any talk about Anastasia and Ryder?" I asked.

Brosco said, "Not a word."

I wasn't sure if that was good news or not. "Really? Not even when we announced we were reopening the investigation?" Hirsch asked.

Brosco said, "No."

"Did anything happen with the Castellanos ten years ago that would've prompted some action against Anastasia?" Hirsch asked.

Deeley said, "I looked it up since you asked me that on the phone. Ten years ago, around when she disappeared, it was the first time we were about to file charges against Big Sal Castellano."

"What were the charges?" Hirsch asked.

"There were several indictments all falling under the RICO laws, but most notable is a murder charge. We had Sal on tape authorizing a hit on a nightclub owner who had refused to pay their protection money. That one hit landed Big Sally murder and racketeering charges. The agents back then were sure they'd finally get him."

"But Big Sal is still a free man, right?" I asked.

Brosco pursed her lips and nodded. "That's the thing. The witnesses disappeared. There were two. One low-level street thug named Vinnie 'the Fig.' Second one was your girl, Anastasia Hall."

I gasped. "Would the mob have taken out a witness and her five-year-old son just to prevent her from testifying?"

Brosco said, "That's one theory, but to be honest, that's not usually how they operate. Yes, they'd kill a witness, but they usually exclude family and children from that kind of brutality. Some families have more of an ethical code than others. The Castellanos are pretty much on the side of don't touch family and kids, and just take out those who they *need* to eliminate. No more, no less. So, although it's a little unusual that they would take out a kid, it's not out of the question."

"And no one talked about taking out Anastasia and Ryder back then?" Hirsch asked.

Costanza said, "Nope. But when we got a hold of Vinnie the Fig, he told us Anastasia had also witnessed the murder. When they both disappeared, it made it obvious there was a hit on both of them."

"Do you have bugs in Jay's office?" I asked.

Costanza explained, "No. We planted the bugs in a couple of key players' vehicles and a dozen restaurants that they frequent. It's not just the Castellanos. All five of the New York families are pretty much under surveillance all the time."

"And they don't know?" Hirsch asked.

Costanza said, "Nope."

We had been told that everything we would hear at the meeting couldn't leave that conference room, and it was clear why. This was the team that was tasked with taking out organized crime in New York City and across the country. It was their life's work, and it had been going on for more than a decade. My guess was they'd only agreed to sit down hoping we had something relating to Anastasia that could point back to the Castellano family and finally indict Big Sal.

"If the family was involved in Anastasia and Ryder's disappearance, do you think they would have used someone local?" I asked.

"My guess is they would have used somebody local to California. There's a pretty big organized crime population in San Jose, San Francisco, and LA. They're pretty much everywhere."

"And you caught that Jay's been going back and forth to California?" Hirsch asked.

Brosco said, "Yeah, he does some legal representation for some of the families out there."

"Does Jay have a license to practice law in California and New York?" I asked.

Brosco said, "He does. He's a smart one. It's a shame he was born into the family he was."

Something wasn't adding up. "Ten years ago, when you were getting ready to indict Big Sal, did you reach out to Anastasia to ask her to testify in the trial?"

Brosco said, "We did."

Nobody mentioned anything about that. Not her husband or her family. Anastasia had kept it secret that she would testify against New York mobsters? Did that mean she'd never intended to testify? "Had she agreed to testify?" I asked.

Brosco said, "She told me she had to think about it."

"Why didn't the FBI contact the CoCo County Sheriff's Department after she disappeared?" Hirsch asked.

Brosco side-eyed Costanza and said, "We thought maybe the mob took her out and didn't want to spotlight the case. It could've jeopardized the entire case."

Bureaucrats. More concerned with closing up the case than helping find a missing woman and her five-year-old child.

Annoyed, under my breath, I said, "That fell through anyway." If the FBI had worked with the original investigators, could the case have been closed all those years ago?

Ignoring my comment, Brosco said, "Did you learn anything from her family or her husband in California about her testifying or maybe running away to avoid the mob?"

Hirsch said, "None of them knew anything about it. They had never even heard of Jay Castellano."

Costanza nodded his head slowly. "You know, it makes sense."

"What does?" Hirsch asked.

"Jay was pretty serious about Anastasia. My guess was after the nightclub murder she witnessed, he sent her packing to keep her, and his unborn child, safe."

Anastasia had witnessed a mob execution, and out of love, Jay broke up with her and ended their engagement? I wasn't sure I was buying this kind-hearted mafioso profile. "Is Jay married?"

Costanza said, "Nope. A confirmed bachelor. He works, he volunteers, and hikes in the Poconos. That's basically all he does."

Then who did he buy the engagement ring for?

"What is it?" Brosco asked.

I said, "Our researcher said Jay bought an engagement ring the last time he was in California."

Brosco said, "Hmm. Maybe he has a girlfriend. Or he's laundering for his family. Sometimes these guys will buy high-ticket items just to launder their money."

I said, "But you said Jay doesn't get involved in the illegal stuff."

Costanza shrugged. "Even the good ones are a little rotten. Maybe Jay has finally turned."

Hirsch said, "Well, we plan to surprise him at his office later today. We'd like to get to know Jay and hear what he has to say about Anastasia."

"Good luck. You want backup?" Deeley asked.

"Is he dangerous?" I asked.

Deeley said, "They're all dangerous. Plus, you told me earlier two guys approached you at the airport."

Hirsch pulled out his drawings and slid them across the table to Brosco and Costanza.

Brosco picked them up and studied the faces. She leaned toward Costanza and spoke too low for me to hear. She sat up and stared at us. "Nice artwork. That there looks like Fat Joe and Four-finger Pete. You'll want back up." She paused. "What did they say to you?"

I said, "They told us they recognized us from the news and the case, and then they told us to have a pleasant visit and to be safe."

Brosco leaned back, as if in thought. She said, "That's strange. It sounds like they knew you were coming and wanted to threaten you."

Hirsch nodded. "That's how we took it. What do you think it means?"

Brosco said, "That you need to watch your backs." She eyed Deeley. "We'll help."

Something was brewing in New York. We knew it and the FBI knew it. But what? What would we learn from Jay?

20

ANASTASIA - SIX YEARS BEFORE SHE VANISHED

THE DOORBELL RANG, AND I HURRIED TO ANSWER IT. I WAS excited and nervous and had all the feels. On my tippy toes, I looked through the peephole and smiled. There he was. My Jay. My future husband and the father of my baby. I opened the door and grinned even wider.

He held a bouquet of red roses in his hands. "You look beautiful, Anastasia. These are for you."

"Thank you, they're so pretty."

He leaned in and put one hand around my waist and pulled me close. He planted a warm, sweet kiss before retreating. "I can't wait to do that for the rest of my life."

"Me too. I'll put these in water."

I hurried to the kitchen and pulled down a vase from the cupboard. As I filled the water, Jay came up behind me, his hands on my waistline. "You know, we could skip dinner and just stay in."

I turned off the faucet and set the vase down on the counter before turning around. "And then what would your family think of me?"

"That you're wonderful."

"And how would they know that if I don't show up for dinner?" I asked.

"Okay. Fine, we'll go to the family dinner."

"Have you told them yet?" I asked.

"Not yet. I think we should give it some time. Let's wait until you're at the twelve-week mark."

"That's what I was thinking too, since at twelve weeks we'll be out of the danger zone."

He nodded. "I know my cousins want to go out for drinks after, so we'll have to slip you a mocktail so it doesn't appear like you're *not* drinking."

"Okay." It was so exciting to have a new life growing inside of me, and it was also kind of fun to keep the secret. I liked that it was something just Jay and I shared.

"Where are we going for dinner?" I asked.

"To one of my family's favorite restaurants. Great food. You'll love it."

I said, "I can't wait," and turned back to the counter to trim the stems off the roses before sticking them in the vase. After, I turned back to Jay. "Okay, I'm ready."

"I have a car downstairs."

I had never dated somebody with money before. Not that I dated people who didn't have any money, but Jay's family had *a lot* of money. He explained they were in the cement business and had contracts all around the city. Apparently, his father had dropped out of high school but still became extremely successful.

When I'd met them at their house, they were so proud of Jay. His father's brown eyes sparkled when he looked at his eldest son. They were such a loving family. They were close and liked to spend time with one another. That night, I'd be meeting his brother- and sister-in-law and a few cousins for the first time. Soon, that family would be mine, too.

Jay hadn't met my family yet since they were in California, but once the semester was over and Jay finished law school, we were going to fly home so they could all meet in person.

I couldn't wait to tell them the news that I was engaged and we were going to have a baby. I thought Mom would be so happy and excited, and my sister would too. Mom had said the greatest joy in her life was her children and that she couldn't wait to be a grandma but that she would because my sister and I were so young. I knew they would be over the moon when they found out there was going to be a new addition to our family.

Jay grabbed me by the hand, and we hurried out of my apartment, ready for a feast with my new family.

***

SEATED NEXT TO JAY AT THE RESTAURANT, I HAD NEVER felt a warmer welcome. I had received kisses on cheeks and hugs from everyone. The dinner was family-style, which was fitting. Jay's mother, Edna, asked, "Will your family be visiting soon? We can't wait to meet them."

I nodded. "We hope to go visit them after Jay graduates, and then I'm sure they'll be happy to fly out."

Jay's father said, "Hopefully before the wedding."

"Of course."

I couldn't wait for my parents to meet the Castellanos and had visions of one big happy family. It sounded silly, like a schoolgirl dream, but really, who was this lucky? The night I met Jay in that nightclub, my entire world changed. I'd been on cloud nine ever since. Other than morning sickness, of course.

The dinner was fun, and people chatted away. Everyone had a nickname which I thought was so fun. In our family, we just called each other by our given names, except sometimes my sister Sophia would call me Ana, but that was just short for

Anastasia. Not exactly descriptive, like Jay's family. Each of his cousins had names like Foxy Johnny and Paul 'the Tiger.' I had quickly learned they all liked to drink and eat and have a great time. It was a fun family, that was for sure.

At the end of the meal, Paul 'the Tiger' came up to Jay and me, slapping down on Jay's shoulder. He said, "Our little Blue Jay. Are you two headed out to the club with us?"

"Of course, the night is young," Jay said.

Paul 'the Tiger' said, "Great, I've got a few buddies who will be there too. They can meet your new girl. Great to meet you and welcome to the family."

"Thanks, Tiger," I said with an apprehensive smile.

He roared with laughter. "Blue Jay, I like your girl. You'll do all right," he said with a grin.

We kissed and hugged our goodbyes before Jay and I hopped into another car with his cousins. As we were chauffeured to Brooklyn, we chatted, and they talked about law school and how they were so happy that Blue Jay had gone to college. They called him the smart one. I had learned that Blue Jays were very smart birds, and that's how Jay got his nickname.

The driver pulled up to the club, and we all exited the black SUV. The bouncer looked at the group and let us right in. We didn't have to stand in line like the group outside of the club. I guessed Jay's family was known about town and well respected. They said it was because his dad had been in business for so long that he was friends with nearly everyone. I stepped into the club and had to adjust my eyes. There were lights flashing and darkness and people dancing. It was the first time I had gone out to a club since I found out I was pregnant. The lights were making me nauseous. It had never affected me that way before the little baby inside of me had arrived.

Jay turned around. "Are you all right?"

"I don't know. The lights are making me a little dizzy and queasy."

"Let's go up to the VIP area. It's darker and quieter."

"Okay, let's try that." We followed Paul and the others up to the VIP lounge, and I took my seat, realizing I was the only female there. They were a great group, but it would be nice to have another girl to talk to. Jay sat next to me after shaking everyone's hand. The lights were still bright, and the music was loud. My stomach continued to churn.

"You okay?" Jay asked.

My discomfort must have shown on my face. "I'm not feeling great."

Without hesitation, he said, "We'll go."

"Are you sure?" I asked, not wanting to ruin his night.

"Of course. It's fine. Let me just say goodbye, and we'll head out."

I nodded. Jay was so great. He was always looking out for me. He was my protector - my knight in shining armor. The man I'd always dreamed of but didn't think was actually real. It took him fifteen minutes to say goodbye to everyone. When he was done, he came up and waved me over. He grabbed my hand and said, "We can go out the back. It's quieter back there."

"Okay." We descended the stairs, and Jay pushed open the back door. The lot was empty except for a few men. Normally, I would've been worried to be there in the dark alley, but I had Jay by my side, so I had nothing to worry about.

He said, "The car should be here any second," before he pulled me close to him. Heaven. The sound of skin being slapped drew my attention to the small group of people in the alley where three men stood. One of them started yelling at the other and then pulled out a gun from inside his jacket.

Bam.

Bam.

Bam.

I gasped, and my body shook. Focused on the man laying on the ground in a quickly forming pool of blood, my instincts kicked in. I was a nurse. Voice shaking, I said, "I should help."

"No. We'll go now."

Just then, the car pulled up, and Jay ushered me into the back seat. He paused before getting into the car and then climbed inside, slamming the door behind him. "Trevor, go now."

He said, "Yes, sir," and then drove away from the nightclub where a man had just been murdered.

Turning to Jay, I said, "Should we call the police?"

"No, we won't call the police."

"We just witnessed a shooting. That guy might die!"

"I need you to forget what you saw. Okay?" Jay asked.

Horrified, I shook my head. "What do you mean, forget what I saw?"

Jay grew serious. "Anastasia, I need you to trust me. Forget what you just saw."

"I don't understand. You need to give me an explanation, Jay," I cried. My body still shaking, he held me tight. I didn't understand his reluctance to get help. Why would Jay want me to forget what I saw? It was too horrible to think about. I cried as Jay held me all the way home.

When we arrived at my apartment, he said, "I'll take care of everything. I'll call you tomorrow." Then he gave me a kiss and hurried me up to the apartment. After making sure I was inside safely, he rushed off without explanation. What did Jay mean he would take care of everything?

21

MARTINA

Hirsch and I stood on the corner, pretending to read a tourist map while we waited for Jay to approach his office building in downtown Manhattan. There was a sea of people in suits of all ages and races rushing up and down the streets. Never having met Jay in person, spotting him may have proved to be a challenge, but then Hirsch tapped my shoulder and said, "There he is."

I glanced up from the map and studied the man entering the lobby of Jay's building - if he wasn't Jay Castellano; he was a dead ringer. We hurried to reach him before we lost him on the inside. By the elevator, we stood next to Jay. He coldly eyed me, and I gave him my warmest, most friendly smile and said, "Mr. Castellano, is that you?"

"Do I know you?" Jay asked.

"No, you don't. My name is Martina Monroe, and this is my partner, Detective Hirsch. We'd like to have a few words with you."

"What is this regarding?" he asked.

"Anastasia Hall."

His face softened, and his body relaxed. "What do you want to know?"

Hirsch said, "We want to know what happened to her and her son, Ryder."

Jay looked at Hirsch and then back at me. "Come with me to my firm. We can speak in a more private area."

The elevator chimed, and the doors opened. Jay stood back. "After you."

I said, "Thanks," and entered. Hirsch followed behind. Once Jay was inside, he pressed the button for the 17th floor.

We silently rode the elevator and ascended to the top floor. On the ride, I wondered why Jay was so willing to speak with us. Did he really have nothing to hide? Did he have any information regarding his ex-fiancé and son?

The elevator halted, and the doors opened. Jay said, "Follow me. We can meet in the conference room. I don't have a lot of time, but I'll tell you what I know."

We followed him down the hall of the upscale New York law firm. There were large windows with views of the city and fresh-cut flowers on the receptionist's desk. We stopped and Jay said, "Good morning. We are going to be occupying the small conference room today, just for a little while, but please make sure that nobody disturbs us."

The receptionist said, "No problem, Mr. Castellano. I'll make sure nobody goes near that conference room."

"Thank you." He turned around. "Follow me."

We continued past large offices with expensive-looking art and cubicles with younger, busy looking folks. Jay stopped and entered a conference room with floor-to-ceiling windows and expansive views of the neighboring sky rises. He flipped on the lights and held the door open until we were both inside. He shut the door behind us. "Please have a seat, Detective Hirsch and Ms. Monroe."

My first impression of Jay Castellano was that he was professional and no-nonsense. That or he didn't like law enforcement or a nosy PI looking into his past. Choosing a chair with my back to the cityscape, I sat slowly, still a little surprised by Jay's willingness to cooperate. Or was it all an act? Once both men were seated, I asked, "Did you know that Anastasia Hall, formerly Anastasia Fennelli, and her son, Ryder, went missing ten years ago?"

He nodded. "I heard."

"Have you talked to her since then?" Hirsch asked.

Jay crossed his arms over his chest. "Look, I'll tell you what I know - off the record. I only have ten minutes before I'm meeting with an important client. A very important client. This will all be off the record. Is that understood?"

Hirsch said, "Yes, all information you provide to us is off the record."

Jay reiterated, "You didn't hear this information that I'm about to tell you from me."

Hirsch said, "Understood."

Jay let out a heavy breath. "Ten years ago, Anastasia was listed as a state's witness in a trial against some very powerful and dangerous people - people who didn't want her to testify."

"You mean your father?" Hirsch asked.

Jay nodded. "That's correct."

"And then what happened?" Hirsch asked.

Jay shook his head and placed his face in his hands. We sat in silence as he composed himself. Emerging from his hiding spot, he said, "Even ten years later, it breaks my heart. Anastasia and Ryder are dead."

Within minutes, Jay Castellano was telling us his dad bumped off his ex and child? There was no way he'd give up that type of information that easily. Something wasn't right about all of this.

"Why do you believe that?" I asked.

Jay frowned. "The boss gave the order to take out all the witnesses. Anastasia was one of the two witnesses. I assumed when they went to get her, she was with Ryder, and he was collateral damage."

"Will you testify to that?" Hirsch asked.

Jay said, "No."

"Why tell us?" I asked, even more suspicious.

Jay said, "To give her family some peace. To end your case and let you find someone else who needs your help."

Was I buying Jay's altruistic reasoning? *No.* "Do you know where she's buried?" I asked.

He nodded.

I certainly hadn't been expecting that.

He said, "I'll give you directions."

Amazed, I watched as Jay pulled a legal pad from his briefcase and began writing directions to where we could find Anastasia and Ryder's grave. Something still wasn't sitting right with me. "Why are you telling us this now and not ten years ago when they went missing?" I asked.

"It was a different time. My family has a strict policy not to cooperate with law enforcement. Even though I wished I could have. I loved them both. And yes, I knew Ryder was mine even though I couldn't be in his life. It was too dangerous for Anastasia. I tried to do what was best for them, but I failed."

Was that anger? Was Jay mad at Anastasia because he couldn't be in Ryder's life? Was it a motive to take out Anastasia and then grab Ryder and... then what?

"How did you fail?" I asked.

Jay gazed out the window. "After Anastasia witnessed what she witnessed, I told her she had to leave New York and not look back. The guilt of not being able to protect them has been eating me up all these years. I don't think the guilt will ever go away."

So, he broke up with Anastasia to protect her. Did Anastasia know Jay's family was in the mob?

"It's okay for you to tell us this now?" Hirsch asked, probably as skeptical as I was.

Jay straightened his posture and returned his focus to us. "You can't tell anyone what I have told you came from me. I'm trusting that you can come up with a good enough story as to how you found their bodies. If you say the information came from me, I will deny every single word of it."

I said, "Hirsch, that sounds like an anonymous tip."

With that, Jay pushed the piece of paper across the conference room table and then lifted himself from the seat. Standing tall, Jay said, "Now if you don't mind, I can't be late for this client, and it would behoove you to move along as well. Good luck, Detective. Good luck, Ms. Monroe."

Hirsch folded up the piece of paper and slipped it inside the pocket of his blazer. He said, "Thank you, Mr. Castellano."

"You can see yourselves out." And then Jay exited the conference room, head held high, and without hesitation.

My eyes met Hirsch's. "Anastasia and Ryder are dead."

Hirsch nodded sadly. "Let's go find them and bring them home to their family."

22

ANASTASIA - SIX YEARS BEFORE SHE VANISHED

A FRANTIC BANGING ON THE DOOR KNOCKED ME OUT OF A deep sleep. Rushing from my bedroom, I wondered who it could be. I ran to the door and looked through the peephole. It was Jay. I opened the door and asked, "What's going on?" I hadn't seen him since the nightclub murder two days earlier, and there he was showing up in the middle of the night.

His eyes were darting in all directions. "Hurry. We need to get inside."

"What is it? What's going on?" I asked again, confused by his urgency.

Inside, he said, "Lock the door."

I turned around, locked the door, and slid on the chain. He grabbed my hand and pulled me over to the sofa. Sitting facing me, he said, "I love you, Anastasia. I love our baby, and that is why I'm doing this."

My heart beat faster. "Doing what? What's going on, Jay?"

"You have to leave New York."

What? "Why? I don't understand. Please tell me."

"It's because of what happened at the nightclub. Those were

some of my family members who did that, and they don't like witnesses. You have to get out of town."

"I won't say anything to the police, if that's what you want." Could I really pretend I didn't witness a man being killed? Could I let someone get away with cold-blooded murder?

Jay shook his head frantically. "I wish there was another way. I really do."

"Jay, what are you saying?"

"You must leave New York and forget what you saw at the nightclub. Maybe even change your name."

I still wasn't quite understanding what he was saying. He wanted me to just up and leave New York, including my job and my apartment, and change my name? And what about my fiancé and our baby growing inside of me? How would I raise a baby on my own? "Where should I go?"

"You could move in with your parents. That would be good. And soon, like in the next couple of days."

He was acting erratic and paranoid. He was freaked out, and he was freaking me out, too. "I don't understand."

Jay sat quietly with both my hands in his, with his head bowed. Tears dropped onto the sofa. He glanced up at me. "I'll always love you, Anastasia, and our baby. My family isn't just in the cement business. They've done illegal things like what you saw. It's not the first time. And they've been talking about what happened at the nightclub, and when witnesses came up, the shooter said it was you and me who saw what happened. They don't have the authority to have you killed. My father would have to approve it."

My jaw dropped. "Killed?"

"Yes. There's a hierarchy within our family, and once they present the situation to my father, he will have to decide whether or not they should have you killed so you can never testify against them. If he agrees and tells them it's okay to take you out, they will. Nobody will ever find you again. So, you have to leave as fast as you can. I can make an argument that you've left town and have no plans to talk. It might be enough to show you're not a threat. You need to book a flight and go home."

His face was blotchy, and he had tears in his eyes. I couldn't believe any of this was real. I sat there staring at the man who was supposed to be my future husband, but the room blurred, and my head spun. My baby was related to killers and criminals. How had I not known? They all seemed so nice. Shutting my eyes, I tried to think back to when something seemed out of place. I mean, sure, they all talked like the gangsters in the movies, but I had just thought it was a New York thing. How had I been so naïve to think I would have a fairytale ending? Opening my eyes, I asked, "What about us?"

He shook his head. "We can never see each other again."

My body shook, and my heart pounded in my ears. Tears streamed down my cheeks. "How am I supposed to do this without you? Our baby, our life."

"I'm so sorry, Anastasia, so sorry. I have money I can give you to live on for a while and pay for your flight - anything you need. We can't be in contact at all. Don't tell anyone the baby is mine. Say it was a one-night stand or something. Nobody can know. It's too dangerous for you and for our baby. I'm doing this to protect you, because I love you so much."

Money? That was his answer? I didn't need money. I needed my partner. He was my partner, or so I had thought. How was this all happening? Would my future father-in-law really have me and the baby killed?

Jay wrapped his arms around me, and we hugged and cried as our bodies rocked together.

What seemed like only an instant later, he pulled back. "I have to go." He removed a white envelope from his pocket. It was nearly bursting open with what looked like cash. "Take this.

It should support you for a while. Book your flight home - as soon as possible. "

In a daze, I accepted the envelope. Had he bought me off? Four days ago, I was marrying a man, who I thought was the love of my life, and having a baby. My new reality was that I was alone, paid off, and forced to flee my home and the life I built in New York. How could he do this to me?

He placed his hands on my face and gave me a delicate kiss. He said, "Remember, don't tell anybody. You never knew me, and that isn't my baby."

As I stared at the man I loved with utter disbelief, he rushed toward the door and stopped. He said, "Lock the door behind me." He hesitated and then said, "Goodbye, Anastasia," and left me forever.

With the only bits of energy remaining inside me, I walked over to the door and locked it before falling to my knees. Sobbing, I wondered how my fairytale ending had turned into a nightmare. What had entered my life in an instant was gone just as fast. Had Jay ever really loved me? Was any of it real? Had I been stupid to believe that we would be together forever? When I met Jay, I knew he would change my life, but I hadn't thought he would ruin it.

Sitting on the ground, I leaned up against the door and calmed myself. With my hands on my belly, I told my baby, "Okay, Jelly Bean. It's just us now. We'll be okay. We don't need him." And we didn't. From that moment on, I would never think of Jay Castellano ever again.

23

MARTINA

WE STEPPED OUT OF THE OFFICE BUILDING INTO THE BRISK fall air. Feeling uneasy about our conversation with Jay, I almost didn't notice two men approaching us from the right. The same men, Fat Joe and Four-finger Pete, who had approached us at the airport. I stopped, as did Hirsch. The larger of the two men, Fat Joe, said, "Hey, what a coincidence. I'm surprised to see yous two still here."

"Is that right?" Hirsch asked.

"Yes, I thought maybe yous be going home by now."

Fists on hips, I stepped toward them. "Why would we do that?"

Fat Joe said, "No need to get upset. It's just that New York's not really a place for the likes of the two of yous."

"And why is that?" Hirsch asked.

The shorter man, who stood around five feet five inches tall, said. "Just thinking maybe it's not safe for some California softies like yous."

"Is that a threat?" Hirsch asked.

Before the small Italian man could respond, footsteps hurried on the pavement behind us. I glanced over my shoulder and saw it was Special Agents Brosco and Costanza. Brosco stared the two mobsters down before she said, "Hey, Joe. Hey, Pete. How's it going?"

Fat Joe said, "It's going pretty good. Thanks for askin'."

Brosco got up in Joe's face. "Oh, really? From where I'm standing, it looks like you're harassing some of our out-of-town guests?"

Four-finger Pete shook his head. "No. No. Yous got it all wrong. We're just out taking a stroll, Special Agent Brosco."

"Really? Because Detective Hirsch and Ms. Monroe here said they also ran into you at the airport. What are the odds of that?" SA Costanza asked.

"Life's full of coincidences. Don't you think, Special Agent?" Pete asked.

While SA Brosco had Fat Joe cornered, SA Costanza got closer to Pete. "No, I don't. I think it would be best if the two of you leave Detective Hirsch and Ms. Monroe alone. Don't you think?"

Brosco gave Joe some space, and he said, "We didn't mean nothing by it. Just seeing how they're getting along. A little birdie told us they're looking for Blue Jay's old squeeze, Anastasia. We're just trying to help."

"Are these two friends of yours?" I asked Brosco and Costanza.

Brosco smirked. "This here is Joe and Pete. They are associates of Jay Castellano's father."

"Yeah, we're in the construction business," Fat Joe said.

Brosco gave us a look as if to say the two were mobsters and obviously did little to hide it. They were a couple of stereotypes. It was as if they'd walked straight out of a movie. Yous this and yous that. I'd thought the funky speech was fake and emphasized for Hollywood. I hadn't realized that was how they actually talked.

Hirsch said, "Brosco, these guys just said we aren't safe here in New York. It sounded a lot like a threat."

"Is that right, gentlemen?" Brosco said as she once again stepped closer to the two men.

Joe shrugged. "We were just saying it's cold here. It's no sunny California."

"How did you know Detective Hirsch and Ms. Monroe are from sunny California?" Brosco asked.

Pete said, "We saw them on the news."

"Oh, really?" Costanza asked.

"It's good to keep up with current events," Joe said.

"Okay, we'll just chalk this up to a coincidence, but I'm gonna tell you nicely. No more coincidences or we're going to have a problem, capiche?" Brosco asked.

Joe said, "Crystal clear, Special Agent Brosco," and the two men turned and walked back down the street they had come from.

When they were out of earshot and far enough away that there couldn't be any sneak attacks, we faced Special Agents Brosco and Costanza. I said, "It looks like you are familiar with those two and vice versa."

Brosco said, "Unfortunately, yes. They're not our favorite thugs. When we spotted them, we figured it was as good a time as any to let them know we're watching. It's not a good sign that they've been following you."

Costanza added, "Yeah. They're threatening you, which means they feel threatened. I haven't heard anything on the tapes that they're surveilling you, but we don't have everything bugged. We'll keep an eye on you until you guys are safely back in California. Those two don't work construction. Both of them are soldiers in the Castellano family. They're real bad guys if you didn't get that. They typically do all the dirty work while the boss keeps his hands clean."

I said, "I didn't think our press conference announcing reopening the case was national news. They had to have heard from someone in the Bay Area."

"I would think so. They have a presence in the Bay Area. It doesn't quite make sense, though. I wonder if it was Jay who told his father and asked to have you followed. His father's the only one in the organization who can actually put a hit on you, and they rarely take a hit out on law enforcement. They don't like the heat that killing a cop brings. They'd rather just let us go. Which is why it's a little surprising they would follow and threaten you."

A lot of strange things with this case. If we understood correctly, the Castellano mob wasn't acting like the mob usually does. Why? I said, "Maybe they didn't realize we were working with you."

"It's entirely possible."

"You know, I haven't been to New York in quite some time, but so far, I don't feel like I've gotten much of a warm welcome," Hirsch said with sarcasm.

Brosco gave a sly grin. Was she flirting with Hirsch, or was Hirsch flirting with Brosco? She said, "Sorry about that. Unfortunately, the city is crawling with organized crime. We'll have to remedy that. Maybe you should take in a show. Did you get anything useful from Jay?"

Hirsch said, "We did. Jay says Anastasia and Ryder are dead."

Brosco raised her sculpted brows. "Really? He told you that?"

Hirsch said, "Yes. And he told us where they buried the bodies."

"You're kidding," Costanza asked.

I said, "It surprised us too. Now we have to go back to California and dig up the site and see if he was telling the truth."

Something inside of me still felt unsettled. It was too easy. Too clean.

Brosco said, "If it turns out to be true, then the theory that Big Sally took out Anastasia to eliminate her as a witness was correct. I'm surprised they would have allowed Ryder to be killed. They don't usually touch kids - especially blood. But it's possibly Sal didn't know Ryder was Jay's. There was no word on the tapes about Jay having a son. We pieced together the timeline after we contacted Anastasia to be a state's witness."

Could that explain the mob's peculiar behavior? I said, "Well, if they're as bad as you say, they're capable of anything."

Costanza said, "Yep. Let's go over the details you received from Jay back at the office. It'll be a good idea to put together the complete story before you head back to California."

"Sounds good." If what Jay and the feds said was true, Anastasia was at the wrong place at the wrong time, and it cost her and her son their lives.

24

HIRSCH

A HEAVINESS FILLED ME AS I APPROACHED THE DIG SITE. Despite the grim circumstances, the sun was shining and there were blue skies with only a smattering of white clouds overhead. Much brighter than the gray of New York. Even with my repeated explanation to Anastasia's mother, sister, and husband that we weren't certain we would find Anastasia and Ryder's bodies, they had insisted on being at the dig site. The three of them had agreed they didn't want to miss the moment we found them, if we found them. Trying to put myself in their position, I supposed if I'd been waiting for answers to what happened to my wife or child for ten years, I couldn't wait for a call either. I wasn't looking forward to unearthing skeletons of murder victims, especially not that of a five-year-old boy. There was just something worse when it was a kid. It was innocence lost, stolen, and taken away. It wasn't right. I waved at Martina, who stood next to the family as I approached the dig site that had been cordoned off by yellow crime scene tape. On the other side of the tape were Brown and the crime scene investigation crew.

Jay had been rather descriptive on the location, but he hadn't explained who gave him the details or why. The circumstances were strange, to say the least. The FBI and I had tried following up with him to ask additional questions, but he dodged our calls and wouldn't let the FBI into his home or office without a warrant. Jay's lack of cooperation had me suspicious of him and his potential involvement in the disappearance of Anastasia and Ryder. It was as if he was protecting the guilty. Would he do all of that for his family? Maybe. People covered up murders for family members all the time. It was pretty incredible, not in a good way. As much as I loved my family, I would never cover up a cold-blooded murder for any of them.

Reaching Brown and the CSI team, I said, "Hey, how is it going?"

"Not bad. We're going as fast as we can but still being careful, which basically means slow. If they are down there, we don't want to disturb them and lose valuable evidence."

"How close are you?" I asked.

"My guess is if they're buried six feet, we should hit on something within the next hour."

I said, "Nice. Thanks," and then walked over to Martina and the family. "How are you holding up?" I asked the group.

Mrs. Fennelli said, "Anxious. Nervous. But hanging in there."

Martina said, "That's understandable."

Sophia, Anastasia's sister, said, "I still can't believe Anastasia and little Ryder may have been murdered by mobsters."

I said, "We don't have any evidence yet, but based on our discussion with the FBI, we believe so."

Demetri shook his head. "It doesn't make any sense. Why would someone now confess who killed them, why, and where they are buried? Why not ten years ago? Any idea who provided the tip?"

Maintaining a neutral expression, I explained, "It's not uncommon for witnesses to come forward years after the crime.

Sometimes it's because of a guilty conscious or they're no longer afraid of retaliation from the criminal. We don't know who the tip is from - it's registered as anonymous."

The FBI and I both believed that keeping the tip anonymous was best. We didn't want the mob to retaliate against Jay, plus we were still hoping to get more information out of him, even though he'd been ducking us.

"How did Anastasia end up at a mob hang out? It doesn't make sense," Sophia cried.

It wasn't part of the confidentiality that we promised Jay, but exposing Anastasia and Jay's relationship was something we planned to explain later and not at their grave. I said, "We're still looking into it."

Sophia shook her head at Martina and me.

"I'm sorry you're having to go through this. I understand what you're going through."

"How could you possibly understand?" Sophia nearly screamed.

She was clearly succumbing to the emotion of the day. Everyone grieves in their own way. I explained, "My older brother was murdered. We were told it was a mugging. He was killed walking down the street in San Francisco. They never caught the guy who did it, and all they have is speculation that there was a robbery and maybe my brother fought back."

Sophia bowed her head. "I'm so sorry for your loss."

Mrs. Fennelli patted my arm. "I'm sorry, Detective. It's a hard day."

"Thank you. You are understandably upset. This shouldn't ever happen to anybody's family."

I glanced over at Martina. Her husband and her best friend from high school had been killed. That was a lot of tragedy for one person. It was no wonder she protected her family so fiercely. It also explained how she had become an alcoholic but then turned her life back around. She was a strong woman, and I was glad she was finally working a little less and taking time to go to her daughter's Girl Scout meetings, dinners at home with her mother, and regularly taking Zoey and their dog to the park to play. It seemed like Martina's life was finally getting some balance. Maybe it was my turn.

We had been home from New York for three days, and I was looking forward to seeing Kim on Saturday night. We spoke on the phone as soon as I was home. The conversation was easy and reminded me of back when I was in high school. I used to talk to girls on the phone for hours, like we never could run out of things to say. It was like that with Kim. Afraid my feelings were moving too fast, I considered pulling back, but then I decided to let things play out naturally. If I scared Kim off with my feelings, then it wasn't meant to be anyhow.

Martina tipped her head toward the family and started small talk, answering questions as we could. It was stilted and uncomfortable, but at least it passed the time.

Brown finally called out, "Hirsch."

I hurried over. "What is it?"

"We've got a skull." I stepped closer to the hole and peered over. Sure enough, there was a human skull peeking out of the soil.

"Do you want us to keep digging to see if there's a second skull before bringing the family over?" Brown asked.

"No, let's let them see now, but you can continue. I'm guessing based on the size of the skull, that's an adult."

Brown said, "Yeah, that would be my guess."

I headed back over to the group and explained. "Brown's team unearthed an adult human skull. They will continue digging to see if there is a second."

"Can we see?" Mrs. Fennelli asked.

"Yes."

Without a word, Demitri ran over to the hole and knelt down in front of it before burying his head in his hands and sobbing. I hadn't thought it was Demitri who had killed his wife and child. This just about confirmed it. Would I ever love somebody that much? Sure, I had been upset after my divorce, but I didn't have grief like that.

Martina escorted Anastasia's mother and sister over to the hole, and they stood next to Demetri, who remained on his knees. They glanced over before turning to each other, embracing, and breaking into tears. Martina glanced over at me. I gave her a look of sorrow. It was the moment they had been waiting for, for ten years.

I knelt down next to Demetri and put my hand on his shoulder. Pain emanated from his body, and I couldn't empathize with him, but I could be there for him. A few moments passed as the family grieved. Demetri paused, looked up, and turned to me. "Where's Ryder?"

I said, "They're not done yet."

He nodded before standing up and stepping toward Anastasia's mom and sister. "I'm so sorry. I should've protected them."

Anastasia's mother shook her head. "Don't say that, Demetri. You were so good to her and to Ryder. None of this is your fault."

As she embraced him, I tried to find a silver lining in all of this. And failed. Sure, at first, they would comfort each other and help each other grieve. They'd be there for each other through the investigation and at the funeral, but eventually, both families would move on, and they'd be each other's history. All because Anastasia witnessed an unspeakable act by a bunch of thugs. It was senseless, and it was stupid. It made me angry and sad.

Brown called me over once again. He knelt down and pointed in the grave. "That there looks like tiny phalanges."

I said, "Like a little kid's fingers."

He nodded.

I said, "Okay, keep going."

The team continued as I tried to distract the family while the team unearthed Ryder. Usually at this point, there would be cheers that we found something, but with the grieving family in attendance, there was no celebration to be had.

Once we were back at the station, I was sure the Cold Case Squad would do their usual hoots and hollers, but I wasn't sure I could. There was something off about all of this. Answers were still needed.

Martina approached and asked, "How much longer do you think?"

I said, "Soon."

She gave me a knowing look. We were called over again by Brown. He said, "We have a second skull. It's strange, though."

"What do you mean?" I asked.

He knelt down and pointed to the two skulls. "There are bullet holes in both of them."

"Why is that strange?" Martina asked.

Brown explained, "There's no staining around the holes."

"What does that mean?" I asked.

Brown said, "Usually with a gunshot wound to the head, there is staining from the brain bleed, but with these, the coloring around the holes is actually lighter than the surrounding bone."

"Could they have cleaned the bodies after they killed them?" Martina asked.

Brown said, "It's possible. Or they inflicted the gunshots post mortem."

That's unusual. Why would the killer do that? To hide the true cause of death? "The autopsy should happen pretty soon since it's a high-profile case."

Brown nodded. "If I were you, I'd request the dental records right away and maybe get a DNA sample from the family for a double confirmation of identity."

Something in my gut stirred. "We will get DNA from Anastasia's mother and her sister. Ryder isn't Demetri's biological son." I wondered if we should request a DNA sample from Jay, not that we needed it if we had Anastasia's. He probably wouldn't give it anyhow.

Martina said, "I'll get the family."

Brown pointed at the skeletons of a woman and a small child as the family surrounded him. The female was on the bottom and the small bones of a child on top. The skull lay where the woman's chest would have been. It was the first time I'd seen a mother and child buried together. Lowering my head, I hoped to never see it again.

25

ANASTASIA - SHORTLY BEFORE SHE VANISHED

HIS SMILE MELTED MY HEART. I FINISHED READING HIS favorite bedtime story, *Goodnight Moon*, and tucked him in. "I love you, Ryder."

"Love you too, Mommy."

"Good night. I'll see you in the morning."

"Good night. See you in the morning," he said, in that sweet little boy voice of his.

I ruffled his hair before walking out of his bedroom and down the hall into the kitchen. Demitri was still working despite the late hour. He'd warned me he had an important report he needed to finish up and that Ryder and I would have to have dinner without him. I didn't mind having a little alone time. A glass of wine and that novel I had been trying to finish for over a month sounded fantastic. While I was walking toward our wine rack, the phone rang. Hoping it was Demitri, I skipped to the wall and picked it up. "Hello."

"Is this Anastasia Hall?" a woman with a low voice asked.

"Yes."

"Maiden name Fennelli?"

I glanced around the room, and my pulse sped up. "Yes, this is Ana."

"Mrs. Hall, my name is Special Agent Brosco with the FBI in New York. Do you have a moment to talk?"

Staring at the wine rack, I thought it may be a two glass kind of night. "What is this regarding?"

Please. Not about that.

"We have information that you were a witness to a crime, a murder, six years ago in New York. We have compiled charges against those responsible, and we'd like you to be a witness in court."

No.

I flashed back to that fateful evening at the nightclub. The man who had been shot dead, with blood pooling beneath him. I tried to block out that scene and that time in my life because both were things I never wanted to visit again. Shame filled me, and I wondered if I had done the right thing all those years ago. My mind drifted to my sweet boy lying in his bed. Yes, I had done the right thing.

"What do you need from me?"

"Will you testify to what you saw?"

Was I willing to open up my family to the wrath of the Castellano crime family? "Look, it's been a long time. My memory is fuzzy."

"Mrs. Hall, a man was murdered in cold blood, and his killers are free, probably planning to kill others. Now we finally have enough evidence to put away a lot of really terrible people. We need you to testify in court that you were there that night and identify the shooter."

"I didn't know him." I didn't, but his face was burned in my memory. The face of a cold-blooded sociopathic killer. He'd shot the other man without hesitation or any reaction, as if he'd just taken out the trash.

"Mrs. Hall, we need you."

"I'll have to think about it." Could I really testify? When I'd left New York, I told myself I would never look back. Not physically and not mentally. As it was, because of that night, I'd had to lie to everyone I cared about. It had started with my roommate, Marcy. I'd told her I suffered a miscarriage and lost the baby, and I was so heartbroken over my breakup with Jay and the loss of my baby, I had to leave New York. She'd been so sympathetic I had felt like a jerk for lying to her. And for lying to my family and to Demitri. He had no idea that Ryder was related to a major crime family. Ryder was the grandson of the boss of the Castellano crime family. *Nobody could ever know.*

Special Agent Brosco said, "Ma'am, we really need your help with this."

"I'm sorry. I can't talk right now. I'll have to call you back."

"Mrs. Hall, we can protect you."

I didn't believe that, not for a second. "I'm sorry, I have to go." I quickly hung up the phone.

It was rude to hang up on a federal agent, but didn't that agent realize what I would be giving up? *Everything. Again.* If the Castellanos found me or learned that Ryder was related to them, what would they do? Would they take him from me? Would they kill me? Kill him? Kill Demitri? No. I had to protect both Ryder and Demitri. Sweet, loving Demitri.

At the wine rack, I pulled a Cabernet Sauvignon from the slot and opened the bottle before pouring the dark red liquid into a large wine glass. I took a hardy drink before setting it down on the counter and steadying myself.

The phone rang again, but I didn't answer it.

Over the last six years, I had done a great job of forgetting about New York. Back then, I was so distraught. Everything seemed hopeless, and I wondered if I could be a single mother or if I should end my pregnancy. Every time I felt the little jellybean flutter inside of me, I knew I had to keep him. Ryder and Demitri were everything to me.

My gosh, I thought I had been fortunate to meet Jay, but even now, I wondered what that really was. Was it love? Was it lust I had confused with love? The last six years with Demitri had felt different. Different good. Sure, he flattered me like Jay had, but with Demitri, it was more than that. He protected me. He cared for me and my son — our son. He supported my dreams and was there every moment I needed him. I could never forget the love on his face on our wedding day.

His hazel eyes twinkled in the sunlight as he said his vows. He'd written them himself and included a line about being excited about future things — big and small. He had paused and gave me a knowing smile. It was his way of telling me he was just as excited about our baby as I was. In that moment, I knew Demitri was it for me.

When I had accepted his marriage proposal, I wasn't as sure. Two months into our relationship, I knew I liked him a lot, and I even thought it may be love. It wasn't a hot burning love like with Jay. It was like a warm and soft love — like home.

On the night Demitri professed his love for me, I realized I had let things go too far without telling him the truth. I was scared it would make him go away, but my time had been running out because any day I would start showing. After he told me he loved me, I hesitated, and he looked sad and worried. I knew in that moment I needed to confess. "Demitri, there is something I have to tell you." I met his pleading gaze and mustered all my courage to do it. "I'm pregnant."

His eyes widened. *Oh, jeez.* Realizing he may think he was the father, I quickly recovered. "You're not the father. I'm almost four months along."

With hurt in his eyes, he asked, "You are? Are you seeing other people?"

"No, only you since I've been back in California. In New York, I had a one-night fling and found myself pregnant. Please don't tell anyone, but I thought you should know."

I was sure it would be the end of Demitri and me. From that point, I was sure it would just be Jelly Bean and me.

"Are you in contact with the father?" Demitri asked.

"No, I don't have his contact information. I don't even know his last name," I lied. I hated lying.

"What are you planning to do?"

"I plan to have my baby."

Demitri sat quietly, looking down as if deep in thought. My heart raced as I thought of the words he would use to break off our relationship, and I thought maybe I did love him. The fear I felt that the relationship would end was making me nauseous. Was that love?

After what seemed an eternity, Demitri turned his gaze to me. "I love you, Ana. Do you love me too?"

"I do. I love you, Demitri." I smiled, tears in my eyes. I didn't know if it was because of the hormones from the pregnancy or genuine emotion, but something in that moment told me I couldn't lose Demitri - I just couldn't.

"I know this is sudden, but if you let me, I will love you, and I will love that baby and raise it as my own. Will you marry me, Ana?"

My mouth dropped open, and I was speechless. I thought he would want to run away when he learned the truth. Instead, he wanted to make a family. No, there wasn't burning desire between us. There wasn't throw caution to the wind and forget my birth control pills kind of passion, but there was love and comfort and safety. Jay nearly destroyed me and ruined my life. Demitri made me whole. With a bit of doubt and tears streaming down my cheeks, I nodded. "Yes, I'll marry you."

We embraced, and we kissed, and we made love like we

never had before. With Demitri, Ryder and I had found home. And there was *no way* I would let any one of the Castellanos take that away from me. The FBI could find themselves another witness. As far as I was concerned, New York was my past, and that was exactly where it would stay.

26

MARTINA

Staring down at the skeletal remains of a woman and child, I wondered if that mother had ever thought she'd be laying on a metal table while detectives watched the medical examiner figure out what happened to them. Would Zoey and I ever be on the ME's table? A chill ran through me, and I shook away the thought. It was too dark, even for me. I glanced up at Dr. Scribner, dressed in green surgical scrubs and wearing glittery eyeglasses. Although in her fifties, the glasses remind me of Zoey, and it made me contemplate whether my little girl would grow up to be a medical examiner. As it was, she loved science and was quite curious about detective work. "Have you made a positive ID yet?" I asked Dr Scribner.

"I'm afraid not."

Hirsch looked puzzled. "Why not? Was there an issue obtaining the dental records? I can make a call if you need."

Dr. Scribner removed her glasses. "I'm afraid that won't help. My assistant called over to get the records from Anastasia and Ryder's dentist and learned there had been a fire at the office ten years ago. All the records were destroyed."

Fishy. "Did your assistant find out what caused the fire?" I asked.

"Once my assistant was told there were no records, he thanked them for their time and told them to have a good day. But I can give you the office's details if you want to look into it."

Hirsch said, "Thanks. We'll check it out. Vincent can pull up the fire investigation report. Did you find anything interesting regarding the manner and cause of death?"

Dr. Scribner nodded. "As a matter of fact, I did." She walked over to a table along the wall and picked up a folder and returned to us. She opened the folder and pulled out a piece of paper and handed it to Hirsch. It was a diagram of two human bodies with pen marks showing wounds and notes about the autopsy.

She said, "You see those two marks on the heads?" Dr. Scribner pointed with her finger. The adult skeleton and the child had a visible wound on their skulls. "Each had a gunshot wound to their head, but those gunshots occurred postmortem - after they were already dead."

That was strange. "Did you determine the cause of death?" I asked.

"Well, based on the postmortem gunshot wounds — sometimes a killer will do that to disguise the actual cause of death — I looked a little deeper. You can see the hyoid bones are intact, which means they likely weren't strangled. There is no other obvious cause. Which leads me to think they were either smothered or poisoned or died of natural causes. We'll have to wait to get the labs back to see if there is any poison in their systems."

"They can get that kind of information just from bones?" I asked.

Dr. Scribner said, "They can if there's enough left of it."

"And it sounds like we'll have to wait for DNA to determine identification?" Hirsch asked.

"Unfortunately, yes. I have sent the samples out to the lab. We asked for a rush since it's a pretty high-profile case, but it could take a few days at the very least. It usually takes weeks."

"Any other interesting findings?" I asked.

Dr. Scribner folded her arms across her chest. "There are a few puzzling things about each of the skeletons. The teeth, for one. The smaller skeleton's teeth show that they may have been rotted out, which typically means they had poor nutrition or they had been sick or taking medication like you would see in chemotherapy patients or the terminally ill. But from what I understand, Ryder was a healthy five-year-old boy when he went missing. Is that correct?"

I said, "Yes, he was. From the photographs, anyhow. His father Demetri said that he was healthy and happy."

"Well, then it's possible this wasn't Ryder."

"Then who was it?" Hirsch asked, but then he paused and said, "So, you're saying it's possible this may not be Ryder and Anastasia?"

"Anything is possible. We'll have to wait until we get the DNA results."

I stared down at the tiny skeleton and focused on the teeth that Dr. Scribner had been describing. She was right. They didn't look like healthy five-year-old teeth. "What about the woman?" I asked.

"Fairly normal, not like the boy."

"You'll let us know when the DNA comes back?" Hirsch asked.

"Absolutely."

Questions and thoughts swirled in my mind. Had we been so convinced the remains found at the gravesite were Anastasia and Ryder that it hadn't occurred to us it might not be them? But if it wasn't, why would Jay have led us there? And if those remains didn't belong to our victims, who were they? The FBI had said it would be very unusual for the mafia to kill one of their own, especially a child. Had they stolen the child and killed Anastasia? Maybe the skeletal remains were Anastasia's, but not Ryder's?

We thanked Dr. Scribner and exited the autopsy suite. Out in the hallway, I said to Hirsch, "What do you make of that?"

"Interesting."

"Yeah, you want to share your thoughts over lunch?" I asked.

"Yes, let's discuss. I have a few theories."

Excellent. I had a few theories of my own. It would be interesting to hear what Hirsch thought. No wonder the case had gone cold. If I was right, somebody was actively trying to cover up what really happened to Anastasia and Ryder. But why? Was it a simple child abduction? Silencing of a potential state's witness? There were too many possible motives.

After lunch, Hirsch and I strolled back through the building. We needed to update the whiteboard with our newfound information. There were so many directions the case could go. We wanted to make sure we had a clear picture. Hirsch pulled his cell phone out of his pocket and stared at it, and a small smile formed on his face. He silenced the call and put it back in his pocket, acting as if nothing had happened.

"Who was that?" I asked.

"Kim."

"How are things going with her?"

"Things are good."

Were his cheeks turning red? "Good?"

He stopped and turned to me. "I really like her."

"Yeah? When do we get to meet her?" I knew my mother would love to have the two of them over for dinner - especially since she'd made the love match.

"Not sure. Maybe after this case is over?"

I knew they had only gone on a few dates, and it was probably a little early, but considering Kim's mother was friends with my mother, maybe not. When I got home, I would have to ask my mom if Kim's mother had said anything about the two of them. It was good to see a smile on Hirsch's face for something other than solving a case or discovering a new clue. I was happy for them. I patted him on the back. "Let's hope it ends soon. Then you can finally have that barbecue at your house. We can all celebrate and meet your new lady friend," I said, half-teasing.

"Deal."

We reached the Cold Case Squad Room and found Vincent sitting at the table, tapping away at keys on the laptop as if he were on a mission. "Hey, Vincent."

Without looking away from his computer, he said, "Hey, Martina. Hey, Hirsch." He continued tapping away before doing a dramatic final tap and pushed away from the laptop. "I have the details on the fire at Anastasia and Ryder's dentist office."

That was fast. We'd texted him from back at the autopsy suite only two hours before.

"And?" I asked.

He said, "Arson."

"Did they catch the people who did it?" I asked.

"Nope, but I found something interesting. Wanna guess when it happened?" Vincent challenged.

No. "Ten years ago."

"Yep. But it was ten years ago on the day that Anastasia and Ryder went missing. Coincidence?"

Looking at Hirsch, I asked, "Hey, did you start believing in coincidences?"

Hirsch cracked a smile. "No, I did not."

"Hey, Vincent, can you get the name of the fire inspector, so we can talk to him about the details of fire?" I asked.

"It's already in your email."

"'Thanks."

Hirsch said, "Well, then, I think it's time to talk to the fire inspector to get the details about what happened at the dentist's office."

"You guys need anything else?" Vincent asked.

Hirsch said, "No, we're good for now. Thanks for acting so quick."

"Any time."

At first, I wasn't the biggest fan of Vincent. I mean, sure, he did a good job, but he reminded me of one of those guys everything seemed to come so easily to yet they acted like they were brilliant. But I had learned he was a good guy. When he stuck his neck on the line to make sure justice was served for a fallen soldier, he gained a lot of respect from me. He wasn't just a cocky know-it-all. He actually cared about the job and those we were helping. That's why he worked so hard. We were lucky he was part of the team. Hopefully, his skills, along with Hirsch's and mine, would help us figure out what really happened to Anastasia and Ryder and why.

27

HIRSCH

Standing in the kitchen of the fire marshal's office, he stood at six feet four inches tall, broad shoulders with a head of thick, dark hair. I said, "We appreciate you meeting with us, Inspector Lang."

He covered a yawn. "Anytime. And I know time is of the essence on this one. Not just for you, but for me, too. I pulled the file for the original investigation into the fire at the dentist's office. I remember the case because I was lead inspector."

Perfect - straight from the horse's mouth - so to speak. "What can you tell us about the fire? Anything strange about it?"

He grabbed his coffee from the machine and motioned for us to follow him down the hallway. He ushered us in, and then we all sat at the table. It looked like an interview room with just a few chairs, a table, and a large window that I guessed was two-way since I couldn't see through it. He sipped his black coffee and then said, "What was interesting about it was the fact that it was obviously arson. There were no signs the perpetrator tried to hide that fact."

"How so?" I asked.

"Well, for starters, they used a bomb. My theory at the time was that somebody broke into the building, placed the bomb in the reception area, and then casually strolled out before they remotely detonated it. It's not something I see every day. Not at a dentist's office anyhow."

"They bombed it?" Martina asked with brows raised.

"Yep."

"Was anyone injured?" I asked.

Inspector Lang said, "No. We were lucky in that respect. The bomb was detonated late at night."

"Did you have any leads in the case?" I asked.

"None. There were no security cameras at the time and no one with a motive that the dentist or her staff could think of. But based on how the bomb was built, I'd say the person who did it was experienced, and they had a unique signature as well. The wires were painted red, white, and green. It's not something I'd seen before."

Red, white, and green. What did it mean? I said to Martina, "The day that Anastasia and Ryder went missing, their dentist office was *bombed*."

She smirked. "Definitely not a coincidence."

"Is there anything else you can tell us about the fire that would help us figure out if there are any more connections to our case?"

Inspector Lang said, "Yeah, I've got one more for you. Late last night, I responded to a fire. A bomb just like the one used at the dentist's office. Red, white, and green wires. Remote detonated. That's why I agreed to see you right away. I had reviewed the file from the dentist's office right before I went home, so it was fresh in my mind. My gut says these two bombings are connected. At the very least, the same person made the explosive devices."

"What building did they bomb?" Martina asked.

"The state testing lab's satellite office in Concord. Any

reason that would be related to your case?" Inspector Lang asked.

Eyes wide, Martina said, "Yeah. We had samples from the remains found earlier this week sent there for DNA analysis. It's the only way to confirm the identity of our missing persons since their dental records were destroyed in a fire ten years ago."

I said, "Somebody doesn't want us to know the true identity of those remains."

Martina nodded. "Exactly."

Something wasn't feeling right. "Why haven't we heard about this on the news?" I asked.

"I haven't released the report yet, so it's not in the press. I wanted to talk to you before we made the announcement. It's better that whomever did this doesn't know we connected them to the other bombing. It's better to make them think they got away with it."

This meant whoever took Anastasia and Ryder bombed the dentist's building and now the testing lab in the Bay Area. Somebody was covering their tracks, and fast. "What else can you tell us about the test lab bombing?"

"Same type of bomb as the dentist's office, but this time, we have security cameras. The team is reviewing surveillance footage now to identify everyone who entered and exited the building in the last twenty-four hours. The bomb was placed in a storage closet and remotely detonated around midnight. Thankfully, there were no staff present. But because of the location of the bomb it means it could have gone unnoticed for a while. It'll take some time to rule out staff, but we'll get there. As soon as we find any suspicious characters, I'll call you."

I said, "Thanks, and best of luck, Inspector Lang."

Martina seconded the notion. "Yes, Thank you Inspector Lang."

"No problem. I have to run, but I'll share any information so we can get the bottom of this. I'd be more than happy to solve two bombings and put a bad guy away."

We nodded in agreement before Inspector Lang hurried off. I turned to Martina. "Okay, now we try to find this bomber before he attacks anyone or anything else here in the Bay Area."

Back in the squad room, we found Vincent clicking away on the keyboard of his laptop once again. I said, "Hi, Vincent."

"Hey, it's the dynamic duo."

I said, "We need your help."

"I'm all ears."

We explained to him the connection between the dentist's office bombing and the testing lab and how we needed every report and piece of evidence sifted through to find similarities.

Vincent said, "Okay, and I'll call the lab right away and ask if they need another DNA sample from the family."

I said, "Thanks, Vincent." I was proud Vincent took on the request without hesitation. His normal responsibilities rarely involved that level of review or activity, but I knew he would be good at it and probably quick, too.

Martina and I marched over to the whiteboard, where we had all the details of Anastasia and Ryder's case mapped out, and updated the latest information. If I didn't know better, I'd say somebody was trying to thwart our investigation. But who and why?

28

MARTINA

Driving home, I thought, *TGIF. What a week*. I couldn't wait to go home for movie night with Zoey, Mom, and Barney. We reserved Friday nights for movies, pizza, and soda. I enjoyed the pizza but refrained from the soda, and Zoey could only have one. All that sugar would not only rot her teeth and give her diabetes, but it made her far too hyper. *No thanks*. She was a kid, and I wasn't a terrible mom, so she got to have it once a week, along with ice cream. It was our end of the week ritual. My Zoey was in fourth grade, and I knew the years we'd be sharing our Friday nights together were limited. She'd be a teenager in just a few years, and I could only imagine what that would be like. She was smart, sassy, and had been since she could walk and talk. I could only imagine what the hormonal teenage version would be like. *Lord, help me*. Thankfully, I had my mom to help because if Zoey was anything like me as a teenager, I was going to need all the help I could get.

This year had been interesting, full of surprises and some heartbreak. But overall, I'd finally found my balance. Between the Girl Scout meetings, Friday movie night ritual, and daily trips to the park with Barney, I felt at peace. When Jared was alive, I had taken for granted all my blessings. I had a loving and supportive husband and a brilliant daughter. We had a loving family and home. Someone had stolen it in an instant. My only regret was that I didn't appreciate it all as much as I should have. That's why I tried to celebrate the small things and remember each day I was lucky to be alive, healthy, and had a family and a job that meant something.

My time with the sheriff's department helped me get that balance, but part of me still missed going into the Drakos Security & Investigations office every day, working with people who were like family. Not that Hirsch and the rest of the Cold Case Squad hadn't become an extended family, but it was different. In hindsight, I had grown up in the offices of Drakos Security & Investigations. It was my first job out of the military, and it made me who I was. Sometimes I felt guilty, like I had turned my back on my family. I was still meeting every few weeks with Stavros, but it was different from seeing somebody in the office every day. As I waited for the light to turn green, I thought I should talk to Mom about hosting another dinner or barbecue before the weather got too cold. We could invite Stavros, Rocco, some of my pals from the Drakos team, and, of course, Hirsch and some of the other members from the Cold Case Squad. And I certainly wanted to meet Hirsch's new lady, Kim. Did I need to do a background check on Kim? Would Hirsch be okay with that? Who knows, maybe he already had.

The light turned green, and I continued down the road and began thinking about changing into flannel pajamas and cozying up on the sofa with my three favorite creatures, Zoey, Barney, and Mom. I glanced in the rear-view mirror and spotted a silver sedan with two men in the front seat. Had I seen them two lights back? They were going the same direction I was, or I was being followed. There was no way I would allow anyone to follow me home - where my family was.

I made a quick left and watched the mirror. The silver sedan also made a left. I drove down a few blocks and made a right. My heart beat faster as I spotted the silver sedan make the same right. Who was following me?

I slowed my speed to get a better look at the driver and passenger. It was fuzzy, but it was definitely two men with dark hair. Could it be? *No, that would be crazy.*

Opting for safe rather than sorry, I pulled out my cell phone and called Hirsch. It rang and rang. Dang, I remembered he had a date with Kim. "Martina, what's up?"

"Hey, Hirsch, sorry I forgot you had plans, but I'm on my way home. I'm almost there, but I think I'm being followed."

"By who?"

"Two men in a silver sedan. Both men are older with dark hair."

"Where are you now?"

"About two miles from my house."

"Where did you pick up the tail?"

"After leaving the grocery store where I stopped to pick up ice cream for movie night."

"All right, go back to the grocery store. I'll meet you there."

"Are you sure? I could head back to the station?"

"Hold on a second." Hirsch must have covered his microphone on his phone because all I could hear was scratching and muffled noises. He said, "I'm close by. I'll meet you there in five minutes. Turn around. You don't want to go to your house."

"I'll turn around now." I wondered where Hirsch was, that he was only five minutes away. Maybe at a restaurant with Kim? Maybe it was a good thing Kim was getting a glimpse of what it was like to be dating a detective.

After I made a U-turn at the next light, I continued to watch the two men who followed my every move. They were decent drivers and could keep up with me, but they certainly weren't particularly concerned with being inconspicuous about it. Did they want me to notice them? I drove back to the shopping center and entered the lot but didn't see Hirsch's car.

It was dark out, and there weren't many people around. I parked far from the entrance of the store and opened my glove box and retrieved my firearm. Spotting the silver sedan pulling into the parking lot with Hirsch right behind him, I climbed out of the front seat with my weapon in hand and strolled to the back of my car. Standing at my trunk, I stared down the two men who'd been following me. My mouth dropped open a little.

Hirsch parked his car and ran over to me. "Martina, are you okay?"

"I'm fine. It looks like our friends from New York decided to visit us."

Hirsch stood next to me, hands on hips. The two men got out of the car and walked up to us. I said, "Gentlemen, what a surprise."

Fat Joe said, "Yous got us thinking maybe California sounded good this time of year."

"Why are you following me?" I asked.

Four-finger Pete said, "No worries. We just wanted to have a chat."

"Have you heard of a telephone?" I asked.

Fat Joe said, "I'm old school. I like a good face-to-face."

Four-finger Pete nodded.

I said, "You came all the way across the country for a chat. Well, then let's hear it. What do you want?"

Fat Joe said, "We wanted to ask yous to drop this whole Anastasia investigation."

"And why would we do that?" Hirsch asked.

Fat Joe said, "Yous two drop the Anastasia thing, and we don't have a problem."

Hirsch puffed out his chest. "Is that so? Are you threatening a police officer?"

Four-finger Pete nodded. "Look, we're just following orders. Just like yous."

"What happens if we don't drop the case?" Hirsch asked.

"Well, it would depend on my instructions. My boss said you're a smart lady and a smart detective, so maybe we just ask nicely that you stop looking into our business. Maybe yous let it go and say yous couldn't find the broad and everybody goes home safe and happy."

Looking them up and down, I said, "This must be pretty important to your boss to fly the two of you out here."

Fat Joe said, "It's pretty important to the boss, that's true. That's why I think it's best to drop it. Yous seem like a real nice lady and nice guy, so do yourselves a favor and drop it. Anastasia and Ryder are gone forever, and nothing can bring them back. Okay?"

I shrugged. "Okay, sure. We'll do whatever you ask."

"See, yous are smart," Fat Joe said, rather sarcastically.

Hirsch stepped toward them and practically growled. "She's plenty smart. And if you don't want to get arrested, you'll go back to New York and stop threatening us."

Fat Joe said, "Okay, we'll go home. Just drop the case and everybody's happy."

Hirsch and I exchanged glances. Hirsch said, "Look, we'll take your request under consideration. We thank you and appreciate all the effort you have made to have a face-to-face talk. Now, go home. Otherwise, things may not work out so good for the two of you."

Fat Joe lifted his hands as if in defense. "Hey, we're not bad guys. We hear yous. We'll go. Yous two have an enjoyable night, and Ms. Monroe, yous enjoy that ice cream."

Hirsch and I stood leaning against the trunk of my car as we watched the two goons drive out of the parking lot.

"Should we follow them?" I asked.

"We'll get them on surveillance. I'm going to call the feds and see what they know about our two new friends' trip to California. I don't want to involve too many people in case it could mess up the investigation."

"Good idea."

"Give me a sec." Hirsch pulled out his phone and left a message for Agent Deeley. It was late in New York, and it wasn't likely there would be anyone in the office. He hung up and put away his phone.

I said, "Hey, thanks for coming out. I know you have a date tonight."

"It's fine. She understands. Are you okay to go home, or do you want me to follow you in case those two New Yorkers are stupider than they look?"

I shook my head. "No, I'll be fine. I'll keep an eye out. Hopefully, when you hear from the feds, they'll be able to shed a light on what these two guys may be doing out here. Maybe they came out to do more than have a chat with us."

Hirsch nodded. "That may be. If Deeley or Brosco call me back tonight, I'll let you know."

"Great."

"You have a good night and have some mint chocolate chip for me," Hirsch said with a smile.

He knew we usually had Zoey's favorite ice cream for Friday movie night. I said, "You have a good night, too."

He waved, and I retreated to my car. After putting away my weapon, I drove home, being super vigilant and checking my mirrors the entire way. I didn't want to lead a couple of hired guns to my home. Why were they so afraid of us finding out what had happened to Anastasia and Ryder? I knew the Mafia didn't like their victims to be found, but this seemed different. What were they afraid we would expose?

29

MARTINA

I strolled into the Cold Case Squad Room, coffee cup clutched in my hand. The weekend had been uneventful, which was nice. No mobsters from New York followed me and nobody threatened my life. We went to the park with Barney for more than an hour and enjoyed the bright sunshine and cool breeze.

Hirsch had already arrived in the office. No surprise. He was always the first person to arrive each day and usually the last to leave. He was the head of the Cold Case Squad and had far more responsibility than the rest of us, with his administrative duties like paperwork and budget reviews. The last item had me a little nervous because I hoped they had the funds to renew my contract for the next year. If not, in a few months, I'd be back at Drakos Security & Investigations full-time. There were worse things. "Good morning, Hirsch. How was your weekend?"

The look on his face told me something was wrong. Very wrong. "It was good, but we just got some news."

"What is it?"

"The DNA is back."

"Already?" I was more than a little surprised at the quick results.

"After the fire inspectors released the site, the lab personnel went back into the lab to salvage what remained. Thankfully, they had already prepared Anastasia and Ryder's DNA samples and had completed the PCR Testing and input the results into their computer, which was backed up to their servers. The fire didn't damage the servers. We would have gotten the results last week if it weren't for the fire."

Incredible. "Is it them?"

"The DNA shows the remains we found at the site Jay directed us to are *not* Anastasia and Ryder."

Mindlessly, I dropped my backpack on the ground and pulled out the chair to sit in front of Hirsch. "You're kidding?"

"Nope. DNA is not a match. Jay lied to us, and I think our pals from New York, Joe and Pete, are working with Jay to keep Anastasia and Ryder's whereabouts a secret."

What did all this mean? Why would Jay not want us to find Anastasia and Ryder? Or did Jay not know it wasn't them? My instincts were telling me I knew exactly why Jay and his goons didn't want us to find them. "Who knows that it wasn't Anastasia and Ryder in that grave?"

Hirsch said, "You, me, Vincent, Dr. Scribner, and the testing lab. What are you thinking?"

I said, "I think we should keep it quiet and tell the press the results aren't back yet."

"But we have to tell the family, right? You were there. They cried over remains that didn't belong to their family members. They have to know it wasn't them."

I nodded. "Agreed, but they have to swear to secrecy. If it gets out that it wasn't Anastasia and Ryder, we may get more visits from the mob's own Tweedle Dee and Tweedle Dumb."

Hirsch said, "Speaking of — I didn't hear from you this weekend. I'm assuming you didn't run into them again."

"Nope, no sign of them this weekend. Any idea if they're still in town?"

"I have Vincent on it, and I'm still waiting to hear from the feds."

I said, "Maybe after the morning meeting, we go to the family and let them know what we found. They'll need to postpone the funerals."

"Good point and good plan."

Vincent walked into the room with a solemn look on his face. He stood between Hirsch and me. He said, "Crazy news, right? But hey, I got a hit on that license plate, and I have been following their movements all weekend. They're still in California."

Nice work, Vincent. "How did you track them?"

"Rental car's GPS."

I realized how different the situation was from my former life. In the past, I would've worked all weekend. I would've been in the office right alongside Vincent and probably Hirsch, working tirelessly until we caught the bad guys. Instead, I could let go and enjoy the weekend with my daughter and my mother and have much needed time off. I supposed that was a good thing. But part of me thought maybe I wasn't that important to the case, considering the investigation went on without me. I shook off the thought. It wasn't true. I was being sensitive. It was because nothing eventful had happened, which was somewhat typical with cold cases. Plus, if Hirsch had heard from the feds, he would've told me, and if there had been a break in the case, he would have called, and I would've come running. Mom and Zoey would've understood.

"What have they been up to?" I asked.

"They hit Monterey, Carmel, and Big Sur. To be honest, it looks like they're sightseeing."

I said, "I wonder if they're waiting for orders."

"That's what I think," Hirsch said.

Vincent said, "I'll let you know if they make any unusual stops."

Hirsch said, "Thanks, Vincent."

While we waited for the other members of the Cold Case Squad to arrive, the three of us discussed the case. I was beginning to agree with Hirsch. Vincent would probably be pretty good in the field, and we could use him more on cases.

Once everybody was inside and Hirsch was about to turn on the projector, I turned to him and said, "It'll be okay."

He nodded and proceeded with the debrief. I could tell the DNA news had really brought him down. But I'd already had my suspicions that something wasn't adding up about Jay's story, and I had a feeling I knew exactly what it was.

30

HIRSCH

STANDING IN THE LIVING ROOM WITH MRS. FENNELLI, HER daughter, and Demetri, I wasn't sure how to deliver the news. It wasn't often that we delivered news that the remains we found didn't belong to their loved one. At least the three of them could gather so quickly. I said, "Thank you for meeting with us today. We've had a development in the case. But what we're about to tell you needs to be kept quiet. You can't tell anybody about this because it could jeopardize the investigation."

"What do you mean, jeopardize the investigation?" Demitri asked.

I said, "Can the three of you agree? It's very important."

Mrs. Fennelli looked at Martina. Martina nodded at the group, as if telling them they needed to comply. She had a way of gaining trust with the family members of victims. The three agreed, and I continued, "We think there are people who are trying to cover up what happened to Anastasia and Ryder. Because of the news we received this morning. This may be difficult to hear, but we received the DNA test results back on the remains found at the park." I paused as Mrs. Fannelli cried. She probably thought she was about to be told once again that her daughter and grandson were dead and we had confirmed it with testing. It was the worst news any parent could receive, but that wasn't what she was going to get today. "It's not Anastasia and Ryder."

Anastasia's sister gasped, and her mother's eyes widened with shock. Mrs. Fennelli said, "What do you mean?"

Demitri asked, "It's not them?"

I said, "No, it's not."

"Why would this anonymous tipster tell you where their bodies are buried, but it's not them? It doesn't make any sense," Demetri said, bewildered.

Martina said, "Those are all very good questions. We're not sure why they wanted us to believe the remains of those two people were Anastasia and Ryder. All we know right now is that it's not them."

A single tear escaped Demetri's eye. "They could still be alive," he said in a nearly inaudible whisper.

Anastasia's mother and sister looked at each other. "That's right. It wasn't them. They could still be alive, right?"

Martina said, "It's possible. Right now, we can't rule anything out. We can't get into it too much, but there's been some other suspicious activity from ten years ago, as well as recently, that makes us believe somebody is trying to cover up what happened to them. Since we don't fully understand the situation, we don't know why. We're following every lead, and we won't stop until we find the truth."

Spoken just like Martina.

"What can we do?" Demetri asked.

I said, "There's nothing you can do except for what you've been doing, which is to cooperate with us. But please don't tell anyone this news. Not yet. We're hoping to resolve this quickly, but in order to do that, we need to keep this information in a tight circle. It's important, so we can find the truth."

Martina and I could feel a shift in the investigation. A lot of the dots were starting to connect. We said our goodbyes and exited the Fennelli home.

Outside, my phone buzzed in my breast pocket. I fished it out and said, "Talk about timing," before answering. "This is Hirsch."

"Hey, Hirsch. I got your message on Friday. Sorry I didn't get back to you earlier, but there's been some crazy stuff going on in New York."

"Here in California, too."

Deeley said, "I'm here with Brosco. I'm going to put you on speaker, okay?"

"No problem." I explained about running into Joe and Pete, the arsons, and the DNA results.

Brosco said, "Hey, Hirsch, it's Brosco. Joe and Pete are both highly dangerous individuals. If they're still in California, it means they are not done with what they came to do."

"That's not good news." I shook my head at Martina.

"Not only that, but do you want to guess how Four-finger Pete got his nickname?" Brosco asked.

"No, how?"

Brosco said, "Rumor has it he blew it off when he was building a bomb."

Dumbfounded, I motioned to the car, climbed in, and shut the door behind me. Martina did the same. I said, "You don't say. Do you know if he has a particular bomb signature? The fire inspector says the signature on these particular explosives is pretty unique."

Brosco said, "I'll send over the full dossier on these guys to your email, but long story short, Pete paints the wires red, white, and green. The colors on the Italian flag."

Shaking my head in disbelief, I wished I wasn't on my cell

phone so Martina could hear this - *it was nuts.* "Have you had any eyes or ears on Jay?"

Brosco said, "No, but he's been pretty quiet lately and hasn't been at the office. This weekend, we rounded up some of the Castellano soldiers. We have a couple of them on murder charges. The team is working on a RICO indictment to get the boss too. Jay's probably tied up representing the family."

"Wow. Congrats on the bust. I don't think Jay will talk to me on the phone. Could you try to get to him and question him about the bodies?"

Brosco said, "We'll go to his office and see if we can compel him to talk. I'll let you know what happens."

"Thanks, Brosco. Thanks, Deeley."

"Anytime. We'll let you know if we get a hold of Jay."

After thanking them again, I ended the call and turned to Martina, who had been staring at me the entire time. "Well, I think we found our bomber."

"Oh, yeah?"

"Want to guess how Four-finger Pete got his nickname?"

Martina smirked and shook her head. "No kidding."

"The feds are sending over a dossier on Fat Joe and Four-finger Pete. They are going to Jay's office to talk to him for us."

Martina said, "Good to hear. Could this case get any stranger?"

"I don't think so. This one makes my head hurt."

Martina said, "I hear you, but I can feel we're getting closer."

"Is it that magic gut of yours?" I asked.

She smiled. "It's rarely wrong."

No doubt. I hoped this wasn't one of the times it *was* wrong.

31

HIRSCH

Fire Inspector Lang greeted us with a smile and a sparkle in his eyes. "Boy, am I glad to see the two of you. This is my colleague and bomb expert, Specialist Wellington."

Martina and I introduced ourselves and sat around the conference room table.

Armed with the files on Fat Joe and Four-finger Pete, it was likely the fire inspector would get to close out two bombings, assuming we could corroborate what we thought had happened and we could find the two prime suspects. I said, "Good to see you too, Inspector Lang."

Martina just nodded and smiled.

Inspector Lang said, "We reviewed the files you sent over, and I had Wellington look, too. He did a comparison from the crime scene photos and description from the bombings in New York to the bombings at the testing lab and at the dental office here in the Bay Area."

Detective Wellington said, "They're a match. Not only that, but the surveillance footage from the lab also caught a couple of characters in the area the day of the bombing, fitting the description of those two. It's not the greatest quality, but it makes Four-finger Pete Manzano and Fat Joe Barberini our prime suspects."

"The only problem is they're only suspected bombers," Hirsch added.

"Yes, but if we can talk to the two of them, we might be able to prove they were the ones who did it."

"How so?"

Wellington said, "Typically, what we do is look for the materials used and then trace them back to where they were purchased and then we can link them to the people who purchased them. But in this case, we have something we rarely see with professionals."

"What's that?" Martina asked.

Detective Wellington said, "On the bombing ten years ago, we have a partial palm print, and a few latent prints found at the scene. They didn't match anybody in the state's files back then. Ten years ago, we didn't have the greatest in fingerprint technology. Today, we can match the palm print and latents to anyone in the country - assuming they're on file in AFIS."

The FBI's Automated Fingerprint Identification System, or AFIS, was a critical tool in most investigations. This one would be no different. I nodded. "That's great. I wonder if that was one of his early bombings, which is why he'd been sloppy."

"That's what we think. Based on the files the feds sent over, it looks like the first suspected bombing from Pete Manzano was about eleven years ago. He's probably upped his game since then and now uses his pal Joe Barberini in his crimes. Since there wasn't a single fingerprint found at the testing lab bomb site, he's gotten better or more sophisticated. Based on the investigation reports we read through for the other suspected bombings, we were lucky that you two connected him to the dentist's office. The one time he screwed up. Now, we can nail him and his accomplice to the wall."

This was very interesting. We get Pete's palm print, and we get him off the streets for good. I didn't like the look in his eyes and could tell he wasn't a good guy. The feds didn't need to tell me that. He had dead eyes - like a true sociopath.

I said, "We can put an APB out on Manzano and Barberini. We believe they are both still in California. One of our team has been tracking their movements using the GPS on their rental car. We could go to the last known car location and bring them in for questioning." Once we had them in custody, maybe we could get them to talk more about what they were really doing in California and why they were trying to kill our investigation.

Inspector Lang said, "Great idea. Let us know if you need us. Any help you need, you got it."

I said, "We appreciate that. Let's stay in touch as the case develops."

We exchanged business cards with Specialist Wellington and said goodbye to both of them.

As we walked out of the building, Martina said, "Looks like we might get lucky on this one."

I responded, "Yes, we could close out a few arsons and put these guys behind bars. I'd call that a win."

Martina said, "Now all we need to do is find Anastasia and Ryder."

"Yep. Still no word from Deeley?" My phone vibrated in my pocket, and I pulled it out. "Speak of the devil." I spoke into the phone, "Hey, it's Hirsch."

Agent Deeley said, "Hey, Hirsch, it's Deeley."

"Good to hear from you. We just met with the fire inspector and bomb expert." I explained the partial print, the connection between the bombings, and that we were about to go look for Joe and Pete.

Deeley said, "Well, I'll be damned. If nothing else, if you can pin Pete and Joe for those bombings, I would call your investigation a job well done."

Eyeing Martina, I said, "Yeah, that would be great, but I'd rather find Anastasia and Ryder. Has your team been able to get any information out of Jay Castellano?"

Deeley hesitated. "The team has been trying for the last couple of days to get a hold of Jay without success. They even reached out to a couple of informants within the family, and nobody knows where he's at. He basically vanished."

"Did anybody trace his credit cards to see if they're being used?" I asked.

Deeley said, "Yeah, we had an analyst go through his financials, and they haven't been touched. Nobody matching his description has taken any trains or flights."

"What do you think that means? Is it possible that he was taken out by the mob?" I asked.

Deeley explained, "I'm not sure what the motive would be, but it's possible. The mob doesn't joke around when they get rid of a liability. Their goal is to take them out and for them to never be found again. If someone found out Jay was talking to you and therefore the FBI, they could take him out thinking that he violated the omerta. The omerta is serious to the mob. It basically means you can't talk to cops, especially not the FBI. But it seems like a bit of a stretch. He's the boss's son. I would think it would need to be a pretty big offense to get him killed."

"Could they have found out that he told us where Anastasia and Ryder were buried, even though it wasn't true?"

Deeley said, "Maybe, but if that's the case, they knew he provided bad information to you and Martina. Unless something big is going on within the family that we're not aware of."

"Is there anybody who would want to get rid of Jay?" I asked.

"It's possible it was a rival borgata. The Castellanos don't always get along with the Ambrosinis."

"Did they have a reason to take out Jay?" I asked.

"Maybe, but we haven't heard any rumblings about the Ambrosinis starting a war. And taking out the boss's son would do just that."

"Well, if he wasn't taken out by any members of organized crime, then he's on the run. What motive would Jay have to run?" I asked Deeley and myself.

"That's a good question. I have no idea."

I said, "If you think of anything, let me know."

"You got it. Good luck tracking down Joe and Pete. I'm glad to hear there's finally enough evidence to get them locked up."

"Same here." After thanking him, I hung up the phone and looked at Martina. "Did you hear that?"

"Jay vanished?" Martina asked.

"Yep. Now not only are Anastasia and Ryder missing - so is Jay Castellano."

Jay was pivotal in figuring out what happened to Anastasia and Ryder. It was as if when one window opened, another was shut in our faces. Would we ever figure out what happened to them?

32

MARTINA

Shaking my head, I hopped into Hirsch's car. I couldn't believe Jay was missing. My instincts had told me that he was the key to finding Anastasia and her son. Without Jay, we had little to go on - unless our bombing pals from New York knew what happened to them. Considering it was most likely they'd bombed both the dentist and testing lab to conceal the identity of the remains buried in the park - they had to have known, right?

As we drove back to the station, I contemplated the case, and quickly, my mind drifted to my time working with Detective Hirsch. Since I had begun working with the Cold Case Squad, I had made all kinds of new contacts. The FBI, the park rangers, the sheriff's department, and now the fire inspector's office. Even though I had taken the job because I liked the idea of helping families whose cases had turned cold without answers, and I had needed a bit of a breather from Stavros, it really had been a great opportunity. I knew Hirsch was reviewing the budget for next year, and I was secretly a bit fearful that the budget wouldn't come through for my contract for next year. I enjoyed working with Hirsch, and I liked working with other branches of law enforcement. It was a pretty unique and cool gig. I didn't want to give it up. Not yet, anyway.

"Any word on the budget?" I asked.

"Not yet. Sarge is still working on moving things around." He glanced sideways at me. "Are you worried about your contract?"

"Not worried. Just curious, I guess."

"Well, no matter what happens, I'm sure we'll keep working together in one way or another. Sarge is pretty crafty. He doesn't want to lose you any more than I do."

I hoped that was true. "Good." Breaking the uncomfortable feeling in my belly, I said, "Boy, this case has more twists and turns than Highway One."

"No kidding. Who would have thought when you received that letter from Mrs. Fennelli we'd be tangled up with the FBI, bombings, and one of New York's biggest mob families? You know, I don't think I had as many complicated cases before you came around," he said with a smile.

"You didn't work cold cases before, either."

"Good point. If they were easy, they wouldn't have gone cold."

I said, "If I didn't know better, I'd think you like a challenge."

"Perhaps."

"Speaking of... have you seen Kim again?" I asked.

Hirsch tried to fight a smile, but his rosy cheeks gave him away. "Yeah."

"Boy. You like her."

"A lot. It's funny, I really didn't think this would be anything. But I've fallen for her. Hard."

A pit formed in my stomach. Was that jealousy? Longing? Sadness? I'd once and only once fell head over heels - and fast. I had married him - and then buried him. "That's great."

"Is it? It's kind of terrifying."

That was sweet. "Have you told her how you feel?"

Hirsch swallowed. "I told her last night that I loved her. I didn't mean to, but it just slipped out."

"What did she say?"

"She said she loved me, too."

Wow. It had only been a few weeks. I guessed when you knew, you knew. "I'm happy for you. Now, I really have to meet her."

Hirsch grinned, and his eyes sparkled. "You will. She wants to meet you, too."

Maybe Kim and I would be friends? It had been a while since I'd had a girlfriend to talk to. My social circle was pretty much Mom, Zoey, and Hirsch - and my sponsor, Rocco, and the folks on the Cold Case Squad. I wouldn't mind a non-work friend added to my life. If she was as great as Hirsch said, I was really looking forward to meeting her. I could only imagine how Mom would react when I told her this news. Not that I was one to gossip, but I thought Mom would be delighted that Kim and Hirsch had hit it off so well. She'd played Cupid, and the arrow struck the targets right in the heart.

By the time we got back to the CoCo County Sheriff's Department, Hirsch and I had planned the perfect barbecue for after we solved this case. We'd both laughed that we hoped it wasn't the dead of winter when it happened for more than a few reasons. One, a cold rainy barbecue wasn't fun and, two, if this case dragged on for several more months, it would be torture. Neither one of us wanted that. I strolled up to the receptionist. "Good afternoon, Gladys."

"Hi there. I have something for you, Martina."

"What is it?" I asked.

"Someone left a letter for you."

Was this becoming a regular thing? Hirsch and I had just

been talking about how the first letter I had received from Mrs. Fennelli is what catapulted us into Anastasia and Ryder's missing persons case. I wondered if Mrs. Fennelli had left another letter. That would have been strange, considering she had my phone number. I accepted the envelope that had my name written on it in block letters. After I thanked Gladys, I walked back to the squad room with Hirsch.

Once inside, he said, "I have to admit, I'm starting to get jealous that you're getting all the fan mail. Who is it from?"

"Don't be too jealous yet." The room was empty, so I dropped my backpack on the floor near the whiteboard.

Hirsch said, "You know, if this case gets too much more complicated, we're going to have to commandeer another whiteboard."

"I hear you."

"Well, are you going to open it?"

I flipped open the flap on the envelope and pulled out a small piece of cardstock and read.

As I continued, my heart rate climbed.

Ms. Monroe.
I appreciate you trying to help the family, but I'm begging you to stop looking for Anastasia and Ryder Hall. Please. From one mother to another. Please, close the case. If you don't, there will be no happy ending for anyone.

My jaw dropped open, and I glanced over at Hirsch. "What is it?" he asked.

"It's a letter begging me to stop looking for Anastasia and Ryder." I walked over and showed him the note.

My stomach swirled with a feeling like no other. Letter still in hand, I realized I should bag it up and send it off for fingerprints. "We need to bag it up and ask Gladys for a description of the person who dropped it off."

Without a word, Hirsch ran out of the room and then returned with an evidence bag. He held it open, and I slipped it inside. "Now let's go talk to Gladys."

We rushed to the receptionist's desk. "I need you to tell me exactly what happened when the letter was dropped off. If you can, I need a description of the person, when they dropped off the letter, and what they said."

Gladys hesitated, as if surprised by the request, and then said, "It was around two in the afternoon. She was tall, about your height. She wore a brimmed hat, sunglasses, and a long coat, which I thought was strange because it was pretty sunny out. Her skin was olive - kind of like yours, too."

"Did she have long or short hair?" Hirsch asked.

"Um. I couldn't tell. It was tucked under her hat, but I think it was blonde."

"What did she say to you?" I asked.

"All she said was that she had a letter for Martina Monroe and then left."

"She didn't ask to talk to me?"

"No."

Very odd. "Is there anything else you can tell me about the encounter?"

"No. Other than her hat, glasses, and coat, it was pretty unremarkable."

"Thanks, Gladys. You've been really helpful."

"Is everything okay?" Gladys asked.

I said, "Everything is fine. Thank you."

Hirsch and I hurried back to the Cold Case Squad Room. I said, "We need to send this for fingerprint analysis, and we need surveillance footage from the lobby and the parking lot."

"What are you thinking?" Hirsch asked.

All kinds of things - as if all the pieces are falling into place. "I don't want to jinx it."

He nodded. "I'll call Vincent and let him know we need his help."

The note had me thoroughly unnerved. What if my gut was right? What did that mean?

33

MARTINA

Huddled around the monitors, Hirsch and I watched as the figure approached the receptionist's desk at the sheriff's station. Like Gladys had explained, the woman was about my height, five foot seven inches, and she was wearing a bucket hat that concealed her hair and big 'Jackie O' type sunglasses that covered half of her face. "Can you zoom in on the hairline?" I asked.

Vincent said, "Sure thing," and he zoomed in to enhance the image. Based on the image, it appeared the figure was a Caucasian woman with olive skin and bright blonde hair. Not typically a natural combination.

I said, "Hey, Hirsch, do you want to go for a ride?"

He said, "Sure. Where to?"

Ignoring him for a moment, I said, "Vincent, can you also get some security footage from outside the station to see where this woman went in the parking lot?"

"No problem. If it's clear enough, I'll record the license plate number to whichever car she gets into. After that, I can get traffic camera footage to track her movements."

Nodding, I said, "Perfect. I want all of her movements before and after she came to the station if you can."

"That will take some time, but I can do it."

I said, "Take whatever time it needs. It's important."

"You got it."

Hirsch said, "If it requires overtime - it's approved."

I hurried out of the surveillance room, with Hirsch following me, and back to the Cold Case Squad Room to grab my backpack. Hirsch said, "I'm happy to follow your lead, but where are we going?"

Stopping, I turned and smiled at him. "We're going to get a handwriting sample."

Hirsch nodded with a knowing look in his eyes. "I'll call Mrs. Fennelli while you drive."

Were Hirsch and I becoming one mind? Most of the time, we didn't have to speak the words aloud to know what the other was thinking. My goodness - was Hirsch my best friend? I shook my head. I couldn't think about these sappy thoughts because I needed to focus on the Fennelli family. "How long do you think it will take Vincent to get that footage?" I asked.

"My guess - all night, if he can get the footage from the city in a timely manner."

It wasn't great news, but at least we had a lead. There were still a ton of questions that needed answers in order to confirm my suspicions, but it seemed as if my gut had been right. But there was still something about the case I couldn't quite figure out... and there was still the possibility I was wrong.

Hirsch hung up the phone. "All right, Mrs. Fennelli's home."

"Did she seem suspicious?" I asked.

"She had questions, but I told her it was best we spoke in person."

"Yeah, that's best. Until we get Pete and Joe off the streets, who knows what could happen? Or who is listening?"

Hirsch said, "I'm reconsidering putting out an APB. All we have is a physical description and a license plate number for our department to look for. If we do a statewide APB, we're likely to find them sooner or... they have some law enforcement on their payroll and will hear about the APB and ditch the vehicle. And then it'll be really tricky to find them. What do you think?"

I said, "Tough call. But you know, they may have already ditched the car."

"That's true. I'll call in the APB."

It was the right the thing to do. If we could scare them enough to ditch the car, maybe they would start making some mistakes, and we could catch them that way.

As I pulled up to the front of Mrs. Fennelli's home, my heart went out to her. She had lost her daughter and grandson and then her husband. Her other daughter was the only remaining member of her nuclear family. That must be awful. She had spent so much time trying to find her daughter and grandson. I thought if something ever happened to Zoey, I'd do the same. Were tracking devices for children illegal?

Once Hirsch finished calling in the APB on Pete and Joe, we hurried up the walkway. Mrs. Fennelli met us at the door. "Detective. Miss Monroe. Do you have some news?"

"Not yet, but we had a development."

"Please come in. My daughter's not here, but I can answer any questions you have."

I said, "Perfect."

"Can I get you a drink?" Mrs. Fennelli asked.

"No, ma'am, we don't want to take too much of your time," Hirsch said.

"What is it? What is this about?"

I explained, "I received a letter."

"From who?" Mrs. Fennelli asked.

This is where I needed to tread carefully. But even if I did that, I was not sure it would help. How would I be able to stop her from having false hope? I didn't think I could. *Here goes.* "We don't know who it was from, but the letter was requesting we stop looking for Anastasia and Ryder."

Mrs. Fennelli's eyes widened, and then she motioned for us to sit. "Why would someone do that? You won't stop, will you?"

I sat on the couch in the living room where Hirsch and I had been a few times before. "We don't know why someone did it, but no, we won't stop until we know the truth."

"Did they say anything else?"

"Just that there wouldn't be a happy ending, and the letter pleaded to me specifically... it stated from one mother to another."

Mrs. Fennelli gasped. Yes, the wording was eerily similar to her own letter to me, begging me to open the case.

I said, "We'd like a handwriting sample from you and your two daughters. Do you have an old letter or something that would have all three of your handwriting so that we can send it to a lab for analysis?"

Mrs. Fennelli stared straight ahead. I wanted to give her time to think about it but not too much time. Hirsch said, "It may be a birthday card or something to that effect, or even just a grocery list... anything."

"You think it might've been Anastasia who wrote the letter?" Mrs. Fennelli asked in almost a whisper.

I said, "We don't know. We have surveillance video showing the woman who dropped off the letter."

Tears streamed down Mrs. Fennelli's face. "If she isn't dead, why didn't she contact me all these years? Maybe I knew it. At that grave site, I was sad, but it didn't feel right. A mother knows. She's alive. I know she is."

So much for not giving her too much hope. But I believed, as a mother myself, we had a bond with our children. Some things you can't explain. If Mrs. Fennelli truly believed her daughter was alive, she may be. I said, "I know this is a lot to take in, Dottie, but if you can get those handwriting samples for us, we can send them to the lab, and we can know more about the person who left the letter for me - it's very important."

She nodded. "Oh, yes, I'm so sorry. I know exactly where they are." She lifted herself off the sofa and hurried through the house.

I glanced over at Hirsch. "Well, now I really hope it was her because her mother thinks she's alive and that we're going to find her."

"What do you think?" Hirsch asked.

Before I could answer, Mrs. Fennelli had returned with a stack of letters in her hand. "Anastasia sent us letters from New York. And I have letters I can give you with a handwriting sample of Sophia's from letters she wrote when she was in college. Do you still have the letter that I gave you? Or do you need a new one?"

Mrs. Fennelli had dried her eyes and appeared to be in action mode. Her renewed belief that her daughter was alive seemed to have energized her.

"We do."

"All the letters are a little older. Does it matter how long ago they were written?"

"No."

"Will the letters be destroyed?"

"No, of course not. We will return them to you after the technician has done the analysis."

"Okay, do you need all of them?"

Hirsch added, "The more samples you have, the better."

"Okay." She handed the letters to me, and I accepted them. She looked me deep in the eyes. "You'll find her, won't you?"

I said, "We will," ignoring any look Hirsch may have been

giving me. He usually warned me against making promises to the families.

"Is there anything else I can help with?" Mrs. Fennelli asked.

"Has anybody tried to contact you in the last couple of days or since we spoke last? Maybe a strange phone call or hang-ups or anything out of the ordinary at all?" Hirsch asked.

She shook her head. "No, nothing out of the ordinary. Should I be on the lookout?"

"Just be aware of your surroundings. If anything strange happens, call us. No matter how small you think it may be," Hirsch said.

Mrs. Fennelli nodded. "I will. Thank you both so much. When I saw you on the news, I knew the two of you would be the ones to find my baby and my grandson."

We showed ourselves out. Back in the car, Hirsch gave me the 'making promises again' look. I knew I shouldn't do it, and I always told myself I wouldn't. But like Mrs. Fennelli's mother's instinct, I had instincts too, and I believed with all of my being that we would find out what happened to Anastasia and Ryder. I just hoped we weren't too late.

34

HIRSCH

Staring at the whiteboard, I tried to make sense of all the clues and connections we had uncovered in the Anastasia and Ryder Hall missing persons case. It was a web that didn't quite make sense yet. The door to the Cold Case Squad Room opened, and I was expecting to see Martina, but it was Sarge. "What's up?" He rarely came to the Cold Case Squad Room. We had weekly meetings to go over progress with the squad and all other administrative tasks I was *fortunate* to be in charge of. I liked the job but didn't like the paperwork and bureaucracy.

Sarge said, "I just got off the phone with the sheriff. He's concerned we have given no updates on the Hall case. What's going on?"

Bureaucracy at its finest. We had to make the public believe we were earning our paychecks, and the sheriff wanted to be the one to tell them, when all we wanted to do was solve cases. "We're on the verge of something big, but we need to hold off on another press release - for now."

Sarge studied the whiteboard. "Is this the case?"

"Yep."

"You still haven't found Joe and Pete?" he asked.

"I put the APB out yesterday, shortly after they found the rental car abandoned. Somebody must've tipped off Joe and Pete that we're after them."

"If they fled California, do we need to have the folks in New York help us out?" Sarge asked.

"We've checked train and flight reservations, and we don't think they left California. We think they're still in the Bay Area."

Sarge stared at the board. "All right, I suppose we don't want that out on the news. But if we put their mugshots on the screen, maybe somebody will see them and call it in."

"Not a bad idea, but I'm a little concerned that if we spook them, whatever information they have, we'll lose if they decide to flee. They could get a new car and drive to Nevada and keep on driving until they hit New York. And who knows, maybe they already have."

"Do you think they know what happened to the Halls?"

"I think they do. Otherwise, why blow up the test lab and the dentist's office?"

"It's a good point. Any word yet on who the remains found at the site belong to?"

"After we got the news that it wasn't Anastasia and Ryder, I talked to Dr. Scribner. She says she has seen this type of thing before. She thinks it's likely they got these either from a morgue or dug them up from another grave and hoped we wouldn't be able to figure out it wasn't Anastasia and Ryder."

"Why would they do that?" Sarge asked.

"That's what we're trying to find out."

"No sign of Jay?"

"Not yet."

"If we can't do a press release, can we at least give the sheriff an update?"

"Right now, we are having the handwriting analysis done on

the note that was given to Martina asking us to drop the case. If the identity of the author of the letter is Anastasia, it means she's still alive, which could be a big problem for her. If the mob thought they had her killed all those years ago and find out she's still alive, they might come back to finish the job. So if they are still alive, we don't want to put their lives in danger."

Sarge nodded. "Enough said. I'll tell the sheriff that you're working hard, and we'll have an update soon."

"Any news on the budget?" I asked.

"Some of the brass are playing hardball, but I'm pushing back. We need you, Martina, and the whole Cold Case Squad. I don't need to tell you that, but I think that's why the sheriff is breathing down my neck about the Hall case. I don't think he wants to get rid of the squad either, but he's a politician and has to make sure that money is being used wisely or at least that it looks like it is."

"When will they make a final decision?"

"I'm hoping to hear by the end of the month, so pretty soon."

If we could solve the case by the end of the month, we would not only save Anastasia and Ryder but maybe Martina and the Cold Case Squad's jobs, too.

I said, "All right. I'll keep you posted on the case."

"Keep up the good work, Hirsch."

Sarge was strutting out of the room when the door flew open, and an exacerbated Martina stood in front of us. "We got it." She stopped and looked at Sarge. "Hi, Sarge."

"What do you have?" Sarge asked.

She shut the door behind her and hurried over to me and the board. "The handwriting analysis is back."

"And?" I asked.

"With 99.9% certainty, Anastasia Hall is the author of the letter that was dropped off at the station and addressed to me."

I looked at Sarge. "This can't get into the press. We need

more time. Vincent and the video guys are still trying to track down all the traffic cameras to get a location on the person who dropped off the letter."

"Understood. Nice work. I've got a meeting with the brass, so I'll see you both later."

We waved goodbye.

After Sarge left, I turned to Martina. "Now what?"

"We find them."

With a smirk, I nodded. It was exactly what I was thinking. Working with Martina, I'd learned to appreciate having a partner - and a good friend. I hoped she and Kim got along. It would mean a lot to me that my girlfriend and my partner were friends too. When I'd gotten married to my ex, I hadn't thought it was a big deal that she hadn't been close to any of my work colleagues or friends. Boy, had I been wrong. I wanted a woman who fit in my life, not one that was kept separate. Who knows, maybe Kim would start going to dinner at the Monroes'. I'd like that. Plus, Kim had to try Betty's famous lasagna. We needed to close out this case before the budget meeting. I didn't want to lose my partner - or her mom's lasagna.

35

HIRSCH

Vincent swaggered through the conference room like he had something up his sleeve. How long would it take for him to tell us what it was? Hopefully, he had received the traffic cams from the city and had a location of our mystery woman or our bombing-mobster pals from New York. "Hey, Hirsch."

"Hey, Vincent. What did you find?"

"I finished researching property records for Jay Castellano."

"And?"

He shrugged. "There are no property records for him in California."

"Bummer." I'd had a feeling there wouldn't be, but we'd had Vincent double check. If Anastasia was alive, she had to be hiding out somewhere, but where? My guess was wherever it was, it was likely funded by Jay. Why else would he lie about them being dead and buried in that grave?

"There is, however...." He wore a devilish grin.

"However, you found something else that is useful, and you want to tell me right now?" I asked with less patience than I usually had for Vincent and his theatrics.

"Nothing for Jay Castellano, but there is a property record for a Ryder Castellano."

Adrenaline pumping, I asked, "When was the property purchased?"

"Interesting that you ask that. Just over ten years ago."

I couldn't believe it. Jay had purchased the property in Ryder's name. It made perfect sense he would put the house in his only son's name. "Where's the property?"

"Lake Tahoe."

"I'm guessing you have the address?" My patience grew thinner by the moment.

"It's in your email. And that's not all I have," he said with a smile.

"What else do you have?" *Please have surveillance footage for the woman.*

"We reviewed the security tapes from outside the station. We have the woman getting into a dark SUV, and we have a license plate number. She appeared alone in the car. We don't have all the footage, but we have the surveillance footage for the woman through town. We lost her on the highway."

Dang. At least we had the license plate number. "When did you find this?"

"I've been looking at the footage all morning."

"Which direction was she heading?"

"South."

As in south toward Lake Tahoe? The woman on the camera had been blonde. Anastasia had dark features, but she easily could have worn a wig or dyed her hair to conceal her true identity. Was it Anastasia or a friend?

"Any word on Joe and Pete?"

"No, nothing. It's like they disappeared."

Not great news, but at least we had a lead on Anastasia and

Ryder. Fingers crossed. "Nice work, Vincent. Let me know if you pick up the woman and her car on surveillance cameras."

"You got it, Boss."

He paused, and his eyes traced over to the door where Martina strolled in. She seemed surprised that Vincent and I were quiet and watching her walk inside. "What is it?" she asked with concern in her voice.

Vincent said, "Should I tell her, or would you like to do the honors?"

Knowing Martina had less patience than I did, I said, "Vincent found property records for a Ryder Castellano."

Martina's eyes widened. "Seriously? Where?"

"Lake Tahoe."

Martina lifted her wrist and looked at her Timex. "Do you really need to be here for the meeting today?"

I looked over at Vincent. "Do you think you can run the meeting this morning?"

His eyes widened slightly. "I can do that."

Martina shot me a reassuring look. Vincent would be in charge of the morning briefing. I believed he was up for the challenge. All he needed to do was ask for updates from the other investigators and lead them to provide input to the others. The meetings practically ran themselves, but it helped to have somebody with the projector up and leading the discussion based on the day's slides.

I said to Vincent, "I'll email you the slide deck, and you'll run the meeting. Martina and I have to go to Tahoe."

"All right, Boss. Good luck."

Martina said, "Let's grab some coffee and go."

"Sounds like a plan." I emailed the presentation to Vincent, shut my laptop, and stuffed it in my bag. "I'm ready."

AFTER A FOUR-HOUR DRIVE TO LAKE TAHOE, MY EYES WERE tired, but my body was pumped. Sitting in a car could drain your energy, but Martina and I had had a four-hour conversation about the case and gone over every likely scenario. We both agreed, all roads led to Lake Tahoe. Assuming Anastasia and Ryder were alive, that had to be where they had been living. If they weren't, we were out of ideas.

We didn't have any leads on the whereabouts of Jay Castellano, Pete, or Joe. They weren't our top concern at that moment. We wanted to find Anastasia and Ryder and reunite them with their family. But if they had been alive all those years, why hadn't they reached out?

If Anastasia had brought the letter in to the station to ask Martina to stop the search for the two of them, why? Why had Anastasia and Ryder been hiding out for the last ten years? Was it to hide from the mob?

Once we hit the first strip mall, I eyed Martina. "Hey, you want to make a pit stop and grab a bite to eat and fill up on caffeine?"

"Sounds good. My stomach is rumbling."

I pulled into a stall right in front of the Starbucks entrance. There, I could grab a salad and some coffee. Salad? Who was I, Martina? What had she turned me into? Her whole healthy mind, healthy body thing had definitely rubbed off on me this year. Between her influence and Kim's, I thought the salads were here to stay. Out of the car, I stretched my arms overhead and then arched my back. More flexible, I walked over to the entrance and held the door for Martina.

"Thank you, kind sir," she said with a silly grin.

Perhaps the road trip had made her a bit loopy.

We stood in line, checking out the small chain café. It looked like any of the dozens of Starbucks I had visited in the past. Just like a trusted friend. I picked up a chicken salad and a cup of fruit while waiting to put in my coffee order. Martina ordered her coffee black, but I still needed cream and sugar in mine.

After putting in our order, we walked over to the pickup counter. Martina said, "There's an open table. Why don't we grab it?"

"Sure."

Seated, I lifted the lid off my salad and munched on the semi-fresh greens. It wasn't too bad. There was chicken, dressing, and even a sprinkle of cheese. They called out my name, and I slid off my chair and headed back over to the counter to pick up my caramel latte. After thanking the barista, I sat back down and took a sip of the creamy, sugary goodness.

Martina shrugged. "At least you're having a salad to balance out all the sugar in that."

"Baby steps, Martina, baby steps."

She smirked.

We were eating lunch quietly when Martina placed her hand on top of mine, as if alarmed. Her eyes were fixated on the door. I turned to look, and my brows shot up. I peeked back at Martina. She gave a slight head nod. We had worked together long enough to not need to use any words. We packed up our lunches and inconspicuously exited.

Both of us moved to the side of the building where nobody could see us. I whispered to Martina, "I'll start the car and wait to see if he has a vehicle or if he's on foot. If he's on foot, you go after him. If he has a car, you sneak back in the car, and we follow him."

She nodded.

When I was sure the coast was clear, I climbed into the car and started up the engine. With my eyes focused on the door, my heart nearly pounded out of my chest. What were the odds?

What were the odds *indeed*? And just like that, the pieces fell into place. The odds were pretty high.

The door opened, and the man in the baseball cap exited with a beverage carrier with three cups nestled inside. I glanced over at Martina and nodded.

She nodded back.

My eyes followed him as he walked toward a dark SUV. I waved Martina over, and she hurried to the car, slipping inside, closing the door quietly behind her.

I slowly backed out of the spot and waited until he did the same. The taillights on the black SUV illuminated, and he backed out of the spot. I did not need to tell Martina to record the license plate number - she was already tapping away on her phone. As he rounded out of the parking lot, I continued on and followed Jay Castellano through the city streets of South Lake Tahoe.

36

MARTINA

A few hundred yards behind Jay on the winding road, I said, "We'll need to follow him on foot."

Hirsch said, "Agreed."

"According to the GPS map, the house should be off the next turn. It looks like that's where he's going."

"How far to the house?" Hirsch asked.

"About half a mile."

After the curve in the road, Jay was out of sight, and Hirsch veered the car off the main road into a turnout surrounded by mature pine trees. "Ready for a hike?"

"Yes, sir." It was times like these that I was thankful I always wore sensible shoes. You never knew when your day was going to turn into a trek through the mountainous Lake Tahoe area.

Hirsch said, "Good. Let's wear our vests just in case."

"Smart." We slowly exited the vehicle, checking out the surroundings before walking over to the rear of the car. There weren't any other souls in sight. Hirsch popped open the trunk, and we grabbed our flak jackets and put them on over our street clothes. "Should we be calling for backup?" I asked.

"Let's check it out first and see if it's needed. We don't want to spook them if we don't need to."

"True. Plus, Jay hasn't actually broken any laws that we know of. There's no reason to arrest him."

Hirsch said, "Exactly. Now, if we see the other two, that's a different story. We'll call it in right away."

I fastened the Velcro on the vest and said, "Ready."

"Me too. Let's go."

We jogged down the main road with the sun shining and the forest trees glistening. At a side road, I motioned to Hirsch to make a right. The property would be the first house on the left. I was sure both Hirsch and I knew it was possible Jay wasn't going to the property, but the likelihood was high, and it was all we had to go on.

We reached the long gravel driveway that led to a decent sized two-story log cabin. There were two dark SUVs parked in front of the cabin. *Bingo.* To avoid being seen, we could squeeze between a thicket of trees on the side of the house to get a better look. I pointed to the left, and Hirsch nodded. We crept as quietly as we could while tree branches brushed our bodies. We hit the end and crouched down in some bushes to have the best cover and view of the front of the cabin. Up close, the log cabin with green shutters and front porch outfitted with comfy chairs was quite charming.

The door to the cabin creaked open, and Jay stepped outside, carrying what looked like a moving box. He walked to the SUV we had just been following and set the medium-sized box on the ground. Jay opened the hatch before picking up the box again and sliding it into the back. He glanced around the property before returning to the home and repeating the task a few more times.

He was moving them. Why? Where were they going? A few minutes later, a tall woman with blonde hair and dark eyes exited the house carrying a box as well. Her hair color was different, but even from this distance, I'd bet it was Anastasia Hall. Following behind her with another box was a teenage boy with dark hair and eyes and a strong resemblance to Jay Castellano. He said, "Mom, which car should I put this in?"

My heart nearly pounded out of my chest. We'd found them both - alive.

"Put it in my car."

Without responding to his mother, the boy walked over to the navy SUV and placed it in the backseat.

Despite being thrilled the two were alive, I couldn't help but have a churning in my belly. Why had they hidden without saying a word to anyone? The turmoil Anastasia's family and husband had gone through was catastrophic.

I wanted to talk to Hirsch about what we were watching but knew we couldn't risk making a noise. We didn't want to spook them.

When we started this case, I knew there was a possibility Anastasia and Ryder were still alive, but it was small, a tiny, less than one percent possibility. Even with receipt of the letter, actually seeing the two of them was amazing and filled me with so many questions. Had they been four hours from their family all these years? Had Jay been hiding them? Why would Anastasia do that? Why would she lie to her family and her husband all this time?

We didn't know the answer to any of those questions. But I knew we needed to confront them before they drove away with all their belongings, and we lost them. Who knows if we would ever catch up to them again. When they went back inside the house, presumably to get more boxes, I whispered to Hirsch, "When should we confront them? We don't want them to leave."

"Let's let them do one last load up. They still have more room in the cars, and if they're moving house, they'll probably take as much stuff as they can." He nodded and stopped speaking when Jay emerged from the house once again with a box in his arms.

The sound of tires on gravel turned my attention to the driveway. Who was that? A green truck with two people pulled up. Movers?

The driver climbed out of the truck, and I had to muffle my surprise. We needed backup, and fast. It was Fat Joe and sure enough, from around the other side of the truck emerged Four-finger Pete. Were they all in on it? Or had Jay's father sent them to take them all out?

Jay said, "Hey, Pete. Hey, Joe. How's it going?"

What the heck was going on? They were working together? Had Jay instructed the two goons to blow up the dentist's office and the testing lab?

Joe said, "Not so great, Jay."

"Why not?" Jay asked.

Joe said, "The cops think Pete and I were involved in a few bombings here in California."

"Why do they think that?" Jay asked with surprise in his voice. Surprised the cops thought that or surprised Joe and Pete were bombers?

"Those two investigators looking for Anastasia are working with the feds back in New York, and they're working with the fire inspectors here in California. They think they've pieced it all together. We're burned, Jay."

"One last job shouldn't hurt, right?"

Jay was behind the bombings, too. What was the last job?

Joe said, "I don't know, Jay. It's a little too hot. We think we should go back to New York. They've got an APB out for us. We need to get lost."

Just then, Anastasia walked out with wide eyes, as if it surprised her to see the two men there.

Jay said, "Go back into the house."

"Who are these people, Jay?" she asked.

Anastasia didn't know the two goons? This kept getting weirder.

Jay explained, "It's okay. You don't need to worry about it. They are part of the plan."

Joe and Pete exchanged glances as if it surprised them to see her as well. Fat Joe stepped closer to Jay. "Who's that?"

"That's Ana."

"As in Anastasia?" Pete asked.

Jay nodded. "Yes, it's Anastasia."

Pete said, "You said you took care of her."

Anastasia, who stood in the doorway, gasped.

"She's the mother of my child."

"You got a kid?" Joe asked.

"Yes. And I'm trying to protect them."

Joe shook his head. "I don't know, Jay. This could go bad for all of us if anyone finds out she is still alive."

"No one is going to find out because you won't tell anyone, right?" Jay asked, rather coldly.

"What is going on?" Anastasia asked.

The teenager peeked out from behind Anastasia. "Hey, what's going on? Who are those guys?"

Jay pleaded with them. "Nothing. Please go inside. Both of you."

The mother and son remained in place.

Four-finger Pete stepped closer to Jay. "We need to take care of this, or we're all dead."

I glanced at Hirsch and nodded before I tapped on my weapon, as if to signal that I could see the gun on Pete's hip.

"It's under control, Pete."

Joe eyed Jay. "Is it, Jay?"

"It is. We're almost done, and then you can get to work. Don't forget who you work for."

Pete pulled his gun from his hip and tapped the weapon on his thigh. "We work for your old man. Not you. We can solve all of our problems if we right the wrong."

Jay advanced toward the men. "No. You won't touch her."

Joe said, "Like I said, we don't work for you, and we don't want to find ourselves at the bottom of the Hudson for this broad."

All three men had their chests puffed out and stances that looked ready for a fight. I knew this could turn deadly fast. Hirsch and I exchanged glances. Both of us nodded. It was time to make ourselves known. I raised three fingers, went down to two and then one. Hirsch and I ran out from the shrubs with our weapons drawn.

Hirsch shouted, "Police. Hands up."

WITH ADRENALINE PUMPING THROUGH MY BODY, I RACED toward the men outside of the house and shouted, "I said put your hands up!"

Jay raised his hands, as did Ana and Ryder, who stood in the doorway. It seemed as if Joe and Pete had a different idea about how to respond to law enforcement. Within moments, Pete raised his weapon and aimed at me. Before I could get a shot off, he went down hard, and blood spattered from his neck. Martina ran over to Pete, presumably to check for a pulse. She put her fingers to his neck, glanced up at me, and shook her head.

Pete was dead. *Better him than me.*

I glanced over at Anastasia, who cried and clutched her son. Ryder stared out with wide eyes. Jay remained stoic. Martina stood and grabbed a handkerchief from her back pocket and then knelt back down to pick up Pete's gun carefully with her free hand. The other still clutched her own weapon.

I said, "My name is Detective Hirsch, and this is my partner, Martina Monroe. Some of you have met us before. This is what is going to happen. I'm going to search each of you for weapons, and then we'll have a chat. Ma'am and young man, please come out here."

The boy said, "Is that guy dead?"

Looking down at the man face down in a pool of blood, I said, "He is. He can't hurt you. Martina will guide you out."

Martina walked toward the porch. Anastasia said, "It's okay, we'll be okay." The blonde woman clasped her arm around her son and walked around Pete and toward Jay and the black SUV.

I said, "Thank you. I'm sorry this has gotten so unpleasant. Now please stay put while my partner and I get to work."

Martina kept her eyes and gun trained on the others while I approached Joe. "We'll start with you first." He remained silent while I patted him down and then checked his pockets. After confiscating his keys, wallet, and cellphone, I was confident Fat Joe wasn't packing any heat. Apparently, Pete was not only the bomber but the gunman as well. Out of precaution, I slipped a pair of cuffs onto Pete's wrists.

He said, "Hey! What are those for?"

"There is an APB out for you and Pete. I'll need to keep you secure."

"But I'm not under arrest?"

"Not yet. But I'd bet my badge that truck is stolen and that you will be charged in relation to the bombing of the dentist office and test lab."

Joe mumbled something I couldn't decipher before I escorted him to a chair on the porch. "Why don't you sit there and get comfortable? This might take a while."

Joe didn't make a fuss.

Next, I went up to Jay. "Do you have any weapons on you?"

"No."

I patted him down. He had nothing in his pockets. His keys, cellphone, and wallet were probably inside. Next, I turned to the blonde woman. "What's your name?"

She lowered her eyes. "Ana."

"Anastasia Hall?" I asked with a heavy heart.

She nodded.

"And you are?"

He said, "Uh, Ryan."

I looked back at Anastasia. She said, quietly, "We changed it when we left."

"This is Ryder?" I asked.

She nodded again.

I peered over at Martina, who gave me a knowing look. It was exactly what we had thought. Anastasia and Ryder had been hiding out for the last ten years, but why? Hiding from the mob?

Calling out to Martina, I said, "I'll search the truck. Can you monitor the others?"

Martina said, "I got it."

Making my way over to the truck, I glanced inside the cab. It was clean. I guessed it was another rental, but most likely it was stolen. In the bed of the truck sat a large plastic container, like one would use for storage in the garage. I pulled down my sleeve to cover my hands and opened up the bin. Somewhat unsurprisingly, I found all the makings of a bomb. But I was no bomb expert, either. In almost every circumstance, this was the point that I would call in for backup, especially the bomb squad, but my gut told me something else was going on that could jeopardize everything - including the lives of the remaining people standing in front of the house.

Anastasia pleaded. "Please don't call anyone. They'll kill us."

From across the car, Jay still stood. "It's true. They'll kill her if they think she's still alive."

Fat Joe gave his two cents. He hollered to Jay, "It's not just yous they gonna kill. They'll kill me too just for helpin' yous."

Jay ignored him. Clearly defeated, Joe grumbled before looking away.

I walked over to Jay, who still had his hands in the air. "Do I need to cuff you, or can I trust you will not harm my partner, myself, or anybody else?"

He nodded. "I would never hurt Ana or Ryan or the two of you. Please."

"Are there any weapons in the house?" I asked.

Jay said, "Yes."

"What weapons do you have in there?"

"There's a rifle in a locked cabinet."

I glanced over at Martina. She nodded. "I can get it." She disappeared into the cabin.

"What else is Martina going to find in the house?" I asked.

"That's all."

"Just the rifle."

Jay said, "Yes."

"I need to call this in."

Anastasia shook her head, crying. "You don't understand. They can't know."

Walking over to Anastasia and Ryder, I asked, "Do either of you have a weapon on you?"

Ryder said, "No."

"Ma'am?"

Ana said, "No, of course not."

Based on their clothing, it wasn't likely, but I did a quick pat down of each before stepping back. "The three of you can put your hands down."

Ana latched on to her son. Jay hurried over to them. I studied the bunch and said, "We'll need to understand what's going on here and what's been going on."

Martina emerged from the house with a rifle. "Found it." She glanced over at the truck. "If the truck is secure, I'll put the weapons in there."

"There's a partially assembled bomb in the back, but the cab is open. I have the keys."

She walked over to the truck and placed Pete's semi-automatic and the rifle across the seats and shut the door, then walked up to me. "Keys?"

I pulled the keys and Joe's cell phone from my pocket. "Here, put that in there too."

Martina concealed the items, locked up, and returned. "I did a quick sweep of the house. There's nobody else inside. I didn't see any other weapons either."

"Nice work."

"You call for backup yet?" Martina asked.

"Not yet. We need to hear what's going on." Turning to Jay, I asked, "Why shouldn't I call backup?" My instincts told me I knew the answer, but I needed confirmation.

Jay said, "They won't just kill Ana. They'll kill me and probably Ryan too."

From the porch, Fat Joe said, "And me!"

After eyeing Martina, I said, "Why don't we all go inside?"

I marched Anastasia, Ryan, and Jay inside and had them take seats on the sofa in the living room while Martina stayed outside with the dead body and Fat Joe.

Martina and I met at the doorway. "What is our game plan here?" she asked quietly.

"We need the feds. I can hold down these four if you want to go back and get the car. I'm interested to hear what Jay has to say. He seems to think his life is in danger if we call the police. Let's give him a little time to explain himself before we call it in."

Martina said, "Okay. I'll let you bring Joe inside."

"Sure. Are you okay?" I asked her. After all, she had just

killed a man. Even when it was a scumbag trying to kill you, it still didn't feel good to take another person's life.

"I'm all right. Better him than you."

"Thanks."

"Any time." She smirked and then said, "I'll be back," in an Austrian accent before running off. I shook my head with a slight smile before returning to the cabin. Who knew Martina had a sense of humor?

38

MARTINA

Adrenaline still pumping through my body, I jogged back to the car. Everything had happened so fast. I hadn't taken much time to process what was going on. I had shot and killed Four-finger Pete. Did I regret it? *No.* Did I wish it hadn't happened? *Yes.* But I knew he would've taken out Hirsch and I could not have lived with that. I didn't know if Pete had a family or children or anybody who would miss him, but it was most likely that he did. Most bad guys weren't all bad.

From what the FBI organized crime task force explained to Hirsch and me, most of these guys had a believable cover for their family and friends in the community. Each one had a legitimate job they claimed to have. Maybe they said they were owners of a fish market or flower shop or in hotel management, but in actuality, they were gangsters. Street thugs who worked in an organized fashion with a hierarchy where the profits were distributed through a pyramid that flowed up to the top to Jay Castellano's father - Big Sally. The low-level guys made the money and gave a cut to the next level, and that repeated to the next level and the next level until it reached the top dog, who sat mostly protected from scrutiny and collected all the money and made all the decisions.

It was clever, and the bosses were nearly untouchable until they passed the RICO laws, mostly to combat organized crime. It was why Anastasia had been a target for murder. She was a key witness in the killing of that man outside the nightclub, which would have traced back to the borgata and Big Sally. Anastasia had been presumed dead long ago. Yet, there she was, sitting in the cabin with her ex-fiancé, her child, and a goon who worked for him.

At the car, I climbed in and had to pull the seat forward so that I could reach the pedals. I wasn't a short woman, but I wasn't six feet tall like Hirsch, either. With the car started, I pulled out of the gravel turnout and made my way back to the road and toward the cabin.

Part of me was excited to find out the story behind Anastasia and Ryder's disappearance. I had a theory, but I also still had a lot of questions too. The other part of me didn't want to see a dead body lying on the ground. We didn't want to move it until the authorities got there, but I was sure Ana wouldn't mind sparing a sheet or two so that we didn't have to look at the deceased man in the front yard.

Easing my way down the gravel driveway, I drove up the path and parked behind Jay's black SUV and the green truck Joe had been driving when he showed up.

Why had they shown up? What was the plan? Jay said there was a plan and told Anastasia that those two were part of it. If that was the case, why did they turn the gun on Hirsch? And why had Joe and Pete seemed surprised to see Anastasia alive? I had assumed they were in on it.

Out of the car, I hurried past the late Four-finger Pete and entered the cabin. To the right sat Ana, Ryan, and Jay on one blue plaid sofa and Fat Joe across on the matching love seat by himself. Hirsch sat on the armrest of a big, beige chair.

Meeting Hirsch's gaze, I said, "Hey," and then focused on Ana. "Do you have a sheet we can have? I'd like to cover up the body."

She nodded nervously. "I can get it, or you probably want to come with me?"

I said, "I'll come with you."

Anastasia got up, and I followed her down the hall, admiring the home. If this was where they'd been the last ten years, they'd been lucky. It was far better than most homes I'd been in. It was cozy and seemed well loved.

We reached a closet at the end of the hall. She opened it and pulled out the linens. I'd checked it earlier for weapons and people hiding, but I hadn't remembered that there were linens inside. She handed me a folded sheet with blue and white stripes.

"Thank you."

"Can I ask you something?" Ana asked.

"What is it?"

With a long face, Ana said, "I sent you a letter asking you to stop the investigation. Why did you keep looking?"

Trying to be careful, I had to choose my words thoughtfully as my heart went out to both her and her mother. "You might find this hard to believe, but I received a letter before yours. It was from your mother, Dorothy Fennelli, begging me from one mother to another to re-open your case. I know if my daughter went missing, it would eat me up, and I wouldn't be able to move on. My partner and I wanted to be able to tell your mother what happened to her baby. I'm sure you can understand that."

Ana raised her hand to her face, and tears fell. "I'm so sorry. It nearly killed me to leave them all without saying goodbye. He didn't give me a choice. He said if I didn't go with him and stay hidden, they'd not only kill Ryder and me but my husband, too. I had no choice." She stared into my eyes. "Do you think they'll understand? Or do you think they'll hate me?"

"My guess is they'll be happy to know Ryder and you are still alive. My partner and I have met with your mother, sister, and Demitri several times now. They love you both very much. My guess is they'll be able to look past that and understand where you were coming from. Assuming you have a good reason."

"Martina," Hirsch called out. We had been gone longer than was necessary.

I replied, "Coming, everything's fine," and said to Ana, "It will be okay. We'll get this figured out."

"I wish I had your confidence."

"Come on, let's go back out there. I need to cover up the body."

Ana grimaced. "Okay."

I followed Anastasia back to the living room, where the group sat quietly. Anastasia re-took her seat, and I waved to Hirsch while I stepped out with the sheet.

Outside, I took one last look at the dead man before I laid the sheet over Four-finger Pete. I hoped whoever mourned him would be okay. The blue and white striped sheet lying on the ground seemed odd and out of place but looked far better than a dead body. After a quick prayer for Pete and his family, I hurried back into the living room and stood next to Hirsch. "He's covered up."

"Thanks." Hirsch turned his attention to the group of people in that room. "First, I need to know what the plan was here. Let's start there and then go backward. It looks like you're moving? What's that all about?"

Jay said, "Yes. I was moving Ana and Ryan because the two of you were getting too close to finding out that the bodies in the grave were not theirs. After we moved our stuff out, Joe and Pete were here to burn down the house to remove any evidence that Ana and Ryan were ever here."

"Who else knew about this plan?" I asked.

"Nobody. I'm surprised you could find us."

Hirsch said, "Our tech traced this address to a Ryder Castellano. With that address in hand, we set out to find it and see if there was a connection. But, actually, we spotted you at the Starbucks in town. You led us straight here."

Jay shook his head as if ashamed that he didn't have a better plan or that he hadn't been more careful. Hirsch said, "Now let's talk about what's happened over the last ten years. I would like to hear from you, Anastasia."

Ana fidgeted in her seat. Her nerves were obviously in overdrive. She said, "Ryan and I have been living here for the last ten years. He goes to school, I go to work. We go by Ana and Ryan Sorensen. We have a good life here. Ryan does well in school. We mostly keep to ourselves."

Hirsch cocked his head toward Jay. "Now, let's hear why you moved them here ten years ago. Jay?"

Jay nodded. "Ten years ago, there was talk about silencing Ana because she was a witness to the nightclub murder. They gave the order that she had to be taken out - killed - because they were afraid she would be a state's witness. It was a pivotal case. The RICO laws were just coming into play, which meant that my father and other key players in the organization would all be tried together for that nightclub murder and another one that happened shortly before that. They were serious about staying out of jail. The order said to kill anyone who impeded eliminating the witnesses."

Martina said, "Sounds like she is a pretty important witness."

Jay said, "Yes."

"So, instead of allowing her to be killed, you hid them away?" Hirsch asked.

Jay's eyes filled with tears. "I couldn't do it. I couldn't let them hurt her or Ryan."

"How did you do it?"

He wiped his eyes. "I approached Anastasia while she was at the park with Ryder. I mean, Ryan, and told her she had to come with me or she and Ryan would be killed. My father had already assigned the hit to some local thugs in San Jose. There was no time for any other action other than to hide them and make it look like she'd run or been abducted." He let out a breath. "I lied to my family and said that she had been killed, and I paid off the hitman to keep quiet about it. I stole the bodies from two different morgues with the help of a few associates of mine. We tried to match the descriptions close enough so they would pass for Ana and Ryan. Pete and Joe helped me cover up the crime by eliminating their dental records. They didn't know the bodies weren't Ana and Ryan. But obviously my efforts to hide them weren't enough."

I glanced over at Hirsch. Jay Castellano had betrayed his family to save the woman he loved. It was touching, although it still didn't explain everything.

Fat Joe said, "Yeah, that's right. I didn't know about the cover-up. And if the boss finds out, all of yous could be killed. And me too. There's no winning here."

Jay nodded. "Joe's correct. In our world, loyalty to the family is to be valued above all others, including wives or girlfriends or any non-blood relative. Loyalty is to my father, the boss of the Castellano crime family. My betrayal could be enough for my father to order my death and anybody who helped betray the borgata. If my father finds out that Ana and Ryan are still alive, he could choose to put a hit out on them or all of us."

I looked at Hirsch. "Let's talk in the hall."

Hirsch nodded. We stepped aside to the doorway where I could still keep an eye on the group, but if we spoke softly, they probably wouldn't be able to hear.

"What are you thinking?" Hirsch asked.

"If Jay, Anastasia, and Joe are willing to turn state's evidence and be witnesses, maybe the feds could help them disappear using witness protection. It sounds like if they go back to New York, or their old lives, it will be a death sentence for all of them."

"I agree. I'll give Deeley a call. After all, we have a dead body in the front yard. We have to figure something out, and soon."

I nodded. "I'll sit with them." I returned to the living room and explained to the group, "Hirsch is going to make a few calls and see what we can do to resolve this peacefully."

"How?" Anastasia asked with fear in her eyes.

"There is no statute of limitations on murder. Maybe the feds will make a deal. We have been working with the organized crime task force at the FBI in Pennsylvania and New York. We'll wait to hear what they want us to do. There is a dead body outside. We can't just leave it there forever. We need to call this in, but we don't want to risk any of your lives." Although there were a few lives I valued a little more than the others.

Joe said, "Violating the omerta will get you killed real fast, and I ain't a rat."

I glanced over at Jay. He said, "The omerta is basically a code of silence within the Cosa Nostra. If you talk to law enforcement, you're a rat, and it's grounds for termination - death. It's a very serious offense. But it's better than dead, don't you think, Joe?"

Joe shrugged. "I didn't know what yous was doing."

"Do you think my father will believe you?" Jay asked.

Trying to ease the tension, I said, "Let's wait and see what the feds have to say," and then looked over at Ryan, who was paler than before. He was clearly traumatized. I knew we shouldn't be talking about any of this in front of him, but it was an unusual circumstance. We couldn't leave any of them alone. It was too risky. "So, Ryan, what grade are you in at school?"

He looked up at me. "I'm a sophomore."

"Do you play any sports?" I asked.

His eyes brightened. "Baseball."

Memories of our conversation with Demitri sprouted in my mind. He'd said that he assumed by the time Ryder was fifteen, he'd be watching his high school baseball games. I said, "Cool. Have you been looking at different colleges or what you want to do after high school?"

Thankfully, the normal conversation seemed to relax the tension in his shoulders. "Yeah, I'd really love to go to Oregon State to play baseball. It would be like a dream to play on a college team. I love being surrounded by the trees, but I also like the ocean, so Oregon seems like the best of both worlds, plus Oregon State has a great program."

I said, "That's great."

A little deflated, Ryan asked, "Are we going to have to move?"

I said, "There's probably not a way to avoid that, unfortunately."

Ryan said, "Oh. Will we be allowed to tell anybody that we're moving? Like to say goodbye? I have friends and... Lindsay."

Having to move schools and lives at fifteen would be tough. I didn't envy Ryan and his situation. He was certainly dealt an unfair hand. Who was Lindsay? A girlfriend?

Anastasia gave a small smile, as if she were reading my mind. "Lindsay is his girlfriend."

Poor kid. His move into witness protection was going to be rough. Hirsch returned. "Did you fill them in?"

"I did."

Hirsch said to the group, "I've spoken with the FBI. They are going to send some local agents to secure the scene and transfer you to a secure location."

"Into witness protection?" Anastasia asked.

"We're not sure yet. The safe house will be temporary. The full witness protection will depend on what kind of deal they can put together for those of you who are willing. We'll need you to sit tight for a little longer."

Ana said, "Okay."

She seemed more relaxed hearing there may be a way out of this. Ana said, "Anyone hungry or thirsty? There's food in the kitchen. I can whip us up something to eat."

"I could eat," Jay said

Joe said, "I'm starving."

"I'm hungry, Mom, and I can help you." Ryan stood.

"Okay, honey," she said and rubbed her son's shoulder.

Although Ana and Ryan had an unusual situation, like living under assumed names and hiding from the mob, they were close. He seemed like a good kid.

Eyeing Hirsch, I said, "Why don't I go with Ryan and Ana into the kitchen, and you can hang out with these guys?" I would much rather hang out with Ana and Ryan than those two mobsters, and I was pretty sure Hirsch knew it. Plus, I needed to call home and let Zoey and Mom know I would miss Friday movie night for the first time in six months.

"All right. It could be a while before the feds get here."

"Do they seem hopeful?" Jay asked.

"We'll have to wait until they get here to see what the law can do for the three of you."

Jay nodded. I wondered if he was torn between his choices.

Would he continue to betray his family and turn states' witness against his own father and the entire world he grew up in? Or would he go on the run? My bet was he'd do whatever he thought was best for Ana and Ryan, like he had ten years ago. I guessed some types of love lasted a lifetime.

39

HIRSCH

THE CABIN CRAWLED WITH FEDERAL AGENTS. They separated each of the witnesses, Jay, Anastasia, Ryan, and Fat Joe, to discuss potential deals for them. The agent in charge, an older man with a receding hairline and a round face, approached. "Hirsch, it looks like you've found yourself in quite a situation."

"We sure did."

"Well, they're going to question all of them separately to see how much information they have and whether they're willing to testify against the Castellano family."

"Hopefully, they will come up with something that will keep them safe." When Jay had confessed that he had defied his family because he loved Ana, I wasn't surprised. When I had considered the potential motives to hide someone for ten years that included risking your own life and family, there was only one answer I could come up with - *love*. I wasn't sure I'd ever known such a deep love. Although my feelings for Kim were getting increasingly stronger - at an alarming rate. Would she become someone I would risk my own life for? *Yes*. Even if I wasn't on the job, where I risked my life every day for complete strangers, I would do everything I could to protect her. "How much longer will they be here?"

The agent said, "Probably a few hours."

Martina approached. "Hey. I just got off the phone with Sarge. He'll be calling you soon, Hirsch."

"I have no doubt. What did he say?" I asked.

"He said he needed something more to tell the sheriff."

I wasn't surprised, but the FBI had advised us not to tell the sheriff's department we had found Anastasia and Ryder in the event that they went into witness protection. It was better the mob did not know she was still alive until they listed her as a witness for the prosecution.

I said, "Thanks for the warning. So, Agent Donavan, what happens after you question them? Assuming they will qualify for the witness protection program."

"We'll move them to a safe house, and then they'll decided their housing situation - whether Ana and Jay will want to be placed together or separately."

I thought I knew what Jay's response would be, but I didn't get the vibe Ana and Jay were together or romantically involved. Based on our research, Jay lived in New York and only came to California one or two times a year. I doubted they were holding a long-distance relationship. Yet the love was obviously still there - at least on Jay's side. It made sense why he had never married. Maybe he couldn't get over the fact that he had to break it off with Anastasia to protect her.

Two agents approached with Ana and Ryan, who sat back down on the sofa. The agents came over to us. "We think we can make a deal with Ana and Ryan."

Martina said, "That's great news."

"It is. Ana knows enough to take down the Castellano Boss."

"What about Jay?" Martina asked.

"He knows a lot more than just the murder at the nightclub, so my guess is he'll go in too."

"What about Joe?" I asked.

"He knows a lot, too. He's basically a hitman for the mob. If he turns, I'm sure the feds will accept it and put him in witness protection."

I wasn't sure if that was fair. He'd killed people for a living and because he snitched on his bosses, he would get to live out the rest of his life a free man. If it meant that Ana and Ryan would remain safe, I supposed I didn't have to like all the conditions.

In the living room, Ana said, "Agent Donavan."

"Yes?"

"We have some questions."

We all approached.

"If Ryan and I are going to witness protection, is there any way we can see our family before we're gone again? They've had to wonder about what happened to us for ten years, not knowing if we were dead or alive. I feel like I owe it to them to explain or at least to see them one last time." Her eyes pleaded with the agent.

Agent Donavan said, "We'll see what we can do. Since the Castellano family already thinks you're dead, we don't need to fake your death. We can say that your missing person's case remained cold. We'll work with Detective Hirsch and Martina to figure out the logistics to make sure nobody sees you except those family members - assuming we can trust them to keep your secret."

It would not please the sheriff that we failed to close the Hall missing person's case. I hoped it didn't mess with the funding for next year. Maybe there would be something I could tell him that would make him keep our confidence. Maybe say the FBI took over the case?

Agent Donavan turned to us. "What do you think? Will Ana's family agree to keep quiet?"

Martina said, "I think Ana's mother, her sister, and her husband would do anything to see Ana and Ryan again, including keeping their secret."

Ana broke down into sobs. It was an impossible situation she was in. I could appreciate that. She'd fallen in love with the wrong man and witnessed the wrong thing. A wrong place, wrong time situation had altered her entire life. Her son sat next to her, rubbing her back. It was sweet. It was obvious the two were very close and looked out for one another. Deep inside of me, I knew I wanted something like that. Did Kim?

Another agent emerged with Jay, who looked at Ana. "I've agreed to testify. I'm going into witness protection as well."

"And you agree to allow Ryan into the program, right?" Agent Donavan asked Jay.

Martina gave me him a strange look, and he explained, "Because Jay is Ryan's biological father, he has to agree for him to go into witness protection."

Martina glanced over at Ana and Ryan with a startled look.

Ana said, "It's okay. Ryan knows. Ryan and I don't have any secrets."

Martina relaxed. "But if I recall, Jay's not listed on the birth certificate, right?"

She bit her lower lip. "Yes, that's correct. We decided to raise Ryan, Ryder, as Demitri's. I listed Demitri as his father on the birth certificate."

"So, Demitri has to agree?" Martina asked Agent Donavan.

The agent nodded. "If that's the case, then yes."

Ana's eyes filled with tears and hope. "We'll have to see Demitri then, right?"

The agent said, "Yes, we will."

Jay deflated. It made me think he didn't realize Ana had

chosen to not list him as Ryder's father, and he must have seen the look in Ana's eyes when she mentioned seeing Demitri. He shook his head and then pulled a small box from his pocket. After a deep breath, Jay sat on the sofa next to Ana and turned her to face him. "Ana, they wanted to know if we wanted to be placed together."

She dried her cheeks with the tissue. "'Together?" she asked, as if confused.

I nudged Martina and then nodded toward Jay and Ana.

Jay said, "Yes. Ana, I've always loved you. There's nothing more I'd rather do than spend the rest of my life with you and Ryan."

Ana shook her head. "I don't know. I can't do that to Demitri."

"You've been gone from Demitri for ten years."

Ana shook her head. "But he's my husband, Jay."

Jay lifted the box and opened it to reveal a rather large princess cut diamond ring. "I want to marry you, I want the three of us to be a family. So, will you... marry me?"

Martina and I exchanged surprised expressions. The mystery behind Jay's engagement ring purchase had been solved.

"Jay. I can't. I'm married to Demitri. We took vows. He loved me and accepted me. He married me and agreed to be Ryan's father without hesitation. I love him and could never hurt him like that." She glanced over at her son and then back at Jay. Lowering her voice, she said, "You know, after I had to leave New York and learned what your life is really like, I knew that although I had once loved you, we weren't meant to be together. If we were, you would have been the man to marry me and have your name on Ryan's birth certificate. It's far too late for us. I'm sorry. My answer is no."

All the color drained from Jay's face. He put the ring in his pocket and said, "Okay." He got up and walked over to the far side of the room. My heart went out to the guy. It was obvious Jay had always loved her, but he also had to realize he ruined her life. If it wasn't for Jay, Ana and her son wouldn't be hiding from the mob, and they wouldn't have to leave their lives behind - for the second time.

Ana looked up at the agent. "If Demitri, my husband, wanted to go into witness protection with me, could he?"

Agent Donavan said, "That can be arranged."

She looked back over at Jay, whose back was to the room and his former love. "When can I see my family? When can I talk to Demitri? I mean, he may not want to go. I'd understand if he didn't, but it would be nice to have the option," she said with excitement in her eyes.

Agent Donavan said, "Soon. We'll arrange a meeting with Demitri and find out what his wishes are. It sounds like maybe you'd like to speak with him first. We can arrange a secure meeting for that as well. I'm assuming Hirsch and Martina can help us out with those details?"

Martina said, "Absolutely."

Looking at Ana, I realized she was an incredibly strong woman. Ten years ago, she had made a gut-wrenching choice to go on the run to protect her son and had left behind her family, her husband, and her life. She had rejected Jay, a man who had loved her and saved her life, in order to keep her vow to Demitri - a man she hadn't spoken to or seen in ten years. It was a bit of a gamble on her part. Would Demitri forgive Ana's absence and drop his whole life to run away with her and Ryan?

40

MARTINA

Ana fidgeted in the back of the van. "Are you all right?" I asked.

"I'm nervous, and I hope they're okay. I can only imagine what they have gone through over the last ten years."

"From what they've told me, it's been pretty awful. However, seeing you and knowing that you're okay will probably make it a lot better for them."

It didn't seem to ease her anxiety. I think I would be nervous too if, after ten years, I hadn't seen my family - especially when you could argue she could have reached out at any time during those ten years. It may have put her in danger, though, so I thought they would understand why she hadn't. "Is Demitri here yet?" Ana asked.

"Yes, Detective Hirsch is inside with your mother and your sister and Demitri. We'll go in once he texts me, and it's clear."

"What is happening in there?" Ana asked.

"The FBI is sweeping the house for listening devices or other indications it's not safe for you and Ryan. Once it's clear, we will tell them you're here, and then you'll go in."

"Do you think we're safe?" Ryan asked.

"I think you are. But in my profession, we like to go with safe rather than sorry. It's a precaution and a good one."

"You said you are a private investigator and security something?" Ryan asked.

"Yes, I'm a private investigator and security consultant. In my job, I help people find loved ones, among other things, and as a security consultant, I have led teams to ensure the safety of celebrities and politicians and perform security assessments to let people know the best way to stay safe. For example, determining whether you should have an alarm system or bars on the windows."

"Will you do that for us in our new house?" Ryan asked.

"The FBI will do that for you."

"How did you get into your job?" Ryan asked.

It was good to see that Ryan was comfortable with me and seemed to be adjusting to his new reality and the situation he was living in. He was a tough kid. I said, "I was in the Army, and a friend of ours from the Army started up the firm and thought we would be a good fit. The rest is history."

"Do you like it?" Ryan asked.

"I do."

"We saw you on the news looking for us. Do you and Detective Hirsch do that for a lot of people?" Ryan asked.

His interest in my job was a good sign, and I hoped it helped ease any kind of anxiety that he may experience on the verge of meeting his grandmother and aunt and stepfather for the first time in ten years. He likely didn't remember them very much.

I said, "Yes. I started working with Detective Hirsch and the Cold Case Squad earlier this year. It's been an interesting journey. And we've met a lot of interesting people along the way. One thing we've learned is that you never know how the cases will turn out until they get resolved. I, for one, was thrilled to find the two of you alive and healthy. I'm sorry for your circumstance, and I'm sure it hasn't been easy. Ana, I'm sure that wasn't an easy decision for you to go on the run."

Ana said, "It wasn't. Jay had come out of nowhere at the park. He told me we were in danger and explained the whole situation. He set up the whole thing. Our new identities and the house to keep us safe. Ryan didn't know - nobody knew Jay was his biological father until after we went into hiding."

"We will explain all of it to them, if that is okay with you?"

"It's fine. I'll be happy to not have to lie anymore." She paused. "I used to be so angry at Jay for putting us in that position, but after all he's done for us, it pains me to turn him away. But my heart is with Demitri." Tears escaped once again.

I said, "I'm sure Jay will be happy if you're happy. He obviously loves you both very much."

Ana said, "I know he does. I just feel a little guilty and felt like I had to make a choice between two loves, but in my heart, I made that choice fifteen years ago, you know? When I met Demitri, he was everything I ever wanted and more. I'm so scared he won't want to be with us, but I would completely understand if he didn't."

After the few conversations we'd had with Demitri, I had a feeling he would be more than happy to drop everything to spend the rest of his life with Ana and Ryan. "In my experience, sometimes people can surprise you in the best way."

My phone buzzed, and I read the text from Hirsch. They were ready for me to come in. "They're ready, but first I'm going to go in, and Detective Hirsch and I will explain the situation, answer questions they may have, and then I'll come back for you. You will stay here with the two agents. I should be back in just a few minutes. Any questions?"

"You'll tell them we're here?" Ryan asked.

"We will."

I put my hand on Ana's shoulder. She seemed to need some

encouragement. "It will be okay. You're one very strong woman. You can do this."

She nodded.

"I'll be back in just a few minutes."

I waved and exited the van. The agent standing outside the home gave me a nod before I hurried up the steps and let myself inside and closed the door behind me. From the hallway, I could see there were multiple agents still guarding the exits and entries.

Hirsch said, "Martina, over here."

"You ready?" I asked.

"Yep. Let's do this."

In the dining room, Demitri sat next to Ana's mother and sister Sophia. We approached and stood behind a set of chairs to face the group. There was no easy way to tell them so I simply said, "We found Anastasia and Ryder." Shocked, nobody said a word. "They are alive and they're healthy."

"Where are they?" Mrs. Fennelli asked.

"They're here, but before they can come in, we need to explain the situation." I turned to Hirsch and let him take over.

"As we told you, we're doing a full security sweep of your home. We didn't tell you why. It's because we needed to make sure it was safe for Ana and Ryder - who goes by Ryan now - to come in here and speak with you."

Mrs. Fennelli and Sophia were in tears.

"What is going on?" Demitri asked.

Hirsch told them the entire story of why Anastasia and Ryder had disappeared and had been living under assumed names with the help of Jay Castellano, her former fiancé and biological father of Ryder. We also explained the connection to organized crime and why their lives were in danger and that the two of them would be put into witness protection.

Demitri shook his head back and forth. "We'll get to see them, but then they'll be gone again?"

"Yes. Except the circumstances could change. But for now, that's all we can tell you. Typically, when material witnesses are put into witness protection, there is no time to say goodbye to loved ones or to reconnect ever again. However, because Anastasia and Ryan are already presumed to be dead, we're able to grant this meeting."

I asked, "Did the three of you have any more questions before I bring Ana and Ryan in?"

Demitri said, "I just want to see them."

I said, "I'll be back." A reference to a few days before, when I had done my best Terminator impersonation. I looked at Hirsch, who I knew was suppressing a smile.

As I walked outside, I thought about the last few weeks. I'd reconnected loved ones in the past, and it was a joyous occasion, but this one was bittersweet. I was a mom, and if my child had been missing and came back, I didn't think I could say goodbye again. Back at the van, the agent guarding it slid the door open. Anastasia climbed out, followed by Ryan. "Are you ready?" I asked.

"Ready." Ana grabbed Ryan's hand and led him to the house. We reached the front step, and I knocked on the door to let people know we were coming in. The door opened, and Hirsch stood there with a reassuring grin.

Ana and Ryan went in first. She stepped inside apprehensively, but then when she spotted her mother and her sister, she quickened her pace as they ran toward one another. The three women embraced, and their bodies rocked as they sobbed. Ana pulled back and added Ryan to their huddle, and they stayed that way for what seemed like minutes. It was probably a moment that they all thought would never happen.

They broke from the group hug, and Mrs. Fennelli and

Sophia studied Ana and Ryan. Mrs. Fennelli said, "It's so good to see you. My gosh, Ryan, look at you." And Mrs. Fennelli ran her fingers through her grandson's hair. "So handsome. I love you so much." She gave her grandson another bearhug.

When she finally let him go, Sophia took her turn hugging her nephew. When that was over, Mrs. Fennelli said, "We want to know everything that's happened."

Looking over at Demitri from the corner of the room, I could see he had tears streaming down his cheeks. He didn't bother to hide it as he approached. "Ana. Ryan. I knew you'd come back."

Ana didn't say a word. Rather, she wrapped her arms around Demitri's neck, and he squeezed her tight. "I missed you so much, Demitri."

They hugged, and Demitri brushed Ana's blonde hair from her face and gave her a sweet kiss. He said, "I'm so sorry for everything you had to go through. I wish I could've helped."

Ana said, "I love you."

"I love you, too."

Watching the emotional scene, I stepped over to Hirsch, trying to keep it together. The amount of love and pain and excitement was a lot, even for an observer.

Demitri pulled Ana to his side, and he looked across at Ryan. He turned to Ana. "Does he remember me?"

She nodded. "He does. I told him about you. I never stopped talking about you, and I never stopped loving you." Ana led him over to Ryan, whose eyes met Demitri's.

There was recognition in their gaze. "Ryder...I'm sorry, I mean Ryan."

"It's okay to call me Ryder."

Demitri stretched out his arms, and Ryan wrapped his arms around both Ana and Demitri.

The three fit together like a hand and glove. As much as Jay had sacrificed for his love and his biological son, I could see with my eyes and my heart that Ana, Demitri, and Ryan were a family.

After they had passed tissues around as well as bottles of water to help hydrate, we got to a more comfortable position seated in the living room.

Demitri said, "Detective Hirsch and Martina, thank you for finding them. Even if we can only have them for today. I'm very grateful."

Ana shook her head. "Demitri, it doesn't have to be for just today."

"What do you mean?" he asked.

"The FBI said, now this is completely your choice, but you can join us in witness protection. You would have to leave your job and everything, so I don't expect you to do that. It's a lot to ask..."

Demitri cut her off. "I'll do it. I haven't had a life without you and Ryder. Where do I sign?"

As much as I had tried to keep it together, this reunion hit me harder than anything I'd seen. I sniffled as I wiped tears from the corners of my eyes.

Hirsch looked at me. "It's beautiful."

I nodded. Their love had lasted ten years apart. Demitri was, without hesitation, ready to drop everything to be with his wife and child. Hirsch was right. It was beautiful.

Agent Donavan said, "Demitri, we can start the paperwork and the plans. We'll take you to the safe house after you're done here today."

Mrs. Fennelli asked, "How long will they be in witness protection?"

Agent Donavan said, "Once we have all the criminals behind bars, and we don't believe there's a threat against their lives anymore, they can contact you. But for the foreseeable future, between now and preparing for trial, there won't be any contact. And the son of the mobster who ordered the hit on Ana is also going to witness protection and testifying."

"Will we be able to talk to each other after the trial while they're in witness protection?" Mrs. Fennelli asked.

"No, not until we feel they're safe."

"So, it's just today that we have," Ana's sister said, sadly.

"Yes, for now."

Mrs. Fennelli said, "Well, then let's make the best of it."

The family made plans for the day, all inside the home, of course. There were photo albums and take-out from Ana and Ryder's favorite restaurants. There was laughter and there were tears.

Ana and her family had a long road ahead of them to get to a new normal once again. But all of them had shown that through their strength and their love, they would be okay because they had each other - even if they couldn't be together physically.

41

HIRSCH

Back in the Cold Case Squad Room, I stared at the whiteboard with the details for the Anastasia and Ryder Hall missing persons case. We had a mostly happy ending for Ana and Ryder. It was great to find them alive and to reconnect them with their family again but not so happy that they had to go back into hiding. All things considered, it was probably as good an outcome as any. It was a win for the Cold Case Squad, albeit a secret one. While I erased the whiteboard, I outlined the remaining activities needed to close out the Darla Tomlinson case. Martina and I had a court appearance later in the day to help ensure that Andy Tomlinson stayed in jail for the rest of his life for killing his wife and robbing their children of their mother.

From the outside, the Hall and Tomlinson missing persons cold cases looked to be similar. Two missing mothers. Two missing wives. But two very different outcomes. One man murdered his wife to get another as opposed to Jay Castellano, who had sacrificed everything to protect the woman he loved and then later, Demitri gave up life as he knew it to be reunited with his wife and child.

Sarge entered. "Hey, Hirsch."

"What's up, Sarge?"

"I saw on the news that the head and several other members of the Castellano family are being indicted on RICO charges. You two did good."

"Thanks. Is the sheriff happy about it?"

I wondered if we could appease the sheriff with the little information we could give him. Sarge said, "He is. He's not thrilled to learn that you didn't find Anastasia and Ryder, but he understands we can't win them all. But the fact you helped the FBI bring down a mob family won a lot of points."

Remind me to never go into politics. Martina and I were both told we couldn't tell anybody that Ana and Ryder were still alive. Not that I didn't think we could trust Sarge, but the feds had warned us that organized crime had a far reach that often included law enforcement. I didn't argue, considering I had seen firsthand how good people could do bad things in moments of desperation. On the books, it looked like Martina and I had failed to close a case. We both agreed we could live with that. One unexpected win out of the Hall case, after mobsters had identified us and tracked us to California, was Martina and I would no longer be mentioned by name or paraded in front of the news cameras.

"How did the budget meeting go?"

"There's one more review tomorrow. I'll let you know how it goes as soon as it's done."

"Thanks."

Martina entered, looking more refreshed than she had in the last few days. It had been a heck of a few weeks, first trekking across the country, discovering our missing persons, and then wrapping up the logistics with the FBI to make sure the family remained safe and out of harm's way. Martina smiled. "Hey, Sarge."

"Ms. Monroe, you're looking well."

Martina said, "Thank you. I'm feeling rested."

"Will I see you at the barbecue on Sunday?" Sarge asked.

"You betcha. I'll be there with my mother, my daughter, and my dog."

"Great. I look forward to meeting them all."

Sarge said, "Well, I better get going. Good luck in court later today."

"Thanks, Sarge."

We waved as he exited. Martina and I sat down at the table. "What a case, huh?" I said.

"I'll say."

"Does it feel weird that we have to keep it a secret?" I asked.

She nodded. "A little. But you and I don't do this for the fame and fortune."

"Isn't that the truth?"

Vincent and a few other investigators strolled in. Vincent swaggered toward us. "Hey, guys. I saw the news about the Castellano family. I'm guessing that was because of the Hall case?"

"Yep. Anastasia and Ryder led us down a path to New York mobsters, and now they've been taken down."

He sat down next to Martina and lowered his head, and said quietly, "Don't worry, I can keep a secret."

"Thanks, Vincent."

Vincent was far more clever than many people gave him credit for, even me. He'd more than proven himself in the past few cases. He was the one who had connected the property in Lake Tahoe and therefore was critical to finding the witnesses who could put the Castellano mobsters away for life. "Good to know. We appreciate it."

"You know, I was excited when I joined the Cold Case

Squad, but it's really turned into something a lot more than solving a few cases, hasn't it?" Vincent said.

Martina said, "It really has."

Vincent continued, "I credit that to the two of you. You didn't make this just about closing cases and upping our stats. I haven't been in this business as long as some of you, but I think if we had more departments filled with Hirsches and Martinas, we would have a lot more cases solved and a lot more families with closure. It's an honor to work with both of you."

Stunned by Vincent's heartfelt comments, I struggled with words to respond. Vincent had been cocky and young and always joked here and there, but this was from the heart. It went to show that the cases we closed didn't just touch the families directly impacted. They touched every single one of us on the squad.

Martina said, "Thank you, Vincent. This is why we do the job. It's not for stats, it's for people. People who need us. I feel pretty honored to work with you too, Vincent. You're one of the most adept and efficient researchers I've ever worked with, and I've worked with people who are known as the best of the best. I'd put you right up there with them."

Vincent said, "Thank you, Martina."

"I agree with Martina. Thank you for all your help, Vincent. I hope you stay with us for a long time."

"Don't worry, I'm not going anywhere," he said with a smirk before he stood up and walked over to the other investigators who'd entered the Cold Case Squad Room. He smiled and gave high fives and nudged shoulders, as if returning to the silly, cocky Vincent we knew and loved.

Vincent was a good example of why you shouldn't judge a book by its cover or its exterior shell. You could be one way on the outside and a different way on the inside. We were all complex creatures which made being human pretty great. The squad room was full, and we were ready to begin the morning briefing. Not only would we be going through previous cases, but we would pick a new one too.

As I turned on the projector, the room filled with hoots and hollers. It was the normal call at the start of our meeting. I smiled as the team filled my being with gratitude and contentment. This was the greatest job a person could ever have. We not only helped people, but along the way, I think it made all of us better, more caring and compassionate individuals. The Cold Case Squad Room full of dedicated, hard-working people proved just that.

42

MARTINA

NEVER THOUGHT I'D SEE THE DAY. HIRSCH STOOD AT A charcoal barbecue with a woman by his side, smiling, with a bottle of beer in his hand. He finally had the barbecue at his new house. It was late October, but the sun was shining, and the leaves were still on the trees. We lucked out with the weather because I didn't think we would have much more sun in the coming weeks as we approached winter. That was the Bay Area for you - nearly year-round sunshine. We were blessed in so many ways. I continued toward Hirsch, while Mom, Zoey, and Barney lagged behind as Barney wanted to inspect some bushes in the back yard. I smiled, "Hey, Hirsch."

He turned around, replacing the lid on the barbecue. "Martina, you made it."

"Of course. Have I ever not shown up?" I teased.

"Well, there was that time you were fighting a bad guy at a gas station, but other than that, you're pretty solid." He chuckled before he turned to the woman next to him. "Martina, I want you to meet Kim."

She was radiant, with shoulder-length blonde hair and wide blue eyes. She smiled like a woman who was in love. Kim extended her hand. "It's so good to meet you, Martina. I've heard so much about you."

"Likewise. And behind me is my gang. The one in the pink sparkles is my daughter, Zoey. The fluffy creature running around is my dog Barney, and this is my mother, Betty."

Zoey waved. "Hi, nice to meet you. Hi, Uncle August. What are you cooking up?"

"Hamburgers. Do you like hamburgers?" Hirsch asked.

Zoey put her fist on her hip. "Of course, I do. You have cheese, right?"

Hirsch cocked his head. "Of course, I do."

Zoey smiled. "Good."

My mom said, "Kim, it's so nice to meet you in person. Is your mom here? She said she was coming."

Kim said, "You too. Yes, she's in the house putting together a potato salad."

"I brought chocolate and caramel buttercream cupcakes. Where should I put them?" Mom asked.

Hirsch said, "Yum! In the house is fine. Make yourself at home."

Mom winked at Hirsch and said, "Okay," before heading to the glass sliders to enter the house.

I knew my mother was more than pleased with herself that she made such a great love connection. I had to admit Hirsch and Kim looked happy to be together, and I was happy for them. Hirsch did so much for other people. I was glad he was finding some joy for himself.

Working this job could be mentally and physically challenging, and it was important to have something else to balance out your life. I had my Zoey, my mom, and Barney.

A woman and my mother emerged through the back slider, chatting and laughing. The woman carried a bowl in her arms. No doubt the two were conspiring about something.

The woman put down the potato salad on the picnic table that had a red and white checkered tablecloth and a bouquet of fresh wildflowers. I guessed that the decor was Kim and her mother's touch, not Hirsch's. The woman with cropped hair and the same wide blue eyes as Kim walked up to me. "You must be Martina."

"Yes."

She said, "I'm Trixie. I play bingo with your mom, and Kim is my daughter, and oh my goodness, this must be Zoey."

Zoey nodded enthusiastically. "And this is Barney. He's the best dog in the whole world."

Zoey and Barney easily stole the show. Trixie patted me on the shoulder. "It's nice to meet you."

I said, "You, too."

Trixie was a bubbly, cheerful person, and I wouldn't be surprised if Kim was the same way.

More people filled the back yard. Lots of familiar faces from the Cold Case Squad, with smiles and relaxed stances, unlike at work. The squad had a good time together, but there was a lot of seriousness in what we did. Vincent and a young lady walked toward us. "Vincent."

"Hi, Martina."

"This is my girlfriend, Amanda."

We shook hands. "It's nice to meet you, Amanda. This is my daughter, Zoey. Zoey, this is Vincent and his girlfriend, Amanda. Can you say hello?"

Zoey looked up. "Are you on the squad?"

Vincent said, "I am. I do all the digging around in the electronic files. I'm kind of like a computer geek."

Zoey's eyes lit up. "Cool!"

"You know, I can teach you sometime."

Zoey looked up at me. "Mommy, can he teach me how to dig into electronic files?"

I nodded. "Sure."

Zoey said, "Cool! Maybe one day I'll be on the squad too!"

Wouldn't that be something?

Zoey ran after Barney, and Vincent said, "I would've never pictured your daughter in head to toe pink sparkles."

I shrugged. "If it doesn't sparkle, she doesn't wear it."

Amanda smiled. "I love that."

Amanda couldn't be over twenty-five. She was tall with long, dark hair and stylish clothes. I said, "Me too."

Hirsch approached. "Hey, Vincent. And you must be Amanda? I'm Hirsch."

Amanda said, "Yes. It's nice to meet you."

Hirsch said, "Can I get you anything to drink? We've got beer, soda, and iced tea."

Vincent said, "Sure, I'll have a beer."

Amanda said, "Me too."

Hirsch said, "Martina, the iced tea is sugar free."

I said, "Thank you."

He knew I didn't drink sugar. He walked off, presumably to get our drinks.

My mom approached. "Who's this? I have to meet everybody!"

I said, "Mother, this is Vincent. He's our top researcher on the squad. And this is girlfriend, Amanda. Vincent and Amanda, this is my mother, Betty."

Vincent smiled. "It's nice to meet you. I've heard so much about your wonderful cooking from Hirsch."

Betty nodded. "He does like to eat. And I would much rather he eat my cooking than all that fast food. Hopefully, Kim will finally get him out of the habit of buying his food in the drive through."

"Is she here?" Vincent asked.

Everyone in the squad knew Hirsch had a new girlfriend.

He was never unpleasant, but since he'd met Kim, there was a lot more pep in his step.

"She is. Go meet her. She's very nice."

My mom said, "I set them up. I'm basically a matchmaker now."

Vincent called out, "Hey, Sarge."

He waved and smiled as he approached. It was the first big social gathering of the Cold Case Squad since its formation. It was nice for the people I worked with to meet my family. It was as if we were already a family, and now we were integrating it with our blood family.

A warmth filled my soul. "Sarge, glad you can make it."

"I always thought you were a miracle worker, Martina, but the fact you convinced Hirsch to have a barbecue — I'd say it's now a fact."

I chuckled. "Sarge, this is my mother, Betty. Betty, this is Sarge."

He looked at my mother with a sparkle in his eye. "You can call me Ted."

Ted? In that moment, I realized I had never known Sarge's given name.

"Ted, it's very nice to meet you," my mother said, with the same twinkle in her eye.

I hadn't seen Sarge wearing a wedding ring, but rumors were that he was a widower. Was there a love connection happening between my mother and Sarge? Stranger things had happened.

Hirsch returned with beers and a bottle of iced tea for me. "Thanks."

Soon, the back yard was filled with investigators and researchers. Even Dr. Scribner made an appearance.

This team had a lot to celebrate. With the help of all in attendance, whether they were active investigators or our emotional support, we'd closed out many cold cases. Thankfully, that included the Darla Tomlinson case. With compelling testimony and indisputable forensics, the trial had concluded the previous Friday. The jury came back within two hours and found him guilty on all charges, including first-degree murder. Sentencing wasn't for a few weeks, but the prosecution was fairly certain he would get life in prison with no possibility of parole. Andy Tomlinson had robbed his children of their mother and Darla's parents of their daughter. He didn't deserve to be free - *ever*.

With full bellies and a lightness in the air, Hirsch and I sat alone at one of the picnic tables. "This is really nice, Hirsch."

"It was, wasn't it? Thank you for pushing me to do it."

"You look happy, and Kim seems great."

"You know, for the first time in a long time, I think I am happy. I forgot what that was like."

That filled me with warmth. He was definitely somebody who deserved joy and love. "Guess what?" he said.

"What?"

"I was talking to Sarge."

"Yeah?"

"It took some finesse, but he just got word that your contract and funding for the squad was approved for next year."

A grin spread across my face. I couldn't help it. "I guess you're stuck with me for another year."

Hirsch grinned. "Looks like it."

Kim approached and then stopped. "I'm sorry. Am I interrupting?"

I said, "No, please come, sit."

She sat down next to Hirsch. Hirsch grabbed her hand and they sat there, happy and in love. I never thought I'd see the day. "Martina, did you see your mom and Sarge? I don't think they've left each other's side all day."

"Interesting. I was there when they met, and I saw a few sparks between the two of them."

"Perhaps another love connection?" Hirsch asked.

I said, "Perhaps," before I sat back and sipped on my iced tea, staring out at our chosen and given families. I realized I too was happy. There were so many days and months and years when I thought I could never find happiness again, but I had. It looked different from what I had imagined, but it was true all the same.

ALSO BY H.K. CHRISTIE

The Martina Monroe Series is a nail-biting suspense series starring Private Investigator Martina Monroe and her partner Detective Hirsch of the Cold Case Squad. If you like high-stakes games, jaw-dropping twists, and embattled seekers struggling to do right, then you'll love the Martina Monroe thriller series.

What She Left, Martina Monroe, PI, Book 1

She's on her last chance. When the bodies start piling up, she'll need to save more than her job.

Martina Monroe is a single bad day away from losing it all. Stuck catching insurance fraudsters and cheating spouses due to a DUI, the despondent PI yearns to return to more fulfilling gigs. So when a prospective client asks for her by name to identify an unknown infant in a family photo, she leaps at the opportunity and travels to the one place she swore never to go: back home.

As the pressure mounts and the temptation of booze calls like a siren, Martina digs into the mystery and discovers many of the threads have razor-sharp ends. And forced to partner with a resentful detective investigating a linked suspicious death, the haunted private eye unravels clues that delve deep into her past... and put her in a dark and dangerous corner.

Can this gritty detective unlock the truth before she's drowned in a sea of secrets?

What She Left is the page-turning first book in the Martina Monroe Private Investigator Series.

If She Ran, Martina Monroe, PI, Book 2

Three months. Three missing women. One PI determined to discover the truth.

Back from break, PI Martina Monroe clears the air with her boss at Drakos Security & Investigations and is ready to jump right into solving cold cases for the CoCo County Sheriff's Department.

Diving into the cold case files Martina stumbles upon a pattern of missing young women, all of whom were deemed runaways, and the files froze with minimal detective work from the original investigators. The more Martina digs into the women's last days the more shocking discoveries she makes.

Soon, Martina and Detective Hirsch not only uncover additional missing women but when their star witness turns up dead, they must rush to the next before it's too late.

A gripping, unputdownable thriller full of mystery and suspense.

If She Ran is the second installment in the PI Martina Monroe series.

All She Wanted, Martina Monroe, PI, Book 3

A tragic death. A massive cover-up. PI Martina Monroe must face her past in order to reveal the truth.

PI Martina Monroe has found her groove working cold cases alongside Detective Hirsch at the CoCo County Sheriff's Department. With a growing team of cold case detectives, Martina and Hirsch are on the heels of bringing justice for Julie DeSoto - a woman Martina failed to protect one year earlier. But when Martina receives a haunting request from her past, it nearly tears her in two.

As Julie's case turns hot, so does the investigation into a young soldier's untimely death. As both cases rattle Martina to the core, she now questions everything she believed about her time working for Drakos

Security & Investigations and with the United States Army. Martina must uncover the truth for her sanity and her own life.

Pushed to the brink, Martina risks everything to expose the real criminals and bring justice for the victim's family and her own.

A gripping, page-turning thriller, full of suspense.

All She Wanted is the third installment in the thrilling Martina Monroe PI series.

Why She Lied, Martina Monroe, PI, Book 4

A missing mother and child. A secret past revealed. Will Martina and Hirsch discover the truth before they meet their end?

In the thick of the current cold case investigation, PI Martina Monroe receives a hand-written letter from a desperate mother pleading for Martina and Hirsch to reopen the cold case of the woman's missing daughter and five-year-old grandson. Feeling a deep connection to the request, Martina knows that Hirsch and she have found their next case.

As the two investigators dig into the life of Ana and her son, Ryder, they quickly find Ana has the life many would be envious of. With a loving group of family and friends, a devoted husband, and a successful career, Ana's perfect life seems a bit too perfect for Martina and Hirsch.

Searching even further into Ana's past, they find a startling secret that leads Martina and Hirsch into the dark world of organized crime. Hot on the trail, the two investigators head to New York City, hoping to find the answer to what happened to Ana and Ryder. However, as soon as they touch down, they realize they aren't the only ones on the hunt.

Will Martina and Hirsch discover the truth before they become victims themselves?

Secrets She Kept, Martina Monroe, PI, Book 5
Release date: June 25, 2022

A ritualistic murder. Multiple suspects. Can the cold case detectives find the truth before the killers strike again?

Ten years earlier, two teenage girls were found murdered by what appeared to be a satanic sacrifice. The case had dominated the news headlines for months before the original investigators failed to arrest the perpetrators of the crime - despite multiple suspects. Without solid evidence to prosecute, and even with the near-heroic efforts of the original detectives, the homicide investigation turned cold. For years, the families of the two victims fought to keep the young women's memory alive and to get the attention of law enforcement to not give up on finding those responsible.

In an election year, and with a stellar record for the CoCo County Sheriff's Department Cold Case Squad, the Sheriff hands cold case investigators Martina Monroe and Detective Hirsch the most notorious decade-old murder case - named by the press, 'The Twin Satan Murders.' Unlike most of their previous cold cases, The Twin Satan Murders were thoroughly investigated by previous detectives. Undeterred by the lack of evidence and answers from the original investigation, Martina and Hirsch investigate the murders as if it were day one.

Knocking on doors, Martina and Hirsch are surprised by the lack of cooperation from the original witnesses. With pushback from the community, the two investigators are forced to dive into the world of the occult. What the two detectives find is more disturbing than any case they've worked on before. Soon, Martina and Detective Hirsch find that some powerful people will go to all lengths to keep the truth buried.

Will Martina and Detective Hirsch find the actual killers before they become victims themselves?

The Selena Bailey Series is a suspenseful series featuring a young Selena Bailey and her turbulent path to becoming a top notch kickass private investigator as led by her mentor, Martina Monroe.

Not Like Her, Selena Bailey, Book 1

A battered mother. A possessive boyfriend. Can she save herself from a similar fate?

Selena longs to flee her uneasy home life. Prepping every spare minute for a college escape, the headstrong, high school senior vows never to be like her alcoholic mom with her string of abusive boyfriends. So when Selena finds her beaten nearly to death, she knows safety is slipping away...

With her mother's violent lover evading justice, Selena's new boyfriend's offer to move in seems Heaven-sent. But jealous rage and a renewed search for her long-lost father threaten to pull her back into harm's way.

Can Selena break free of an ugly past, or will brutal men crush her hopes of a better future?

Not Like Her is the first book in the suspenseful Selena Bailey series. If you like thrilling twists, dark tension, and smart and driven women, then you'll love H.K. Christie's new dark mystery series.

Trigger warning: This book includes themes relating to domestic violence

---

One In Five, Selena Bailey, Book 2

A predator running free and the girl determined to stop him.

After escaping a violent past, Selena Bailey, starts her first semester of college determined to put it all behind her - until her roommate is attacked at the Delta Kappa Alpha house. After reporting the attack, police refuse to prosecute due to lack of evidence, claiming another case of 'he said, she said'.

As Selena and Dee begin meeting other victims, it's clear Dee's assault wasn't an isolated event. Selena determined to take down the DKA house, takes matters into her own hands in order to claim justice for Dee and prevent the next attack.

Will Selena get justice for the women of SFU or will she become the next victim?

One In Five, is the second book in the suspenseful Selena Bailey series.

On The Rise, Selena Bailey, Book 3

A little girl is taken. A mysterious cover-up. One young investigator determined to find the truth.

Selena Bailey, a sophomore at the local university studying criminal justice, returns from winter break to jump into her first official case as a private investigator with her stepmother's security firm.

Thrown into an undercover detail, Selena soon discovers a much darker plot. What seemed like a tragic kidnapping is revealed to be just the tip of the iceberg. Will Selena expose the truth before not only the little girl's life, but her own is lost forever?

On The Rise is the third standalone story in the suspenseful Selena Bailey series.

Go With Grace, Selena Bailey, Book 4

A dangerous stalker. A desperate classmate. Will one young investigator risk everything to help a stranger in need?

Selena Bailey returns in her senior year of college determined to keep her head down and out of other people's lives with the sole intent of keeping them safe and out of harm's way.

Selena is focused more than ever, with three major goals: graduate with her bachelor's degree in Criminal Justice, obtain her Private Investigator's license and find her late boyfriend, Brendon's, killers.

Her plans are derailed when a desperate classmate approaches Selena for her help. At first, she refuses but Dillon is certain his life is in danger and provides Selena with proof. With no one else to turn to, Selena reluctantly takes the case.

The investigation escalates quickly as Selena soon discovers the woman stalking Dillon is watching his, and now Selena's, every move.

Will Selena be able to save Dillon's life and her own?

Go With Grace is the fourth story, and first full-length novel, in the suspenseful Selena Bailey series.

Flawless, Selena Bailey, Book 5

A young woman clinging on to life. A desperate family fighting for answers. Will Selena be able to discover the truth in time to save her?

Selena Bailey returns with her Private Investigator license in one hand and the first official case for Bailey Investigations in the other.

When the sister of a young woman, fighting for her life in the Intensive Care Unit, pleads with Selena to explore her sister, Stephanie's, last days before she slipped into a coma, Selena must go undercover in the billion dollar beauty industry to discover the truth.

The deeper Selena delves into Stephanie's world, the more she fears for Stephanie's life and so many others.

As Selena unravels the truth behind an experimental weight loss regimen, she finds it's not only weight the good doctor's patients are losing. Selena now must rush against the clock to save not only Stephanie's life, but her own.

Flawless is the fifth story, and 2nd full-length novel, in the suspenseful Selena Bailey series.

———————

A Permanent Mark: A heartless killer. Weeks without answers. Can she move on when a murderer walks free?

Kendall Murphy's life comes crashing to a halt at the news her husband has been killed in a tragic hit-and-run. Devastated and out-of-sorts, she can't seem to come to terms with the senselessness of it all. Despite, promises by a young detective, she fears they'll never find the person responsible for her husband's death.

As months go by without answers, Kendall, with the help of her grandmother and sister, deals with her grief as she tries to create a new life for herself. But when the detective discovers that the death was a murder-for-hire, suddenly everyone from her new love interest and those closest to her are under suspicion. And it may only be a matter of time before the assassin strikes again...

Can Kendall trust anyone, or will misplaced loyalty make her the next victim?

If you like riveting suspense and gripping mysteries then you'll love *A Permanent Mark* - starring a grown up Selena Bailey.

JOIN H.K. CHRISTIE'S READER CLUB

Join my reader club to be the first to hear about upcoming novels, new releases, giveaways, promotions, as well as, a free e-copy of the **prequel to the Martina Monroe series**, ***Crashing Down.***

It's completely free to sign up and you'll never be spammed by me, you can opt out easily at any time.

Sign up at
www.authorhkchristie.com

THANK YOU!

Thank you for reading *Why She Lied*. I hope you enjoyed reading it as much as I loved writing it. If you did, I would greatly appreciate if you could post a short review.

Reviews are crucial for any author and can make a huge difference in visibility of current and future works. Reviews allow us to continue doing what we love, *writing stories*. Not to mention, I would be forever grateful!

Thank you!

ABOUT THE AUTHOR

H. K. Christie watched horror films far too early in life. Inspired by the likes of Stephen King, Dean Koontz, and a vivid imagination she now writes suspenseful thrillers featuring unbreakable women. *Why She Lied* is her 14th published book.

When not working on her latest novel, she can be found eating & drinking with friends, walking around the lakes, or playing with her favorite furry pal.

She is a native and current resident of the San Francisco Bay Area.

ACKNOWLEDGMENTS

I extend my deepest gratitude to my Advanced Reader Team. My ARC Team is invaluable in taking the first look at my stories and spreading awareness of my stories through their reviews and kind words. To my editor Paula Lester, a huge thank you for your careful edits and helpful comments. To my cover designer, Odile, thank you for your guidance and talent. Last but not least, I'd like to thank all of my readers. It's because of you I'm able to continue doing what I love - writing stories.

Made in the USA
Monee, IL
10 April 2022

94497700R00156